What Happens Next

Books by Christina Suzann Nelson

More Than We Remember
Shaped by the Waves
The Way It Should Be
What Happens Next

What Happens Next

Christina Suzann Nelson

BETHANYHOUSE
a division of Baker Publishing Group
Minneapolis, Minnesota

© 2023 by Christina S. Nelson

Published by Bethany House Publishers
Minneapolis, Minnesota
www.bethanyhouse.com

Bethany House Publishers is a division of
Baker Publishing Group, Grand Rapids, Michigan

Printed in the United States of America

Library of Congress Cataloging-in-Publication Data
Names: Nelson, Christina Suzann, author.
Title: What happens next / Christina Suzann Nelson.
Description: Minneapolis, Minnesota : Bethany House, a division of Baker
 Publishing Group, [2023]
Identifiers: LCCN 2022034463 | ISBN 9780764240409 (paperback) | ISBN
 9780764241376 (casebound) | ISBN 9781493440689 (ebook)
Subjects: LCGFT: Christian fiction. | Novels.
Classification: LCC PS3614.E44536 W48 2023 | DDC 813/.6—dc23/eng/20220721
LC record available at https://lccn.loc.gov/2022034463

This is a work of fiction. Names, characters, incidents, and dialogues are products
of the author's imagination and are not to be construed as real. Any resemblance
to actual events or persons, living or dead, is entirely coincidental.

Cover design by LOOK Design Studio
Cover image by Blue Collectors / Stocksy
Old bike image by Marta Locklear / Stocksy

Author is represented by Books & Such Literary Agency.

Baker Publishing Group publications use paper produced from sustainable for-
estry practices and post-consumer waste whenever possible.

23 24 25 26 27 28 29   7 6 5 4 3 2 1

To Jodie

Whose friendship has been one
of the greatest blessings
along my writing journey.

1

Faith

Faith Byrne's carefully laid plans took advantage of unplanned distractions and skipped town, never to be seen again. She stood outside her comfortable suburban home, one hand on the mailbox, the other holding a thick envelope from her attorney. Her line of sight did a dance around the yard as if one of her neighbors might be watching and somehow witness this moment of humiliation. Faith didn't have to open the seal to know what the package contained. Inside would be her copy of the final divorce decree. She hadn't wanted the dissolution of their vows, so she certainly didn't need to read through the corrosive words—again.

Tucking the mail under her arm, she straightened her posture and walked past the tulips just beginning to open in the early spring weather. With Easter only four days past, their appearance should have been predictable, but like those who witnessed the death of Jesus, she wasn't prepared for life to return after tragedy.

A horn honked behind her, startling Faith from her pathetic comparison between crucifixion and being dumped by Neil.

She turned to find Kendall, a friend she'd made through Neil but managed to keep in the settlement. The side door of Kendall's green minivan slid open, with Harlow and Ava piling out and lunging toward her.

"Mom, I can't believe you're okay with this. Thank you!" Ava hopped up on her toes, still not stretching quite to Faith's chin. She clutched the phone that Neil had purchased for her, even though they'd decided the girls could wait until their thirteenth birthday for that kind of responsibility. Apparently in his mind, divorce gave her a nine-month advancement in age. "This is going to be the best summer ever."

Faith kissed the top of Ava's head. "I'm sure it will be." She shifted her gaze to her fourteen-year-old. Harlow was skilled at nonverbally cluing her mother in on all things Ava, and what Faith was getting from her older daughter sparked flames in her chest.

The delight melted from Harlow's face. "Stop, Ava. He didn't ask Mom."

Ava's mouth hung open as her body stilled. "So, we're not going to Hawaii for the summer?"

Hawaii? For the summer? Faith's stomach became a jagged boulder. *Thanks a lot, Neil.* "Daddy and I are still working through a few details about your vacation. Let us talk, and I'm sure we'll get everything worked out."

Ava's eyes filled with tears.

"Don't be such a little kid," Harlow snapped.

"None of that." It would serve her husband—ex-husband—right to have an entire summer with the girls. They'd hit ages where they seemed to forget they were sisters, not mortal enemies. "Head into the house and get started on homework. I'll be there in a minute."

As they shuffled inside, their nasty whispers back and forth met Faith's ears. She'd had such a different vision for her children, her family.

Kendall pushed the passenger door of her van open a few inches. "Hey." She patted the seat. "Take a load off."

A quick look in the back seat verified that Kendall's middle school-aged son was in a nearly hypnotic state as he poked and swayed with his video game. She couldn't blame him. Being in the van with her girls could be a bit much. Kendall's offer to bring them home each day after school so Faith could get more time to work was a sacrifice for him too. Plopping onto the seat, Faith let her ponytail drop against the headrest. She breathed out a stale sigh.

"I take it you didn't know about Hawaii." Kendall turned to face her.

"Two weeks. That's what I was told. They'd have the *wedding*, then the girls could spend some time with Neil's parents. They don't get to the mainland very often anymore, and the girls miss them. Maybe there was a miscommunication."

The gentle touch of Kendall's fingers on her arm nearly undid her. Faith let her head loll to the side. There was no mistake. Neil was being Neil, all *I'm in charge here* Enneagram eight, and not a healthy eight. Neil only knew one way—his way—and everyone was expected to move over and let him by. But Faith didn't have to bend to his wishes anymore. That was for Wendy to deal with.

"I'd love to give that man a few of my thoughts." Kendall's lips formed tight lines.

"It wouldn't do any good. He hears what he wants to hear and tosses the rest." Faith patted the package on her lap. "And he's free to do almost anything he wants. The kids are the only area he can't control, so he pulls stuff like this, getting them all excited so I'm the bad guy by saying no."

"The girls will get over it. You're the one who's steady in their lives. You've never let them down."

"They're teenagers, or nearly. We're in the midst of the Mom-ruins-everything stage. And don't forget, he's marrying an attorney. He's reminded me a hundred times how lucky I am that I have joint custody." She shrugged. "Listen, I don't want to be one of those moms who talks bad about my kids' father. He's a good dad, and he loves the girls. I'm glad he wants them around, even as he starts his new family. None of this is their fault, and they shouldn't be punished for our problems."

Kendall rubbed the back of her neck. "You are a far better woman than I am."

If her thoughts were out on display, Faith doubted anyone would see her as holy. How could he take this away from her without a discussion? Harlow and Ava were her kids too. He had no right to give them fantasy-worthy hopes for a summer full of adventures that she couldn't dream to produce for her children. Neil knew better than anyone else that eventually she'd crack.

"Mom." Ava hung out the front door. "I'm starving."

Faith must have checked her Fitbit a thousand times throughout the evening while time ticked away like it was struggling through waist-high tar. After the final plate was stacked in the dishwasher and it hummed with spraying water, she went down the hall, listening at each of her girls' bedroom doors.

Ava stomped around all evening, as if her preteen power play would get her the results she was after, while her sister had taken to her room as soon as she could get away. Both reactions were like punches to Faith's heart. She hadn't chosen the divorce, but there were plenty of things she'd said and done along the way that had served to hurt her kids. Touching their doors, she said a silent prayer for peace, especially for the call she was about to make to Neil.

But when she unlocked her phone, there were four missed

calls—from him. She wrinkled her brow. Once again, she'd forgotten to unmute after finishing a podcast recording session. The last few weeks had been crazy, with Faith trying so hard to get extra episodes researched and ready to air so she'd have the summer to focus on her girls.

Grabbing the stack of mail from the counter, she stepped into the garage. She dropped the envelopes on the washer and plugged in her earbuds, stuffing one in her ear so hard, she felt the air pressure push against her eardrum.

Before she could tap his name in her contacts, the phone buzzed. It was Neil. Great. He even got the prize for making the first move.

"Hello." Her voice was flat. She wouldn't scream at him, but she certainly wouldn't let him off easy either.

"About time."

"Excuse me?" Faith flung the dryer open, the hinges screaming out their abuse.

"Be careful with that machine. It will cost a fortune to fix it."

Her jaw throbbed with the tension. "I don't see how that's any of your business."

"You're right. I'm sorry."

Faith searched her mind for a smart comeback, but he'd silenced her with these words so foreign from his vocabulary.

He cleared his throat. "Listen. I wanted to call and apologize. Wendy thought we'd talked when she mentioned the summer plans to the girls."

"I was fine with two weeks. Why do you need to have them all summer? Neil, that's a long time." Loneliness seeped into her bones even now, weeks before the scheduled departure.

"It's my dad. He's not doing well. He's got cancer in his bones, Faith."

"I'm so sorry." Neil's dad was a dear man who, along with his wife, had welcomed Faith with open arms. The divorce had hurt them deeply too. She blinked back tears. "How is your mom?"

"She seems lost in all of it. Dad is refusing treatment. He just wants to spend his last days feeling the best he can and enjoying family."

Faith leaned onto the washing machine. The last statement hit her like a missile. A year ago, she'd been part of that family. Now, she was the only one not included. She tugged towels from the dryer and began folding. "What can I do?"

There was a long hesitation, followed by Neil clearing his throat. "You can let me take the girls for the summer."

It was her turn to pause, and she took it, folding three dish towels as she considered her response. Saying no to Neil, that was easy. She'd become a professional in that department. But his parents were a different story. When Neil moved out, it was his dad who called to see if she was okay. He'd continued to check in regularly, though the time between calls had been lengthening. Now she knew the true reason why, and it broke her heart. She pulled the last towel from the dryer. "Okay."

"Thank you. I really owe you one."

"Yes. You do. And I'll take that in the form of Thanksgiving and Christmas." Her fingers began sorting through the mail without thought to what she was doing.

"Faith."

"And I want regular communication with both girls through-out the time you're in Hawaii. This is my final and only offer." The first sense of control she'd had in a year felt like a warm wave over her skin. Neil had taken everything away. Now, he was taking her summer too. But she had made the choice to say yes on her terms and for reasons that felt right, not because it was what he wanted.

"You've got it. My dad will really appreciate this. I do too." The tenderness in his voice started to eat away at her anger.

She ripped open an envelope. "Give your parents my best."

They hung up, and she leaned against the washing machine, the letter still in her hand. What was she going to do with herself for three months on her own? How fast the time had gone from the days she would have done anything for even ten minutes alone.

Faith tugged the paper from the envelope.

Faith,

I don't know if you'll remember me. You were friends with my sister, Heather. I'm sure you recall that Heather went missing in September 1987. My family is in great need of closure for Heather's case. We need to see justice for what happened to her. While I know your podcast focuses on people who go on after tragedy to do remarkable things, I wonder if you'd consider looking into Heather's case without any of us qualifying as healed or doing remarkable things. I believe bringing attention to Heather again might be the catalyst to finding out what happened to her.

> *Thank you,*
> *Brooke (Crane) James*

A photograph was paperclipped to the back of the page. Three girls, one in her early teens and the other two at the final stages of girlhood, sat on a curb, ice cream cones melting in their hands. The girl in the middle was Faith.

Faith's father had been developing a neighborhood nearby prior to their next move. They'd spend the summer of 1987 with her dad's mother in the little town of Deep Valley, Oregon. Faith hadn't been back there since. Her grandmother was now in an assisted living facility an hour from the house she still owned, and before that, she'd come to visit them, rather than Faith and her mother making the trip.

Though Faith had nearly forgotten the details of that summer they'd lived with her grandmother, she hadn't misplaced the memory of Heather. They'd built a bond over those warm months, one she thought would follow them well into adulthood, but after Faith left, she'd never heard another word from her friend. Letter after letter was sent, but not a one came back until Faith had given in to the thought that Heather didn't want to be her friend any longer. It was Faith's first true introduction to rejection.

Wouldn't her parents have told her if something happened to Heather?

2

Heather

THEN

When Mrs. Ferdon called me across the street to her house, I assumed it was to complain about my brother's new muscle car. Greg thought he was all that, and he wanted the whole neighborhood to hear him coming and going, as if they would come out of their homes and cheer like he was the grand marshal of the Fourth of July parade.

My summer was already off to a boring start. My best friend, Amy, had gone off to Japan with her sister for the entire vacation, something to do with her dad's work. That left me, on the first day of freedom, walking alone to and from the IGA for a Big Hunk and grape soda.

I folded the crinkly wrapper over my candy and stuffed the remaining half into the pocket of my Bermuda shorts, then crossed to Mrs. Ferdon's yard.

"Well, don't you have the most perfect timing?" Mrs. Ferdon waved me up onto her porch.

I didn't know about that, but my mom would be expecting me home soon. And that was the timing I didn't want to mess with. "What can I do for you?" I figured she needed help with some kind of chore, seeing as how she was all alone since Mr. Ferdon's heart attack last fall.

"Faith."

I squinted up at her wrinkled face. Did she think I needed an extra Sunday school lesson? My fingers grazed the candy bar in my pocket, while the other hand clutched the pop can. I hoped it wasn't the gluttony talk. My mom was big on that one.

Then a girl stepped out of the house. She was taller than me, but most everyone I knew, even the kids a grade younger, had me by inches. Blond hair fell over her shoulders in waves, the kind that meant she wouldn't have an older sister after her all the time to get her look together.

My first reaction was to step back. I wasn't looking for a new friend. I still had Amy, even if she was in a different country, but then the girl smiled, and I felt like she might be okay after all.

Mrs. Ferdon put her hand on the girl's back and pushed her my way. "This is my granddaughter, Faith. She's here for the summer, and I thought the two of you could be friends."

My eyebrows did that thing that drove my mother crazy, jumping up and giving away my feelings. But I caught it quick and dropped them back into place. "Hi." I thrust out my hand. "I'm Heather. What grade are you in?"

"Going into fifth. How about you?" She looked down at the porch.

"Same here. Awesome. Do you want to hang out at my place?" I pointed down the road four houses. "It's the one with the flag in the front yard. I bet my mom will let us have popsicles."

I caught Mrs. Ferdon glancing at my pop, but it was only an hour or so past lunch. It wasn't like I was spoiling my dinner. Still, I lowered the can.

Faith's shoulders rose and fell, but I could tell she was the kind of girl who would be a lot of fun once we got away from the grown-ups.

I grabbed her hand and ran down the street, her footsteps thumping behind me. When we reached the corner, I dropped her hand and checked for cars. "Want to go to the swimming hole?"

She shrugged again, but I was up for the challenge. "Let's go tell my mom. You can borrow one of my sister's suits." Brooke would have a cow, but Mom was all about hospitality, and Mom's word ruled.

We ran through the door and to the back of the house where our kitchen was. Mom stood at the yellow Formica counter, scooping Cool Whip on top of a bowl of Jell-O. I hoped she'd turn toward the sink so I could sneak a taste out of the tub, but I didn't get lucky.

"Hello there. Who do you have with you, Heather?" It was her way of pointing out my failure to give proper introductions.

"Mom, this is Faith." I held my open hand out toward my new friend. "Faith, this is my mom, Mrs. Crane." I swept my palm toward my mom, knowing if I didn't do this right, she'd have me start again.

Mom wiped her hands on a checkered dish towel, then held one out. "Faith, it's so nice to meet you. Do you know Heather from school?"

"No. My family is staying with my grandma for the summer. She lives just down the road."

"Of course. I should have known. Mrs. Ferdon talks about you all the time. I understand you're quite the swimmer."

Faith's face flamed as red as Michael Jackson's jacket, but I couldn't have asked for a better setup. "We want to go down to the swimming hole, and since Faith is such a great swimmer, I didn't think you'd mind."

Mom's mouth tightened into a line. She wasn't one to let me

go too far without supervision, even if my older brother and sister had done this very thing at my age. Being the youngest could really be a bummer. "If you take Brooke with you, I think that would be fine."

I caught myself just before my eyes rolled. Mom did not tolerate faces. "Okay. But what if she says no?"

"Then have her come talk with me."

That was all I needed to forgive my mother for treating me like a baby. "Come on." I motioned for Faith to follow me and ran down the hall, my mother's voice trailing behind with a command to slow down.

Bursting through the door to the room I shared with Brooke, I caught her staring at a poster of George Michael, as if he'd ever give my sister a second look.

Brooke jumped off her bed, snapping a button on her boom box. "What are you doing? Don't you have any respect?"

I shrugged. "Hey, we want to go to the swimming hole, and Mom says you need to come too. Can Faith borrow one of your suits?"

She looked over like she'd just noticed my new friend standing in the doorway. "Whatever." Brooke yanked open her top drawer and flung a swimsuit at Faith. "Why do I have to go with you?"

Another shrug.

"Greg never has to babysit you. It's not fair."

I slipped off my shorts and started changing for the water. "Maybe because he has a job . . . and a life."

"You know what? You are so immature. Ah. I just wish you'd grow up already." She turned toward the door, no doubt to whine to Mom about having to take us.

Faith still stood there, clutching the borrowed suit.

"The bathroom is right there." Brooke pointed on her way by.

By the time Faith and I entered the kitchen, our towels rolled up and tucked under our arms, Brooke had given in.

Mom pulled three popsicles out of the freezer. I eyed the red one but knew better and offered Faith her pick first. Our friendship was confirmed when she chose the purple.

Brooke ripped the plastic off her orange treat, and we went outside.

We sat down on the curb to eat our popsicles, the heat burning my backside until I inched back to the narrow strip of grass. I'd missed this, hanging out with my sister. Until a year ago, we'd hung out all the time, but then, well, she got all boy crazy and obsessed with her hair and makeup. She didn't look anything like herself or the magazine models she tried to mimic.

By the time we got to the edge of the neighborhood where the path led through cut-back brush to the water, I was so hot I could have melted. I showed Faith the tree where we tucked our towels so they wouldn't get wet and muddy. The crashing sound of bikes going over roots and bumps took our attention away from the water. Mike, Brian, and Nathan, three boys from my grade, skidded to a stop just before the short cliff over the main swimming area.

I shook my head. Boys had to make everything loud and weird. "Come on, Faith, let's go." She had her arms wrapped around her middle like she was cold, but there was no way. Then I realized she was staring at Nathan. Just what I wasn't looking for, another girl in my life who only wanted to talk about boys. I ran toward the edge and jumped into the hot summer air, then splashed down into the chill of the cold mountain water.

3

Dora

NOW

Dora Crane pressed the button to close her garage door. It rumbled all the way to the cement while she stayed behind the wheel of her old car, its engine running. Beside her sat eight small Dairy Queen Blizzards, all of them M&M. Eight of them fit snuggly into two brown cardboard drink carriers.

Sometimes it was like this. Time froze harder than the ice cream, holding her tight into a place she didn't want to move forward from. It would be easier to sit here and let the last thirty-six years slip away. It's what she'd been wanting all this time, a chance to be whole again. No one understood. How could they? Dora didn't know another mother who lost what she'd lost, who hoped like she hoped, and who had to keep that candle in the window while everyone else moved on with their lives.

That's why she finally shut off the engine when the garage had filled with enough fumes to make her head ache. Someone had to be there, to be ready when the day came. Someone had to be waiting for Heather.

Inside, she placed the Blizzards in the freezer. Brooke and her family hadn't arrived yet. It wasn't surprising. They never arrived on time. It gave Dora an opportunity to start the spaghetti. It was Heather's favorite. Dora made it each year the exact way she had back then.

"Mom?"

Dora started, spinning around with a mustard yellow pot in one hand. "Brooke. I didn't hear you all arrive." The burner scratched as she pushed the pot into place. "Where are the kids? They're so quiet today." Dora's grandbabies were a light in a dark, dark world. They were another reason she didn't stay in the garage today or any of the other thousands of days before this one. "Sybil?" she called, stretching her neck to see into the living room.

"She's not here, Mom."

Dora reached into the refrigerator and retrieved the ground beef. She looked back at her daughter, taking note of Brooke's sudden need to examine her fingernails. "What do you mean she's not here?"

Beef sizzled as it hit the hot pan.

"I left her at home."

Alarms went off in Dora's chest. "Alone?"

"No. She's with Erik . . . and Charity and Connor. You know, your first two grandchildren." A sour note made its way into Brooke's tone.

"I'm very aware of who my grandchildren are, thank you very much. The question I have is, why aren't they here? This is a family event. We celebrate birthdays together."

Brooke anchored her fists into her sides the same way she had as a snotty teenager. "That's not true. Greg hasn't been here for one of Heather's birthdays since the first one Heather missed. But we're not supposed to talk about that. And we don't celebrate Grandma and Grandpa Crane's birthdays."

Dora cocked her head. "Don't be smart."

"Well, I'm just curious why we don't celebrate them every year."

"You know why." Dora slapped a spatula onto the hamburger. "Your grandparents are dead. We don't need to remember them every year. And your brother would be here if he could." Though she couldn't even force herself to believe Greg would have any desire to return for this tradition.

"Mom. We've been doing this for too long. It scares Sybil. I'm pretty sure it scares Connor and Charity too, but they don't feel like they can say anything." She stepped closer. "Heather isn't coming back. She's with Grandma and Grandpa. We need to let her go."

Dora's body filled with a hot pour of mother's rage. "Could you just let Sybil go? If she were to go missing, would you give up on her?" She crossed her arms tight across her chest, forming a barrier between them. "Of course you wouldn't, but that's what you all want me to do. And then what happens when Heather walks back in that door? Would you have her come home to a family that moved on like she was a fashion that went out of style?" Tears gathered on her lower lids. Their presence intensified her anger. "Heather is my child."

Paul entered the room, a man who should understand her pain better than anyone else, but his large hands instead settled on his daughter's shoulders. "What's going on in here?"

"Brooke refuses to celebrate her sister's birthday."

"I didn't say that." She leaned into her father. "Dad and I have talked about this. He understands. Why can't you?"

The scent of hamburger searing drew her attention. As Dora stirred the mess of beef, the feeling of abandonment by her family started another fire she had no way to control. She spoke without turning, without looking at the faces of the people who should be in this with her. "So, you're having little chats about your crazy mother behind her back. That's just great."

"It's not like that." Brooke's tone was breathless, so much like it had been as a teen, always wanting something else.

"You're free. Go home and be with your family. I don't need you here." She blinked away the tears, keeping her chin tucked, her emotions hidden. "And, Paul, why don't you go with her?"

"Mom, don't be like this. I want to stay for dinner." Brooke's hand reached for the spatula, but Dora flung it away, spraying grease across the backsplash. "We aren't trying to hurt you. Dad and I've been talking to someone, trying to understand your point of view."

"How dare you." Dora shoved the pot off the burner. She whirled, facing her betrayers. "What right do you two have to talk about me behind my back?"

"Whoa." Paul held up a hand. "I've asked you a hundred times to get counseling either on your own or with me. Brooke and I have both attended the grief class at the church more than once. We always ask you to join. You continually refuse."

"And that gives you the right to make me the topic of your discussion? I don't think so."

"Honey, it's not all about you. We need to live. Heather is gone. If she wasn't, we would have heard something during all of those years. You know I'm right about this. Heather wouldn't want us to throw our lives away because she . . . died."

"No. She's not dead. You don't know what you're talking about." Dora pushed past them and ran to the bedroom she'd shared with Paul until a couple months ago, when her husband had started sleeping in the room that had once been Greg's, then Brooke's. She twisted the lock, then fell into the unmade bed and let the tears flow. One of these days she'd cry herself dry.

At 11:32, Dora could take it no more. She eased off the bed, unlocked the door, and padded through the dark house. In the kitchen, she searched the refrigerator and found the spaghetti had been completed without her, obviously a work of Brooke's guilt. She served up a helping and placed it in the microwave. While that reheated, she pulled one of the many Blizzards from the freezer.

Dora took a candle out of the drawer and tried to stick it into the ice cream, but Paul insisted on having the freezer set to the coldest possible temperature, so the Blizzard was now as hard as the sidewalk.

A minute in the microwave alongside the spaghetti left the Blizzard melted along the edges and splattered with red sauce, but this would do. Dora couldn't let Heather's birthday go by without the tradition that had somehow become a ritual.

She set the food on the counter, pushed the candle in along the edge of the cup, and started the flame. In a low voice, she sang to her little girl. "Happy birthday, dear Heather. Happy birthday to you."

Somewhere out there, her child was turning forty-six. Did she know where home was? Did she remember her mother? Was it possible that Heather had children of her own?

Heather had never been the kind of girl who fussed over her baby dolls. That had been Brooke. Heather preferred to play in the dirt, climb trees, create using her imagination. Heather was the kind of person the world needed more of. How could someone take her away?

Brooke's words broke into Dora's thoughts.

There'd been a hundred times when she'd wondered for herself if it wouldn't be better for Heather to have died that night. At least Dora would know her daughter was at peace. But they didn't know. They couldn't say definitively that Heather wasn't out there somewhere. Children don't just disappear without a trace.

The spaghetti sat like a rock in her stomach, and the ice cream only made the feeling worse, but this was what she did each year, and she wouldn't stop until she had her baby back. Why couldn't the rest of the family understand that?

4

Faith

With the girls dropped off at school, all the unanswerable questions tumbled to the front of Faith's mind. If she could only call her mother, but the news of Heather's disappearance came three years too late.

She couldn't help the tendril of irritation pointed toward her mom—not that she had died, but that she'd abandon her own family years before to establish and run an orphanage in Guatemala. She'd only seen her granddaughters a handful of times. At least once a month, Faith had to check her jealousy and remind herself that the kids her mother had cared for deserved attention, love, and compassion, even if that came with the loss of the grandmother and mother she could have been here in the States.

Faith pulled into line at the coffee drive-through.

As a mother, she could almost understand the choice her parents made not to tell her about Heather's disappearance. Almost. If she put herself in that situation, she might be tempted to protect her daughters, but the truth would most definitely win out. It would be a betrayal to keep that kind of information from them. That's what Faith felt. Betrayed.

The line moved forward, and Faith drove closer to the window. As she waited, Faith pulled the photograph from her purse, staring into the eyes of the first girl who had been as close as a sister, even with their short time together. Circumstances had woven them tightly together in the swirl of impending changes, both physically and those outside of themselves.

Why hadn't she pushed her parents to let her make a phone call to Heather? Why hadn't she insisted on a visit to Grandma's, where she could run down the block and reconnect with her friend? Blame had a way of spreading out, covering anyone within reach of a tragedy.

That year, 1987, had been a series of storms in Faith's life. Until last night, she'd thought no one could understand the losses she had experienced that year. But she'd been unaware, completely unknowing, that Heather had been ripped away from her family. And her parents . . . it must have broken them not knowing where their child was, when or if she'd ever be in their arms again.

Just imagining the summer without Harlow and Ava nearly cut Faith in half, but they would be back. Neil may not be her favorite person, but he did love his daughters, and he'd do anything to keep them safe.

Her turn arrived without Faith giving a thought to her coffee order, as if she'd stray from her regular choice. "Half-sweet salted caramel latte, please. Sixteen ounces."

"Mrs. Byrne. How are you?"

Faith's gaze swung up to the window. "Camy, I didn't see you there. I'm so sorry."

"No worries. You looked lost in your thoughts."

Faith passed her phone out the window to be scanned. "You caught me."

In a flourishing movement, the young woman waved her hand through the air, a sparkling diamond ring glittering in the sunlight.

"Is that what I think it is?"

"Tucker finally asked me. We're getting married at the end of summer. I hope you and your family can be there."

Faith swallowed down the sourness that flavored her mouth any time someone mentioned her *family*. Did Camy even know that Neil had left, that he was himself planning a wedding—with another woman? "I wouldn't miss it."

Another girl leaned through the window, handing Faith her coffee.

"Thank you. I'll see you all soon." She shifted the car into drive and didn't look back.

By the time she pulled into the driveway, her hands shook and her coffee was still untouched. She sat there, taking turns sipping the lukewarm drink and practicing deep yoga breathing.

The letter from Brooke Crane seemed both unreal and urgent all at once, a tug-of-war between her past and reality. And in the middle sat a giant lake of quicksand able to pull her under.

Faith had left her career as a television news reporter when the girls were little. Getting up before dawn each day to report on murders and other violent crimes had cut through her ability to enjoy the magical days of early childhood with her kids, instead replacing it with fears and obsessions. It wasn't until Neil announced his intention to leave that she even wondered about going back to the stress-filled days that came along with the steady paycheck.

It was Kendall's idea to launch the podcast, *What Happens Next*, as a way for Faith to use her journalistic skills to highlight the great endurance of the human spirit. Week after week, she shined a light on stories of resiliency, on people who found a way to go on even though they faced devastating situations, making positive impacts on the world.

There had to be some kind of redemption lurking in the

event and the consequences of Heather's disappearance. Hearing those thoughts in her head was enough to make Faith want to ditch the podcasting life permanently. How could anything good come out of losing a child? It couldn't. Faith hadn't even managed to spin a positive for her daughters being gone for the summer—and she knew with whom and where they'd be.

The letter felt as though there was urgency tied to the words, but in fact, Faith was under no obligation to get back to Brooke soon, or at all. She could take some time to look into the case and see if there was a story she could tell to bring attention to Heather's disappearance while not abandoning the promise she made to her audience each week.

What Happens Next wasn't a true crime show, at least not in the traditional sense. Her listeners expected stories of hope and healing, of people who fought through loss to come out stronger and still maintaining compassion and wholeness.

Brooke's own words clarified the point. This wasn't a success story.

A week wasted away with Faith staying focused on her production schedule. There was no real need to rush through now that Harlow and Ava wouldn't be home for summer vacation, but once she had tasks on the calendar—well, they needed to be checked off. Her Enneagram was a three. A solid and unshakable, needs-to-make-the-list-and-finish-it kind of three.

The last episode she'd recorded was the story of a girl, Shelby, who survived a house fire that killed her parents and twin baby brothers. With no suitable family member to take her in, she went to live with her pastor and his wife, a couple whose children had long since grown and moved out on their own. Shelby became their pride and joy and was treasured by her new, much-older siblings. But the amazing piece of her story was the career Shelby had chosen. She was a firefighter. Each day, she was prepared to step into the grabbing arms of the thing that took her family from her.

Faith had gone into this episode hesitant and unsure if it would make the final cut. That all changed when she interviewed Shelby over Zoom. There was no self-punishment in her career choice, no survivor's guilt ruling her thoughts and dreams. Shelby knew she remained on earth for a purpose, and she felt this was a piece of that design.

What kind of purpose could Faith be a part of? The question had sat on her shoulders, growing heavier with each passing week that Neil moved on without her. It was like his steps took away the plan her day-to-day purpose depended on. Every year from then on was open. All the goals and expectations for the rest of her life had been scratched out, leaving vacancies where she'd scribbled her life's carefully chosen paths.

Rage stepped into Faith's path as her thoughts walked straight into questions neither of her parents were here to answer. How could they have let her cry herself to sleep over a rejection that had never happened?

An image overcame the anger as it flashed in her mind. That had been the summer her mother was far along in her pregnancy, the long-wanted baby they'd all wished for finally coming to join their family. Mom had been sick, on bed rest most of the time they'd stayed with Grandma Ferdon.

Faith opened her planner to a new goal sheet. She sketched out a strategy, starting with initial questions for Brooke and the online searches she'd need to do to get a better idea of what had happened and what was already known.

Her toes were curved over the diving board, in the ready position to take the plunge, but the real action would only take place when she made the call to Brooke, committing to her sister's case. Grief, disappointment, and regret waited for her entry, but maybe there'd be healing in the depths too. Healing for a family who'd shown her all the kindness a ten-year-old girl could have hoped for.

There was a feeling of doing something wrong that took over when Faith typed the names of Crane family members into her Google search bar. With all the other cases she'd shared with her listeners, she'd felt a surge of power as she dug into the internet mine of information. But she hadn't known any of those people. She hadn't slept in their backyards, eaten with them at dinnertime, or gone to church with them.

Before she could look directly into the case, she wanted to know a bit about where the family was today. Had Heather's older brother, she couldn't remember his name, gone to college like the family planned? Had Mr. Crane's work at the lumber mill resumed a normal schedule? What about Mrs. Crane? Did she remain employed as a receptionist or return to the life of a stay-at-home mom?

Faith leaned back in her office chair, the hinges squawking for a drink of WD-40. What had Mrs. Crane's first name been? She could almost hear it spoken between her parents. Daphney? Donna? No, it was Dora. She remembered with a jolt how she'd thought of Heather's mother when her own girls discovered *Dora the Explorer.*

A Google search for Dora Crane of Deep Valley, Oregon, popped up with a list of results, the top two being advertisements for information about Heather.

But the image that stared blankly from the screen was a shadow of the woman who had seemed like the perfect mother all those years ago. Dark circles and the loss of weight and youth made her eyes appear sunken and dull. The style of her hair hadn't changed from 1987, but the color was salt-and-pepper rather than shiny mahogany.

The cat jumped onto the keyboard, sending the article spinning upward.

"Crouton, you nearly gave me a heart attack."

He meowed and plopped his oversized body onto the desk.

Faith printed out a flyer with information about the case and an age-progressed photo of Heather, pulled a clean file from the shelf, and tossed it in. This ritual was something she did with every case she'd worked on, but none had the personal consequence of Heather's case.

Why hadn't she been told about her friend's disappearance? Wasn't that the kind of thing you shared with your child, no matter how hard it would be? Even Grandma had never uttered a word about it.

Faith slapped the file against the edge of her desk. She must have asked her grandmother about Heather and the rest of the Cranes, but she couldn't remember. The more she tried to retrieve the memories, the further they seemed to slip. Grandma had started visiting them in their new home rather than the family going to her. Faith had tied everything to the death of her father later that year, but maybe there'd been more.

Grandma Ferdon had moved into an assisted living center four years earlier to be with her sister. Though her mental acuity remained intact, Grandma's body was slowly becoming less stable, even if she adamantly denied it. At least once a month, Faith brewed a cup of tea, curled up on her sofa, and gave her grandmother a call. Grandma Ferdon would go on for an hour about the church she attended with friends she'd made in her community. She kept Faith up-to-date on the Skip-Bo tournament standings and the latest from the one soap opera she'd remained loyal to for fifty years.

Two or three times a year, Faith made the drive to see her grandmother in person, but she never drove on to Deep Valley. The rejection she'd felt from Heather had cut deeper than Faith ever acknowledged. How could she ever reconcile her childish disappointment with what had really broken their friendship apart?

In her bedroom, Faith opened her jewelry box. She didn't own anything of value. Even her wedding and engagement rings had been sold to pay her attorney. She dragged a finger along the back compartment, hooking a thin chain and pulling it toward her. Emotion crowded her throat as she looked down at her palm, at the half-heart friendship necklace. Heather had the other half. She'd considered throwing it out once or twice, but something always stopped her.

Faith owed it to Heather for so easily assuming her friend didn't care, that she was self-absorbed and couldn't be bothered with a mess like Faith. She'd pay back that debt by doing whatever she could to bring Heather home.

5

Dora

Dora placed the flyer in a box and covered it with the lid. She looked around the house, so empty now that Paul had moved from their spare bedroom to an apartment downtown. One by one, the family was abandoning her, leaving her alone to keep up the fight. Greg never had returned after college, instead moving around the country doing field research and rarely coming home for a visit.

Three raps on the door, then the squeak of the hinges. Always the same when Brooke came by. "Mom?"

"I'm in the dining room." Dora rubbed at the tension at her temples. Paul must have told her about the separation by now. They were close, probably the only two people in the family who still were.

"Hey." Brooke dropped her bag into a chair. "I was wondering if you were available for lunch. I thought we could try the new Thai place on Seventh Street."

"Don't forget the children who are still here." Paul's words as he left. He hadn't yelled them, Paul never yelled. Even so, each syllable stung. "Okay. Let me get my purse."

Brooke's eyes were round, as if she'd never expected a yes.

When was the last time they'd gone out to lunch together? Dora couldn't remember. Had it really been so long? What young people didn't seem to understand was the speed at which life flew by. In a minute, years were gone, yet every night since Paul had left seemed to drag on for an eternity.

They decided to take separate cars, Brooke needing to return to her work as a dental hygienist and Dora wanting to stop at the grocery store after lunch.

The inside of the restaurant smelled of curry and all the exotic places Dora and Paul once planned to visit when they were old empty nesters. As it turned out, seventy didn't feel as old as they thought it would, she and Paul wouldn't be going anywhere together, and life had succeeded at crushing all those dreams.

"Mrs. Crane? Is that you?" The voice was still familiar though matured, where the face was like that of a stranger. "It's Amy. You probably don't remember me. I was a friend of Heather's." A quick shadow crossed her face.

"Oh my." Dora leaned forward, peering into Amy's eyes, where she could see glimpses of the child she'd known. She had been Heather's best friend. Her family had been in Japan that last summer, which ended up turning into a permanent situation. Heather had never known about the move. That news came after she was gone. "I didn't know you were back in Deep Valley."

"I am. My husband and I own this restaurant. We inherited my grandparents' farm and thought this would be a fun new adventure."

Dora gave her daughter a quick glance. Had Brooke known about Amy before the invitation? "Well, it's so good to have you here. And we always welcome a new restaurant."

Amy dropped menus in front of them. "One of our servers will be right with you. I really hope you enjoy your meal."

"I'm sure we will, thank you," said Brooke.

When Amy left, Dora lowered her menu. "Did you know she was back in town?"

She shook her head. "Not a clue. I hope that's going to be okay."

"Why wouldn't it be? She has the right to live here as much as anyone else." Even as the words were leaving her mouth, she wanted to draw them back. Not everyone. The person who abducted her baby didn't have that right.

For months after Heather disappeared, mothers all over Deep Valley kept vigilant watch over their children. Then, slowly, they returned to normal living, as if once again they were insulated from horrible dangers.

Brooke shrugged. "I just thought it might be hard, seeing as how she and Heather had been such good friends."

Something was up. One thing was always true with Brooke and her father—they didn't bring up Heather's name. Instead, they did whatever necessary to act as though she'd never existed.

Dora skimmed the menu and decided on basil chicken with green beans, an easy decision. "Okay. What's going on?"

Brooke looked up, then set her menu aside. "What do you mean?"

"I know you. You're up to something. Why don't we just get it out in the open. I assume you've talked to your father."

"I have." Lines stretched out from the edges of Brooke's eyes. When had those appeared?

"Can I get you anything to drink?" A girl who had to be right out of high school came up to the table, staring down at them with a grin so perky it made Dora cringe.

"I'd love a Diet Coke. And I'll take the basil chicken with green beans." No need for waiting. This lunch had a strong whiff of awkwardness already.

Brooke rattled off her own order, and the girl left.

"So, you were about to tell me what's really up." Dora clasped her hands below the table.

"It's not like that." Brooke pulled her cell phone out of her bag and set it between them, as if she were about to record their conversation. "Have you ever heard of the podcast *What Happens Next?*"

"What's a podcast?"

"You know. Shows you can listen to through your phone. Dad listens to about a hundred basketball podcasts."

She waved her hand. "No. I would have noticed him listening to his phone. The man can't hear anymore. He'd have it blasting like he does the television."

Brooke made a few swipes on the screen. "His phone connects to his hearing aids through Bluetooth. He's almost always got one playing."

Well, that answered a lot of questions. She'd been afraid he was losing his mind, not that it was any of her business now. "Does your dad listen to this story show?"

"He's never mentioned it, but I plan to tell him about it too."

Dora sat back, crossing her arms. "Oh, so you came to me first. Huh. I guess I should feel honored."

Brooke held the phone in front of Dora's face.

"Is that . . . No."

"It is. That's Faith Byrne, used to be Ferdon. *What Happens Next* is her podcast."

"She never seemed like the kind of girl who'd be into sports."

Brooke took the phone back, her face showing her confusion until a sudden lightbulb effect took over. "No. Mom, not all podcasts are about sports. They're about everything. You can learn about the economy, politics, religion, even true crime. It's a smorgasbord of all the things you're not supposed to talk about in polite company, plus more."

"I don't understand. Are you trying to find me a new hobby?" Of course. Brooke was known for trying to distract her into moving on. "I'm doing just fine, Brooke. You don't need to worry about me."

"Here we go, ladies." The girl, who at second glance must still be in school, set hot plates of food in front of them. "Let me know if I can get you anything else."

"Thank you." Dora sipped her Diet Coke. "I think we're good."

"I'm not any more worried about you than usual, Mom." Brooke scooped red curry chicken over a mound of rice. "I've been listening to Faith's show. She tells stories of tragedy, then gives these hope-filled updates on where the people are now. It's inspiring, and it's become very popular."

Dora's fork stopped just before her lips. "You aren't suggesting we be on this podshow, are you?"

Brooke had made great strides when it came to controlling her eyerolls, but a mom could still tell. "I'm *suggesting* that Faith could look into Heather's case."

"Is she a detective of some form?"

"No. She's more like an investigative reporter. Her show gets thousands of downloads every day. She's influential."

"What are you talking about?"

"Mom, we've got to get you into this century. Do you ever feel like your life pressed pause when Heather disappeared?"

Brooke brought up that awful day as if it were any other. To Dora, it was like calling up a curse. "What's your point, Brooke?"

"I want to make a deal with you. If I can get Faith to come out and do a thorough investigation, getting national attention on Heather's case, you will agree to attend a twelve-week grief therapy group at my church and clean out Heather's room." She held up a hand. "I know I'm asking a lot, but Faith is the best chance we have of finding the truth before it's too late."

Dora dropped the fork holding a green bean back onto her plate. "Don't be ridiculous. I do not need a grief class."

"There's nothing ridiculous about it. Dad and I have both gone through this program. Mom, it helps."

"I've told you a thousand times that I don't need to spend time with a bunch of people mourning their dead family members. You and your dad may have counted Heather out, but I haven't."

"It's not just bereavement they talk about, it's grief. Grief can be about all sorts of things. You can grieve for a relationship that's lost, a marriage even." Brooke's words grew quiet, as if she were realizing what she was saying as the words settled into the space between them. "You know what I mean. It doesn't have to be about death."

"Fine. I'll take your class, but only if Faith comes here to Deep Valley and tells the entire story."

Brooke bit at her bottom lip. "It's a deal."

As far as Dora could tell, the girl hadn't been back since the summer she and Heather were inseparable. If she was as big a deal as Brooke seemed to think, she wouldn't pick up a case this old that had no silver lining.

6

Heather

Every year, the whole neighborhood came out to celebrate the beginning of summer with a block party. All us kids looked forward to it, like an official opening to our three months of freedom. My mom could be counted on to make her red, white, and blue Jell-O poke cake. Patriotic *and* delicious.

I ran in the house, breaking a ton of my mom's keep-the-house-in-order kinds of rules. "Mom. Mr. Hansen brought out the tables. Mrs. Hansen wants to know if you still have the tablecloth they used last year?"

She tipped her chin at me. "Of course I do. The thing wouldn't get up and walk away on its own, would it? It's on the shelf next to the dryer. Take it out to her, will you?"

I jogged down the steps into the basement, where the air was cool and still all year long. The red-and-white checkered plastic tablecloth was right where she'd said. I probably could have found it on my own. Mom had a place for everything, and everything was put back into its assigned place as soon as it was done being used. This thing would probably live on this shelf longer than I would be alive.

Tucking it under my arm, I ran up the stairs, stretching my legs to take two at a time.

"Slow down, Heather. There's no one chasing you." Mom stirred sugar into grape Kool-Aid, my favorite.

I grinned. "How do you know?"

"Because I go up and down those stairs a hundred times a day, and I never see anyone else using the washer and dryer."

Before she could give me a follow-up job, I headed for the street.

All around me, garage doors hummed and clanked up as dads drug out tables, some made from sawhorses and plywood. I jogged over to the Hansens and set the tablecloth next to Mrs. Hansen.

"Thank you, sweetie. Your mama must be proud of you. You've grown into a regular young woman."

I smiled, feeling a little awkward and also sure neither of my parents would agree. "Thank you, Mrs. Hansen."

"Hey, Rowdy, give me a hand with these chairs."

My shoulders did that tense shrug that happened when I was uncomfortable. It's not that I hated my dad's nickname for me, I just didn't care for him using it in public. I wasn't ashamed at all that I was considered a tomboy. The only one who seemed to be bothered by that was my sister. There's more to a person than what they like to do, I guess, but I still wanted people to see me as a girl . . . maybe even a kinda pretty girl.

"Rowdy?"

"I'm coming, Dad." My face tipped down, and I watched my feet skip over the lines in the sidewalk. I loved the way the yards came to perfect cliffs at the edges. It was a thing around our neighborhood. The dads made lawn maintenance into something like a competition. All but Mr. Potter. Ever since his wife died, he didn't seem to care about things like that so much. Mom and Dad had discussions sometimes about helping him out a bit, but Dad insisted it would be insulting to a man who was only just at retirement age. To me, Mr. Potter seemed ancient, a man on the verge of the end of his life.

"Took you long enough." Dad tapped the end of my nose like I was still a toddler. "Let's get these chairs set up along the curb."

I swiped my hand across the back of my neck, which was damp with sweat already. A glance across the way at Mrs. Ferdon's closed garage disappointed me. I thought for sure I could get Faith to help, and at least it would be fun if we were working together.

At the back of the garage, we'd stored enough metal folding chairs to start our own little church in the driveway. Dad had gotten a deal on them when some store downtown went out of business. He loved the opportunity to tell anyone about this find, as if he'd found a real treasure. Each time, I felt myself wanting to grow up a little less.

All around our block, voices began filling the air. Moms brought food out, as well as paper plates and napkins. Coolers were placed in the thin strip of grass along the road, some labeled *Pop* and others *Adult*.

As if God Himself was excited about the party, a breeze wove through the street, cooling my skin and giving me a burst of energy. "Can I go get Faith now?"

My dad ran a rag over the last chair. "Okay, but hurry back. There are a few more things to get done before it starts."

I nodded as I jogged down the road.

Mrs. Ferdon was opening the door as I came up the driveway. "Are you looking for Faith?"

"I sure am."

She hollered over her shoulder for her granddaughter.

I hadn't noticed before, but Mrs. Ferdon was really very pretty for an older lady. I wondered if she and Mr. Potter ever talked, them both being without a partner anymore. Maybe if Mr. Potter had a nice woman like Mrs. Ferdon to talk with, he'd get his energy back and edge his yard.

"Hey." Faith jumped off the porch into the yard. "I'm super excited about the block party." She wore a neon pink T-shirt with denim shorts, the kind of thing you could look cool in but still be able to have fun.

"Me too. This is the best part of the whole year." I gave my words a second thought. "Well, maybe not the best. We have another on the Fourth of July with tons of fireworks."

Faith's face lit up. "I love fireworks. We were in a place last year where they weren't allowed because of forest fires. I'm glad we're here for the summer."

"Where is your regular home?" I'd never been gone from Deep Valley longer than a week, if that. Vacations for our family were usually camping trips. My mom's parents passed away before I was born, and my dad's parents lived one town over. No reason to take long trips to see them.

Faith's answer was a grunt and a shrug.

"What do you mean?" I led her across the street to where my brother, Greg, was setting up a boom box for our father. "You have to be from somewhere."

"My dad builds these suburbs. We've been moving around with him since I was five. But it's possible we might get a house here in Deep Valley. My mom's having a baby, and she's had enough of all this moving around."

"I wish my mom would have another one. It's not so great being the youngest. Everyone in my family treats me like a little kid." I planted my hands on my sides.

"I'm sure it's not that bad. Your parents pay a lot of attention to you."

My head bobbed up and down. "I know. It's too much sometimes."

Music burst from the speakers, announcing it was four o'clock and the party was starting. It was a song by Madonna, one I really liked, but Mr. Crammer stomped over to his son and my brother, shaking a finger at them. A moment later, the tunes switched to some oldies station that the adults loved.

I took Faith's hand and dragged her toward the growing crowd. It was a free-for-all with delicious foods and yummy desserts, all while parents were too busy talking to pay any attention to how much pop you guzzled.

From a red cooler, I snagged an RC Cola, then held the lid while Faith rummaged through until she found a Squirt. We popped our cans open at the same time and tipped them back, letting the cold bubbles run down our throats. When I could take no more, I leaned forward, laughing, the fizz tickling my nose and watering my eyes.

Faith collapsed on the grass, laughing so hard she turned bright red.

I took a seat next to her. The Larsen boys were taking turns riding their big yellow Tonka truck down the slope of the driveway. One of them would be screaming bloody murder soon, but for now they were all squeals and giggles.

Our little neighborhood wasn't fancy or new, but I loved the way everyone seemed to really care for one another. I think it must have been like having a very large family with reunions and stuff like that.

Faith nudged me. "Here come my parents."

I followed her gaze to a man dressed in a pair of slacks and a polo shirt walking alongside a very short and embarrassingly pregnant woman. My first thought was how strange it really seemed that she was just finally having another kid, and that Faith's dad was not going to fit in with the other men if he didn't change out of those boots and dress clothes.

Something didn't make sense. If her dad was building neighborhoods, it seemed like they must be rich, like Donald Trump rich, but they were staying in the spare bedrooms at Mrs. Ferdon's house. I shrugged. Mom would tell me to mind my own beeswax, or maybe not to look a gift horse in the mouth. Whatever brought them to our street brought Faith too.

I turned to Faith. "Do you want to get another pop?"

She crossed her legs crisscross applesauce on the grass. "Let me finish burping this one."

We both cracked up.

That's about the time Brooke walked by with one of her I'm-too-cool friends. They both had headphones over their ginormous hairdos and were bobbing their heads to whatever played on their Walkmans. Huge neon earrings swung back and forth, and the stink of Love's Baby Soft was enough to make a dog gag. Seriously, I'd never understand how she could find me embarrassing.

"Hey, look." Faith pointed to where my parents were talking with hers.

"Let's go see what the parental units are up to." Just then a cap gun went off behind my head. I whipped around, the remaining odor clinging to the air. "Knock it off, Nathan." I waved my hand in front of my face and grabbed Faith's arm with the other one. "You are so immature."

I gave Faith an extra tug when I noticed her looking back at him. The guy was a jerk who just happened to have eyes like George Michael. He'd never change, and he wasn't worth our time.

"Come on, guys. I was just messing around." Nathan pocketed his pistol. "What are you doing?"

"We're going to see what our parents are talking about." Faith stalled and turned toward him.

"It's never good when parents talk to other parents. Mind if I tag along?"

I rolled my eyes. "Suit yourself."

Faith's dad stood three or four inches taller than mine. When he talked, he rubbed his palms back and forth against each other, making a friction noise that drew attention away from his words. "I'm looking for a woman to help out with office stuff at the building site." Faith's dad looked from my mother to my father, not seeming to even notice we were there. "You wouldn't know of anyone looking, would you?"

A strange look passed between my parents, ending with a resigned nod from my dad.

"I would be. If you think I could do what you're looking for." My mom seemed smaller than ever before, like she needed this, yet she'd never once mentioned working in front of me.

A million thoughts went through my head. Who would make my lunches? What about laundry? Honestly, I didn't know how to run the machine. And I was sure my dad didn't, even if he was around. Lately, there'd been a lot of days when the mill wasn't running, but he was still gone, working somewhere else I assumed.

I squeezed in between my parents, suddenly needing them on either side of me. They were warm, but in a way that felt like safety, like a favorite blanket.

"You must be Heather." Faith's dad looked down at me, as if evaluating my ability to be a decent friend to his daughter.

Mom gave me a slight push.

"Yes, sir. Nice to meet you."

"Nice to meet you as well." His gaze rose away from me back to my mom. "I'd love to talk to you about the position. I'm sure, being that you seem to run your home very well, that you'd be a perfect match for what I'm needing in the office." He pulled out his wallet and handed a small card to my mom. "Call me on Monday morning and we'll talk details."

She thanked him, then excused herself to get something from the kitchen.

I had the very strong feeling that something in my comfortable world was about to change.

7

Faith

Faith arranged a fresh ice pack against Harlow's jaw. The swelling from her wisdom tooth removal was already evident, but she made the wise decision to keep her observations to herself.

A knock at the door surprised her, but she didn't startle. Amazon would be delivering her upgraded microphone today. She swung the door open, but the face she was met with was not that of a delivery driver.

Time had made many kinds of changes in the woman who stood before Faith, but in her eyes, she could see the young teen. Heather's sister, Brooke. The shock sent Faith into a kind of fight, freeze, or flee response, her go-to being freeze even if she knew it did nothing to truly protect her. She could feel the minutes ticking by with the pounding rhythm of her heart as she stared at 1987, unable to look away.

"I'm sorry to show up like this." Brooke broke the connection by sweeping her gaze to her feet. "Please hear me out. Then I'll go. I promise."

Faith looked over her shoulder at Harlow, her face tingling as blood rushed toward her core in a mismatched effort to survive.

Harlow asked who was at the door in her mumbled, gauze-filled way, but Faith gave her a bright smile and looked away from her inquisitive daughter. This was the absolute worst time for a surprise visit from Brooke. Neil would be by to visit Harlow on his lunch break.

"How did you get here?" It was a stupid question, but those were the only words that were willing to leave her mouth.

Brooke looked back at her car pulled tight to the curb. "I tried to get here before your kids were out of school. I'm so sorry. I thought I might be able to catch you alone." She wiped a hand along the back of her neck.

The sun cooked Faith's face and the front of her chest. Seeing her was the sole reason Brooke had traveled to the suburbs of Portland. This woman wasn't going to give up easily.

"Mom?" Harlow tried again.

"It's a friend." Though the feeling coursing through Faith was more like an intruder had shown up for the attack.

"Can I come in? I've come a long way, and it's very hot out here. I won't take too much of your time."

Faith paused, evaluating the weather. "Okay. But follow me."

"Sure."

They passed Harlow on the couch, who offered a friendly yet still groggy wave, but Faith wasn't stopping for introductions. "Harlow, I'm going to talk with my friend while I get that soup going. Please text or holler if you need anything."

"You got it." She slurred as she scrolled through Netflix options.

In the kitchen, Faith turned sharply. "What are you thinking, coming to my house? If this were any other case, I'd have the police here." It wasn't anger that peppered her words. It was the reality of Heather's disappearance standing before her where she couldn't push the hurt and regret underground.

"I know. I'm sorry. I've invaded your privacy and I'm taking advantage of a long-lost friendship, but you have something I don't."

"What's that?"

"You can call attention to Heather's case. We need this to end. Can you imagine what it would be like if your daughter went missing and years—decades—went by without knowing what happened to her?" She tapped her fingers in a rhythm along her clavicle, producing a hollow thud deep in her chest. "I can tell you exactly what happens. I've watched it with my mother every day since September 17, 1987."

Faith pulled a barstool away from the counter and stepped back. "Have a seat. I'll make some tea, and we can talk while I get tonight's dinner going for my girls."

Brooke leaned onto the wooden seat. She didn't seem able to look away from Faith.

If Faith felt she could get away with it, she'd stare too. People from the past had a way of remaining unchanged in the memory. The undoing of the long-held image rattled her. Brooke had kind eyes, more curves than before, and the beginnings of gray highlights along her temples. She looked like the other mothers at Ava and Harlow's schools, the teen from 1987 long ago vanished.

Faith placed carrots, celery, and a red onion on the counter, then pressed her palms into the cold granite and took a deep breath. "I didn't know." She shrugged, as if that could dislodge the guilt that had been clawing at her skin since the moment she found out the truth. "I thought Heather rejected me when she didn't return my letters."

"You must have been shocked when you received my letter then."

"More than I can tell you." With the cutting board in the center, she started the task of chopping the celery. "I've done a bit of research into the case." She shivered as the coldness of cinching Heather's life down into four words had the same chilled effect on her as it must on Brooke. "I'll be honest." She stilled her knife. "I started by looking at where your lives are now. I'm sorry if that feels intrusive. Usually, I work on stories with happy endings despite the horrific traumas. I wouldn't even touch this if we didn't have a connection."

Brooke pulled her purse from the floor onto her lap, unzipping the pocket on the side and retrieving the small envelope. "I understand. And, really, I do know that I'm asking you to do something outside of your typical scope, but please." She slid a photo out and pushed it toward Faith. "Please try for Heather."

Wiping her hands on a kitchen towel, Faith's heart softened. She held the photo up, staring at it as if she could see the time long gone, feel the summer heat and hear Heather's voice again.

"This is the last photo of Heather before she was gone. I think that's the day you left."

The nod was barely there.

"She was so sad when you drove away." Brooke pulled her hair over one shoulder, twisting it into a rope. "I told her she should stop whining. That it wasn't like she'd never see you again."

"You couldn't have known." Faith covered her mouth with three fingers.

"True. But it doesn't stop the remorse. I wish I'd have done so many things differently that summer. I'm sure you remember. I was completely wrapped up in myself, wanting to be grown-up, seen. After she was gone, nothing else mattered." Brooke blinked rapidly until her tears were controlled.

Faith slid the photo back. "That was the best summer of my childhood. More and more of the little details have been returning to me since hearing from you." Peeling away the papery skin of the onion released the scent into the heavy air and added to the burn she already felt in her eyes.

They had that in common. When someone disappeared so

suddenly, the times you had, those moments that were supposed to be trivial, became lifelines to the one you loved.

Brooke tucked the photo back into the envelope. "These are copies. I brought them for you." She set the thin package near the coffee maker.

A sound from the front room broke the connection with the past.

Faith's hands stilled and her eyes narrowed. "That would be Neil."

"Your husband?"

"Ex."

"I'm sorry."

"I used to be too." She moved around the counter. "I'll be right back." She held up a hand, hoping Brooke would understand that she didn't want company.

In the living room, Neil sat on the couch with Harlow. Her eyes had sagged shut, and she breathed heavily. Neil had a balloon in one hand, while the other stroked hair off Harlow's face. It was sweet, but the hole he'd left was so filled with her disappointments and grief that there wasn't room for him to step back in. For a moment, she watched, in awe at the shift in her feelings. "Sorry, I guess she's still tired from the medications. You're welcome to come back this evening and try again."

Neil lifted the remote from Harlow's hand and switched to ESPN. "I still have time. I'd like to be here when she wakes up." He leaned into the couch cushion, as if he still had rights under this roof.

"Okay, then. I'm working on the girls' dinner and chatting with a friend. I'll be back in here soon." Faith's footsteps were heavier on her return to the kitchen. "Sorry about that. Harlow just had her wisdom teeth removed. I guess he's hanging out for a bit."

"That's got to be tough. I have three kids. A boy and two girls."

Faith cocked her head.

"Yes. Just like when I was a kid. Trust me, it wasn't planned that way."

"Are you married?"

Brooke's smile lit up her face. "To Erik. We met at church."

"Do you still go to the one on the corner by the park?" She sliced through the center of the onion, then stepped back, blinking.

"Dad and I do, and my family. Mom stopped about a month after Heather was gone. She said she couldn't stand one more person telling her they were praying. Oddly, I couldn't live without that assurance."

"Tell me, were there any leads, any suspects the police looked into?"

Brooke began the hair twisting again. "Mr. Potter was their prime suspect. They even searched his house with the entire neighborhood looking on. They didn't find anything but Heather's flannel shirt. He said she must have left it there when she was caring for his cat, but to the rest of town, that was as good as a conviction. He passed away a couple years ago. Not once did he waver from his story, but I don't know. I mean, if you're the kind of person who will abduct a kid, truth is probably not your biggest priority. Yet, he was always such a kind man. I don't remember ever feeling afraid of him. Shouldn't I have felt something if he was a monster?"

"Nothing really surprises me anymore, aside from your letter." She couldn't help but smile.

"I'm sorry about that. I didn't want to shock you, but," she shrugged, "maybe I did. I need you to do this for me. For Heather. I ran out of ideas years ago, but this . . . you . . . I feel like there's some hope here. Please."

The alarm on Brooke's phone sang out, breaking the moment. She swiped dismiss. "I've got to get going. It's a five-hour drive to get home."

"I can't believe you came this far. Thank you. Seeing you, it helped me understand." Faith reached across the table and laid her hand over Brooke's. "I'll do whatever I can to help. My girls are with their father this summer. So I'm all yours for three months."

It was a commitment, a solemn promise to do the impossible. Likely, all she would be able to give the Crane family was another disappointment, but if there was even the slightest chance that she could give something back to the family who'd shown her what love could look like, she had to make every effort.

The only choice Faith had was to walk Brooke right past Neil to exit the house. Making her go through the backyard or the garage would have been awkward and only lead her husband—ex-husband—to ask questions.

Brooke didn't linger with good-byes, but she did hesitate, for the flash of a second, as if she wasn't sure how to end their reunion. They fumbled around, landing on a stiff hug with limited contact.

Faith stood on the tiny three-by-three cement slab that served as the front porch and watched Brooke's car drive away until it disappeared around the corner. Life could change in an instant. Her marriage was tough, but she'd believed they were both committed until the minute Neil said he was moving out. Heather was a happy ten-year-old with a great family, then she was gone.

In the living room, she found Neil, shoes off, nestled onto the couch with Harlow's feet on his lap. The two of them stared at the television where a superhero movie now played, as if nothing had changed. As if that was still Neil's spot on the couch and he hadn't reached into her chest, torn out her heart, and tossed it in the trash.

As though her gaze had weight, he turned to her. His spine straightened, and he rubbed his index finger across his chin like he'd always done when he felt trapped. It gave her a bit of a thrill to see him squirm until she saw the effect this had on Harlow. Her daughter had felt the tension that came in like a gust whenever she and Neil were together. It wasn't planned or purposeful, but it was there, destroying the peace of their home.

With care, he moved Harlow's feet from his lap and kissed the top of her head. Neil was an amazing father who loved his girls without condition and treated them with deep affection. She was the one who made them clean their rooms, eat a healthy dinner, and refused to let them take their phones into their rooms at night. She couldn't compete with him.

Ava's words from weeks earlier still clung to her. *"Why do you have to be so mean all the time?"* After they spent the summer in Hawaii with their dad and his parents, the girls would have nothing but disgust left for the real life that meant chores, school, and household rules.

Neil stood and motioned toward the kitchen, like this was still his home and he was paying the mortgage each month. Once there, he pulled out a barstool for her to sit. Instead, she rounded behind him and took a position leaning against the stove, her arms folded across her chest.

"Who was that?"

"What do you mean?"

"The woman who just left. Who is she?" The volume of his words rose.

"Hush. Harlow doesn't need to think we're in here arguing." She squeezed her fingernails into her palm.

"If you'll answer my question, we won't have anything to argue about."

Prickles poked along the back of her neck. "I don't see why that's any of your business."

"It's my business when people come in contact with my girls."

The look on his face made her wonder what she'd ever found so attractive about this man. Deep lines formed between his bushy eyebrows, and the bit of stubble he carefully maintained had begun to look less rugged and more like a middle-aged man in serious need of a shower. "Hmm. I believe that who comes and goes from *my* house is no longer any of your concern. You made that perfectly clear when you divorced me."

"Cute, Faith, but you know what I mean. I didn't divorce the girls, just you."

She held herself upright, not allowing him to see how the words pierced her. "Say what you need to say so you can leave." The fire had burned out of her words, leaving them flat.

"I heard some of your conversation with that woman. She's one of your podcast people, isn't she?"

"What if she is?"

"I won't have dangerous people near my kids."

"Have you ever even listened to my show?"

His lip lifted in a condescending sneer. "That's not the point."

"I think it is. You clearly have no idea what *kind* of people I profile." Brooke wasn't like any of the guests she'd had on the show, but there was no need to feed Neil's righteous anger. "That woman happens to be an old friend of mine. I haven't seen her in years."

"And that's why you were talking about evidence and case research?"

"Oh my goodness. How long were you eavesdropping? Did you stand in the hall, hoping to catch some juicy news you could use against me? If that's the case, I think you've given me plenty on you at the same time. Neil, if you wanted so badly to be in my business, you never should have walked away from our marriage." She stomped right up to him. "It's time for you to leave." Her left arm shot up, finger pointing the way toward the front door.

"I've tried to make this friendly. You just remember that."

Even in their worst fights, he'd never looked at her with such deep disregard. Despite her commitment to stand firm, he scared her. Not because he would ever hurt her physically. But because he had the power to take her children.

When he was finally out the door, Faith took the place he'd vacated on the couch. She breathed purposefully, letting the tension ease with her exhales.

As if he could sense her relaxing, Faith's phone buzzed with a text from Neil. She pushed herself off the couch with more effort than it should take a woman in her midforties and didn't read it until she was in the kitchen.

> I want to be clear. I will go back to court and
> take full custody of the girls if you put them in
> any kind of danger.

Faith clicked away on her phone, not in response, but to forward this threat to Kendall. They had an agreement. Any time she received a text or email from Neil that made her want to scream, she'd let Kendall read it first and wait until they talked before responding with emotion. This plan had saved her so many times already that she didn't hesitate to follow it again.

Another ding. Kendall.

> He's trying to scare you and to control you.
> Does he have any reason to say the girls are in
> danger?

He didn't, did he? But Brooke had found her address without any trouble, come right to the house. Many of her podcast subjects had been harmed deeply in violent ways. Most of the perpetrators were in prison or dead, but not all. What if one of these times she called too much attention to someone who didn't want to be named? She didn't even have a security system. She couldn't afford one.

> I don't think so, but I can't predict everything. What if he's right?

> Coffee tomorrow morning. My treat. I'll meet you there at nine, k? We'll talk this whole thing out.

> Thank you.

Kendall was her lifeline, a friend in all circumstances. But even a friend as wonderful as Kendall couldn't fix all the hurts and anticipate the ones to come.

Only a couple precious weeks remained before Ava and Harlow were off for a summer in paradise with their father. She had to keep believing that this was going to be fine, that Neil was blowing off steam and stress. He couldn't really be considering taking the girls. His schedule was crazy half of the year, and he'd be a newlywed. The brand-new husband of someone else. Someone he enjoyed being with, who he found attractive.

A new attractive wife who just happened to be a powerful and well-known family law attorney.

If it came to her job or her children, she'd pick the girls every time. She'd spend the summer doing whatever she could to find Heather and bring her back to her family one way or another. But when August came to an end, so did the podcasting, the research, and the risk. Faith would take whatever job she could find to pay the bills. Her dreams could wait until Ava's eighteenth birthday.

8

Heather

Faith and I had a slumber party that night in our backyard. Dad helped us make a lean-to, which was supposed to keep the dew from covering us some time in the early morning. We rolled around in our sleeping bags, laughing about all the teenagers who thought they were so cool and grown-up at the block party. My sister, Brooke, was one of the very worst. I couldn't believe how she snubbed us and acted like she didn't have a brain in her skull when she talked to that boy in the pink polo shirt. I made Faith promise to punch me if I ever got that stuck-up.

Sometime after all the neighbors' lights had been turned off and Faith was sound asleep, I felt the uncomfortable need to use the bathroom. I'd lost count of how many pops I'd managed to chug before my mom caught us sloshing around, and I may have snuck another couple into the backyard.

I lay there, trying to make myself fall asleep and forget about needing to go, then suddenly I had the worst thought. What if I wet my sleeping bag? Faith would surely ditch me if I was a bedwetter at the age of ten. I couldn't take that kind of chance.

I flopped a leg out of the open zipper. The night was cold, a shock after the heat of the day. In bare feet and summer pajamas, I jogged across the yard, with the moonlight giving enough light to keep me from stepping on something gross like a slug.

When I got really close to the steps leading to the sliding glass door, I heard my parents' voices. Their bedroom window was just above my head. I knew better than to listen in, but that rarely stopped me. Parents didn't talk about anything that mattered when kids were around, even ones who were no longer babies.

My dad wasn't doing much of the talking, which usually meant he was too mad to speak, but Mom was a nonstop ramble of words.

"You know we need the money. You've done a great job supporting our family, and none of this is your fault. The kids aren't small anymore. I really want to do this."

"What are people going to think if you go off working for that guy?"

"They'll think I'm helping my family. The lumber mill shutdowns are no surprise around here. It's affecting everyone. Do you think we're the only house on the block wondering how we're going to help our kid with tuition and still feed the other two?"

Silence dragged on so long I started to wonder if I'd been caught, but then my mom spoke in a hushed tone. "It's not forever."

"He said they'd be done in four months, right?"

"That's right. It's really just the summer. By the time my job is finished, your work will be running consistently again."

"But you know you don't have to do this. I'm taking on odd jobs wherever I can."

"I know. I really want to."

"Okay."

I listened a while longer, in case there was more, but soon my dad began to snore like a chainsaw. My bladder couldn't wait another minute, so I snuck inside as quietly as possible and took care of the immediate issue.

Back in the lean-to, I thought over what I'd heard. I'd had no idea we had money trouble. It wasn't something we talked about at the dinner table. The issue with the mills laying off workers wasn't anything new, but having a brother leaving for college soon was. My dad had always taken extra jobs doing things like cutting firewood in the mountains that he would sell and deliver. Lately, he had been doing more than usual, but I thought he was just helping people out.

I couldn't believe it. My mom was really going to take a job outside of our home. She hadn't been gone a day in my life, in any of us kids' lives. I wondered how much I'd taken her for granted.

Peeking out from under the tarp, I watched the stars twinkling above me. When I caught sight of a shooting star, I made a wish that I'd remember the things my parents were always telling me, like to turn off the lights when I left the room and to not stare into an open refrigerator. Then, I asked God to make everything turn out okay.

9

Dora

Dora had no intention of clearing out Heather's room. There wasn't a reason for it. She was living alone in a three-bedroom house, a woman left by everyone who was supposed to love her. Why should it matter to anyone that she kept Heather's belongings just how she'd left them?

When it had become clear to the police that Heather wasn't messing around at a friend's house and had forgotten to tell her parents, they'd searched the room. Dora still didn't understand what they thought they'd find in there. Heather was a little girl. She wasn't part of some crime syndicate that was exacting revenge for a heist gone wrong.

Maybe if Paul hadn't given up on their marriage and their youngest daughter, then she'd be able to go through Heather's things. It was his fault. He'd left her behind in this home, with only her memories of Heather to keep her company.

If she couldn't pack up Heather's things, she knew what she could do. She'd collect Paul's things and give him what he clearly wanted—his freedom. Everything in this house that was his needed to find a new home too.

Dora flipped on the television for company while she decided what to get rid of first. The news was playing a story about another cold case solved with the use of DNA science. How wonderful for them. She really did mean it, even though it felt like Heather's disappearance continued to move farther and farther down the growing mountain of old crimes.

She'd learned a few tricks over the years, one of which was to stay busy when the grief tried to worm its way in. She took five paper bags from the gap between the wall and the refrigerator and went into Paul's room.

Dora flung the top drawer open so hard it nearly jumped off its runners. She yanked out Paul's socks, dumping them into a bag until she reached the bottom of the drawer. A worn construction paper card lay against the wood. On the front was a child's drawing of a giant man and a little girl. They held hands.

Her fingers trembled as Dora picked up the fragile gift. She opened it to find Heather's kindergarten handwriting. "I love you, Daddy, and Jesus loves all of us." Only about three of the words were spelled correctly and the sentence crawled up and down an invisible hill, but it was perfect.

Heather and Paul had such a connection. How could he let her go?

10

Faith

Coffee with Kendall provided a nice caffeine boost, along with a plan of action. Faith would hold off on her decision about ending the podcast until the completion of the summer. She'd give her all for the three months the girls were gone to Hawaii, doing whatever she could to raise awareness of Heather's disappearance and hopefully finding answers.

Faith took her own road trip, but she didn't go as far south as Brooke had come north. Instead, she stopped at Sparrow's Nest Retirement Village, a quaint little community nestled into the base of the Cascade Mountains. While it wasn't fancy, Sparrow's Nest managed to create its own sort of town here, with a barber shop, a tiny grocery, a park, and trails. Care here started at the level of complete independent living in small cottages that dotted the edge of an expanse of deep green grass. In the larger building, residents could move up to levels of assisted living, nursing care, and memory care.

Her grandmother lived in the first sprawling multi-unit complex. For assistance, she only required help with household chores, but Milly Ferdon also enjoyed having her meals prepared and her laundry done for her. It freed up time to play cards with her friends, a group she usually referred to as "the girls."

Faith usually made it to Sparrow's Nest every couple of months, but time had gotten away from her with the podcast taking off and the other responsibilities that came with raising her girls without a husband.

Climbing out of the car, Faith stretched and took in the sight. Sparrow's Nest was a paradise for her grandmother, but Faith couldn't help thinking the place could have come right out of that movie *The Truman Show*. Every building was painted in the same muted lemon yellow with white trim. The cottages were only differentiated by the yard décor placed by their owners. Even the way the people acted all seemed so . . . content and similar. Of course, that had to be expected. Everyone here was midsixties and older.

At the front desk, Faith signed in, then walked down the hall to her right, passing rooms with doors decorated with family pictures and other personal items. At 17b, she stopped, noticing the photograph taken years before Neil moved out. It still hung in the center of her grandmother's door, the image of a family with no serious troubles visible, a lie in bright and matching colors.

She tapped her knuckle against Neil's smiling image.

A moment later, the door swung open, and her grandmother stood in front of her, always a few inches shorter than she appeared in Faith's mind. "Well, if it isn't my long-lost granddaughter."

"You talked to me on the phone three days ago." Faith drew close for a hug.

As they released, her grandmother held her soft hand to Faith's cheek. "It's not the same as having you right here in front of me." She wrinkled up her nose with an excited grin. "Get on in here before some old guy tries to scoop you up." She shuffled back, one hand remaining on the door for stability.

The apartment was small, with one main room that contained two recliners and a kitchen area with a two-burner stovetop and half-sized refrigerator. Off to the right were two doors. One was the bathroom, large and open and extremely institutional, and the other was her grandmother's bedroom.

"Have a seat. It won't be long before they call us to lunch, and I want a few minutes with you alone before the whole place crowds around us."

Milly Ferdon had a habit of talking her granddaughter up as some kind of celebrity. It had occurred to Faith on more than a couple occasions that the popularity of her podcast could very well have begun in this community.

Her grandmother sat in her old recliner with the hand-crocheted afghan over the back, while Faith took the newer chair saved for company.

"Now, I know you didn't come down for a regular visit when Harlow and Ava are about to leave for the summer. Tell me, what's on your mind?"

Faith hesitated, picking at a rough patch on the side of her thumb. "It's Heather Crane."

"Oh, that dear girl. I pray for her mama every single day."

"Why didn't you tell me what happened to her?"

Her grandmother's face seemed to age ten years in that moment. "We were all torn up about it. Your dad, he was still at my place during the week to finish up the subdivision . . . he took it hard. Probably because of everything else that was happening with the baby and all." She shook her head. "I knew we should tell you, but he was afraid it would be too much to burden you with, so I went along."

Faith placed her hand over her grandmother's. She wasn't here to dish out guilt, only to find out what she could from someone who'd been there at the time of the disappearance. "Brooke contacted me. She wants me to look into the case and give it some new life on the podcast. It's not the kind of case

I usually do on *What Happens Next*, but it feels important. I want to help them if I can."

"That's commendable, and I think you should, but I want you to keep one thing in your mind as you move forward."

Faith cocked her head to the side, eager for anything her grandmother would share.

"You, though wonderful, are not the Savior."

She felt her spine go rigid. "What does that mean?"

"It means you can't fix what is broken in the hearts of the Cranes. You weren't designed for that task. Yes, you can bring attention to the case. And that may bring forward someone who knows what happened, but then another kind of grieving begins, no matter how Heather's case is resolved."

The words settled over Faith like a lead apron, pressing too hard on her shoulders. "If you're right, then why even try to help?"

"Because I believe this is something you need to do. I've suffered over the guilt from not telling you. Many nights I've wondered if that first feeling of rejection you felt that fall when Heather didn't return any of your letters was what started the thread of insecurity you've been weaving around yourself."

Faith had never considered herself insecure. She was deliberate. She planned her life carefully, not taking extra chances, but that was being responsible, prepared.

Electronic chimes echoed through the room.

"That will be lunch." Grandma pushed herself up with a sound that was becoming all too familiar to Faith. "We can't lollygag, or we won't get our table."

Faith followed behind her, the accusation of insecurity flanking her from both sides.

The dining area was a large room with well-spaced tables seating four to six at each. Milly maneuvered with precision to the one in a far corner. "It's quieter back here. People can chat without having to holler over those who refuse to wear their hearing aids."

Before Faith could respond, another woman joined them. Her hair was sparkling white and fluffed like a cotton ball. She wore seemingly mandatory polyester pants, but hers were the color of Pepto-Bismol. On top she wore a collared sweatshirt with the word *DIVA* printed across it in glittery silver.

"Bev, this is my famous granddaughter."

Faith cringed. "Nice to meet you. And I'm not really famous."

"Oh, there she is." Milly waved like she was bringing in a plane. "Connie, over here."

A slender woman with a walker shuffled to their table. "Hello again, Faith. I'm so glad you've come to see your grandmother. Did she tell you how we stomped on her in bridge last night?"

"She didn't mention it."

Milly waved off Connie's comment. "You don't know what you're talking about, old woman."

Plates were set in front of them. Nothing looked like it needed a great deal of chewing.

"My Faith here is going to be staying in my house for the summer. She's digging into a new case."

A green bean lodged in Faith's throat. She swallowed a gulp of water. "I am?"

"Of course you are. You said you'd be working on the case for the summer. Where else would you stay? There hasn't been anyone in it for months."

The urge to run away from this plan was strong. Faith hadn't stepped foot in Deep Valley since the day they packed up the van and moved on. Being in her grandmother's house, where she'd spent the summer before Heather disappeared, was bound to bring back memories she didn't want to face, memories of the family she'd wanted and the fragile one she'd been stuck with instead.

11

Dora

Dora had gotten a cell phone as soon as they became available. The first thing she'd done was give her phone number to the police detective in charge of Heather's case. In all the years since, she'd never seen a reason for a phone that did all the fancy things Paul liked his to do, but times were changing and maybe she should move up a bit.

At the corner of Eighth and Lion Street, she pulled into a six-car parking lot and took the one space that was still open. She checked her purse as she got out of the car, being sure her flip phone, which she almost never used, was still tucked in the outer pocket.

Once inside, the wall-to-wall displays of technology reminded her of watching *Back to the Future*, the scene with the family at the theater.

"Hello, ma'am. Can I help you?" This kid could be her grandchild. He had one hand deep into his pocket, while the other swung back and forth with a computer tablet, completely unconcerned about the potential for damaging equipment with his carelessness. His name tag read *Bryan*.

Dora pulled the phone free of its pouch and held it up. "I'd like to replace this with one that has the podcasts, please."

Bryan took the flip phone and turned it over and over, as if he'd never seen anything quite like it. "How long have you had this?"

"I don't know. Maybe ten years."

His eyebrows shot up. "And it still works?"

"Of course it does. I've had the same phone in my house for over thirty years, and it's never had one issue. Ten shouldn't be worth mentioning."

"Ma'am, there's a whole lot of difference between a cell phone and a landline." He did some odd twisting with his mouth. "You say you still have a home phone?"

"Yes. I need that phone number to stay intact." She bit down on her bottom lip before "the verbal vomit," as Brooke called it, rolled out. She'd been telling people about Heather for so long, it felt natural, but nothing had come from any of those random interactions.

"It's easy to keep that number and move it onto your cell phone. That way you don't miss any important calls."

He was speaking to her heart now. "Can I get a podcast phone that has my home number?"

"I'm not sure what you mean by a podcast phone, but any of the smartphones here will indeed play your podcasts. Which ones do you like to listen to?"

"I've never heard one."

"Is the phone for someone else?"

"No. I want to listen to a podcast. I need a phone that will do that. I want to keep my home phone number." She was talking slow now, as if his brain was the size of a peanut. She couldn't be any clearer. "My husband has one of them, but I don't want hearing aids."

"Hearing aids?"

"Yes. His phone sends the podcasts into his hearing aids. I

want the kind that uses headphones." She tapped her ear to make her point.

"Ma'am." He set his device on the counter.

"Can you call me Mrs. Crane, please? You're making me feel old."

"Mrs. Crane, all the phones we have here, the smartphones, work with headphones. Now, there are a few differences. For most Androids, you can plug in a cord and play your podcasts that way, but if you get an iPhone, you'll need to get AirPods. They work like your husband's hearing aids." He guided her over to a display, where he popped open a small white case and displayed two things that looked suspiciously like hearing aids.

Dora waved her hand in the air. "No. Not that kind. I want the plug-in ones with the wire."

A moment later, he was showing her five different minicomputers. With all the abilities he rambled off, they could hardly be called phones anymore. She let him go on for ten minutes about pixels and memory and an assortment of other things she didn't understand.

"Do you have any questions?"

Dora ran her fingers through the side of her short hair. "No. I want the one in the middle. Please put my phone number into it and let me pay for the thing before I change my mind."

His eyes were wide, but he reached for a boxed version of the phone.

"I'm sorry. I don't mean to be rude. This is overwhelming, and well, I want to listen to my daughter's friend. She has one of those podcasts. My daughter is gone now. She disappeared. It was a long time ago." The words kept falling out, leaving her as unable to stop them as she would be able to stop a speeding car. "My daughter, the other one, she's still here, she contacted this girl who does the podcast. She thinks she can help us."

Bryan's face was blank of reaction.

"It was a lot of years ago."

"I'm sorry."

"Thank you."

They stood there in the silence for a few too many beats, only saved by the electronic buzz as the door to the shop opened.

"I'll get my buddy Jeff to ring you up and get that number switched over." He led her to the counter where the new guy took over.

Dora had never been the kind of woman who chased the next thing, and she definitely wasn't the kind who felt it was a personal accomplishment to figure things out on her own. She'd always been content with her husband and her three kids. They were the source of her joy and fulfillment.

If she hadn't been distracted that day in 1987, she could have gone on with her happy life until it ended one day with a sense of peace that came from completing a long task. Instead she lost Heather, then Greg, who only called once a month or so, and then even Brooke had distanced herself from Dora.

She pulled up to the curb that afternoon, hoping her grandson could untangle the mysteries of this new phone before Brooke got home and gave her that "poor little old lady" look she'd been sporting so often.

Charity opened the door before she could reach it. "Grandma. What are you doing here?"

Dora shrugged. "I thought Connor might help me with my new phone."

Charity held the door open and stood to the side so Dora could pass into the living room. "He's still at baseball practice, but I could take a look."

"It's mighty complicated. I'm not sure you'd understand it."

Her smile dropped a degree. "Can I try?"

"Of course." She was so much like her mother had been as a

teen, fighting for her own independence, not wanting anyone to lend a hand.

In the dining room, Charity took the phone out of the box. "Oh, this is the same kind I have. It's easy."

Dora rolled her eyes.

Charity pressed the button on the side and flew through a series of questions so quickly that there was no way she'd read them before answering.

"Okay. You put your email address in here. I can type it in."

"It's FindHeather@gmail.com."

Charity lifted her head from the screen. "Is that your main email?"

"It's the only one I have." She'd gotten this when a newspaper reporter had asked about all the ways to contact her if anyone had a tip. Dora checked it every night before bed. She rarely got an email, and when she did, it was advertising.

"Okay." Charity passed her the phone. "You need to type in your password."

The letters on the screen were about as big as pin tops, but she managed to get the letters and numbers all in.

"Now we can download some apps. You'll need Facebook. All the . . . older people love it. And you said you wanted podcasts. I'll get you the Spotify app. Do you have accounts already?"

"Accounts?"

"No worries. It will just take a minute." Charity clicked, swiped, and took a quick picture with the phone, then handed it back to her grandmother. "Okay. This is your Facebook. You can see you don't have any friends yet, but all you need to do is look up the people you're interested in and tap on friend request. And this." She made the Facebook screen go away and tapped a green circle with curved black lines. This is your Spotify. You have the free version, so if you listen to music, you'll have to put up with the commercials. It's no big deal, really."

Dora leaned close to Charity. "How do I find *What Happens Next*?"

"Oh, Mom loves that podcast. She listens to it all the time. I guess the host was a neighbor. That's so cool."

"Yes. Very cool."

A minute later, Faith's voice spread out from the phone. It was such a strange mix of feelings. She sounded so much the same, older, but still the Faith from 1987 was in there. It had never occurred to Dora that Heather's voice would have changed over the years. She probably had strands of gray in her brunette hair by now. The world kept spinning, no matter how much Dora needed it to stop and let her catch up.

12

Faith

Faith dangled her key ring from her index finger. On it hung her house keys, car keys, and the spare key to her grandmother's house that had been pressed into her palm before she left their visit.

Life was about to take another big curve in the road. She was off to pick her girls up from school, then they'd go to a special end-of-the-year dinner, but that was it for her time with them. Neil would arrive at seven and steal her children away for the summer.

Walking out of the house meant going by the evidence of her reality. Harlow and Ava had been packed for days, their suitcases and carry-ons stationed by the door as if the girls couldn't wait to get out. Could she blame them? It was Hawaii. Their mother wasn't the center of their world any longer, and that was the way it should be. They were becoming young women. They needed space to become independent, while still needing a mother there to bandage them when they fell. Who would do that this summer? Wendy?

Outside, the sun shone down, promising another of the hot

73

days Faith cherished. Instead of climbing into the van, she pocketed her keys and started down the sidewalk. Days like this weren't to be wasted, especially in the Pacific Northwest.

Along the way, she passed homes that matched the ones on either side. The yards were all maintained by the neighborhood association, with nothing to show the character of the family that lived behind the closed curtains. What had happened to lively blocks filled with children and laughter?

She rounded the corner, the school off in the distance. The thought of moving had occurred to her, but she couldn't make it further than that. Their home had been carefully selected with the layout exactly what she'd wanted and the minimal maintenance Neil desired. They'd been a family in those walls.

As she approached, the noise volume doubled. Parents waited outside while kids spilled from the school doors. Harlow was easy to spot even from a distance. From her neck hung at least ten leis, much like the ones she and Ava had in their childhood dress-up box. Her friends must be sharing in Harlow's excitement.

Faith took one of those cleansing breaths she'd learned in childbirth class. If she didn't muster matching enthusiasm for the trip, Harlow and Ava would leave feeling the divide of divorce that Faith had promised herself to minimize.

As the girls headed to the line of cars, Faith waved, getting their attention.

"What are you doing?" Ava asked, her backpack hanging off one shoulder. "Where's the car?"

"It's such a beautiful day. I thought we'd walk."

She dropped the bag with a thud. "And I'm supposed to carry this with me?"

It would take more than a cleansing breath to tackle the irritation Faith was feeling. Yes, she hadn't thought about the extra stuff brought home on the last day of school, but this attitude . . . Couldn't they have one nice afternoon before her daughters were gone for three months?

Harlow arrived, her eyes asking the same question Ava had already posed. A horn beeped behind them.

"Hey there." Kendall reached across her center console and waved. "Did you walk?"

Faith crossed her arms on the window frame, looking in. "Yep. Parental failure seventy-two for today. Could you give us a ride?"

"No problem. Hop in." She pressed a button and the side door slid open. The girls climbed in without a word.

Faith buckled her seatbelt, then rolled her head toward her friend, where she found understanding.

The van adjusted as Kendall's boys joined the group. "So, Ava and Harlow," Kendall began, "I bet you're excited to spend some time with your mom before you leave. Three months is a long time to be away."

Harlow shrugged. "Not so long. Lots of kids my age are gone for the summer. Some are on exchange programs or working at camps. They don't have either of their parents around, and they seem fine."

Great. Was it better that her daughter didn't think she needed her or Neil? Didn't Harlow understand they only had a few years left before she was off on her own? Didn't she know what they had right now was never going to be again? Maybe she knew it all too well. Neil had ruined everything.

At home, the girls dove into their rooms, making sure they hadn't missed anything important in their packing.

They'd never been away from her for more than a week. Faith had spent hours that morning crafting letters to each of her daughters before tucking them deep inside their suitcases, reminders that they still had a mom at home.

When they finally left for dinner, time was growing short. They wouldn't be able to linger over full stomachs and settle into deep conversation. It would be the business of eating, saying good-bye, and returning in time for Neil to take her babies away from her.

They decided on an Italian chain restaurant that didn't have a line, likely for good reason. Faith allowed them to get whatever they desired on the menu.

"So, Mom." Ava twirled her fork on the napkin after the server walked away with their orders. "What are you going to do all summer? Work?"

Faith took a moment to swallow a long drink of iced tea. "No. Well, sort of. I'm helping an old friend try to find out what happened to her sister." Alarm bells sounded in her head. She shouldn't be telling her girls about this. They might share her plans with Neil. "It's nothing. What are you excited to do first in Hawaii?"

Harlow set her phone down. "You're changing the subject. Why?"

"This dinner isn't about me." She almost said she wasn't the one leaving, but that wasn't altogether true. She would be driving away from the house the next morning herself.

"Should we be worried?" Harlow's serious tone had gotten her sister's full attention.

"No. Listen, I just don't want your dad to make this into more than it is. I'm helping a friend on a cold case. It's basically a research assignment."

Harlow bounced her straw up and down in her pop. "So that's what you were arguing about a few weeks ago."

"We weren't arguing." Heat crawled over her skin. Hot flashes. As if she needed another reminder that she was moving rapidly toward fifty with no husband and children who wouldn't be around much longer. "He was concerned, but there's no reason to be."

Ava tore a hole through the middle of her napkin where she'd dripped water from her straw. "You'll be safe?"

"Absolutely. I'm actually going to stay at Grandma Ferdon's for a bit. It will be like a vacation down memory lane."

"You mean at the care place?" Ava's eyebrows wrinkled.

"No. Where she lived when I was a kid. She still has the house. It's used off and on by a missionary group for people on furlough, but other than that, it's empty." Faith fingered the key ring in her pocket. "I'm looking forward to seeing places I haven't been since the summer I was ten."

The server arrived with plates of steaming, cheese-covered pasta. Something didn't smell quite right when the dish was set in front of Faith, but she scooped up a bite and filled her mouth so she wouldn't have to keep talking about what came next.

Faith stood on the cement porch and watched Neil and Wendy drive away with her daughters. They looked like a family, the four of them, all off on an adventure together. Neil had promised her forever, but now he was giving the life they were supposed to have to another woman. Was she the only one who saw how wrong all of this was?

Back inside, the house was hollow and empty. The quiet cut into her heart. A rush of panic swept over her, much like the first night after Neil walked out. It had taken months before she could fall asleep without the aid of medications. Even now, his empty side of the bed woke her multiple times a night.

Faith curled up on the couch and turned on the television. Crouton jumped onto her lap, kneading her thighs with his sharp claws. This was promising to be a long night. She lifted the cat onto the floor. "Let's get our packing finished." The sooner they were on the way to Deep Valley, the better.

Deep Valley was about as far south in Oregon as Faith's home was north, but Faith and Crouton were determined to make the trip in six hours with as few stops as possible. She felt ridiculous walking a cat around on a leash, especially because her cat wasn't used to that kind of thing and bounced back and forth like a paddleball, not once taking advantage of the opportunity to relieve himself. After the second stop, Faith poured kitty litter into the litterbox and left the cat loose in the car while she drove.

Twice she nearly jumped out of her seat when Crouton cried in her ear.

"I get it. Traveling isn't a cat thing, but it was this or you spend the summer with Kendall. She has boys who play ball in the house. You really wouldn't like that. And they have a dog."

The cat hopped onto the dash, pawing at a fly near the vent.

She wouldn't have left him behind no matter what. Crouton was going to be her sidekick this summer, possibly the only friend she'd have in Deep Valley.

As she drove into town, Faith checked the directions to the house. After so many years, she couldn't remember a thing about how to get to her grandmother's. Even if she did, the once tiny community had grown, with new housing spread out past the main area. Some of this was her father's doing, though she didn't remember much about the subdivision he'd developed that summer.

It wasn't until her navigation app told her to take the final turn that Faith found herself back in another time.

They called it a block, but the neighborhood was more of a horseshoe, with the road looping all the way around and back to the main street. Her grandmother's place was near the middle of the loop, and Heather's home was only a few lots farther down and across the street. Exteriors had changed colors, turning to a more modern palette, but her grandmother's house and the Crane's were exactly the same.

Faith pulled into the driveway and let her gaze rest on the other house. Its mustard yellow paint that was once popular now stood out like a throwback to the seventies. Memories of Grey Poupon commercials came to mind. She looked at the cat and mustered her best English accent. "Pardon me, would you have any Grey Poupon?"

The response wasn't any better than she would have received from her girls—a blank stare. They may have all the electronics now, but they'd missed so much by not growing up in the eighties. It was sad, really. Today's kids didn't need to use their imaginations the way she and Heather had that summer. Maybe that wasn't fair. There were drawbacks too.

Faith snagged the cat and climbed out of the car. Crouton positioned his paws against Faith's chest and pushed, wriggling to escape. She tightened her grip. "Just calm down. I'll let you loose in the house."

The deadbolt rolled open easily, but the heavy door needed a solid nudge with her hip. By the time she was inside, Crouton was hanging from her arm, his front paw straight in the air. She closed the door and let him go.

The cat ran into the center of the living room, turned a circle, and meowed as if he needed to make her aware that they'd come to the wrong house.

"I know, buddy. I'm having second thoughts too."

13

Heather

Monday morning, Mom was up and out the door before I woke up. I felt bad that I hadn't thought to get up with her like she did for me each day before school. The more I thought about it, the worse that feeling got. Mom not only was dressed and ready for the day when she came in my room to wake me, but she also made sure I had a lunch prepared and breakfast ready to eat, then she'd stand on the porch and wave good-bye as my sister and I rode off on our bikes.

My brother was too cool for that kind of thing. He hitched a ride with some of his friends. For the last year, Greg worked at the local grocery store, the IGA, to pay for that ridiculous car. I couldn't believe he would actually use his money that way while my parents scrimped to save for his tuition, but I didn't understand much about what went on in Greg's brain.

I wanted to do something special for my mom, something that would let her know that I noticed all the things she did for me, that I really appreciated her. Maybe a bit of it was already wishing she'd quit and come back, but I wasn't a little kid. I understood a lot of what I'd overheard a few nights earlier. We were in money trouble.

In the kitchen, I twirled the corner cupboard until the cereals were pointed out. A box of Count Chocula surprised me. We rarely had the really good stuff. I poured it in my bowl until a mountain of chocolatey goodness formed, then covered it with a shower of milk.

The flavor was better than I'd imagined, and the milk really did turn chocolate within minutes. When I finished, I shoved my whole arm into the box and wiggled it around in there until I located the prize, a pouch of temporary tattoos. Before anyone saw, I stuffed them into my jeans pocket.

Dad entered through the door to the garage. He looked around the kitchen. I hadn't noticed the mess until I saw him looking. Cereal had slopped over my bowl, leaving a lake of chocolate milk with a line of Count Chocula islands. A stack of envelopes soaked up the excess. When he took another step, it crunched on what I could only imagine was the cereal I'd spilled during my armpit-deep treasure hunt. "Sorry, Dad. I'll clean this all up."

He replied with a grunt, but I caught his meaning. Dad was a pretty cool guy, but he got really bothered by messes. We were in big trouble with Mom gone all day.

The doorbell rang with this really awesome chime sound. It was a Christmas present that Dad got for Mom. I swiped the cereal into the sink and ran water down the drain, then jogged to the door.

Faith was there, but she didn't seem happy. Her eyes were kind of puffy, like she'd been crying or something. This was not my specialty. Usually, if someone was upset, I pointed them toward Mom. But there was the problem again—no Mom. I suddenly regretted making fun of that after-school special about the latchkey kid.

"Hey, come on in." I stepped to the side. "I was thinking about baking some cookies for my mom's first day at work. Want to help?"

Down the hall, music started pumping. I placed my hand on the wall and actually felt the beat.

"What are you doing?" Faith stepped closer.

"You can feel the music. It's Brooke's way of warning the entire neighborhood that she's in a bad mood." Brooke had been driving me crazy with her whining and complaining since the block party. She could be so dramatic. "I should flip the breaker switch."

A throat cleared behind me.

"Sorry, Dad. Just kidding."

"You keep your hands off the electrical box, you understand. That can be dangerous."

I nodded.

"I've got to run to the hardware store and get a piece to fix Mr. Potter's lawn mower. Will you be all right here?"

I was so embarrassed I could feel my cheeks heating. "Dad, I'm not a baby."

"I know, I know." He stepped up beside me and messed up my hair. "But you'll always be my baby girl."

"Dad." I looked at Faith, who didn't seem to be aware of how horrible this was. "Please ignore him."

"Okay, Rowdy, I'll see you later. I'd give your sister plenty of space, if you know what I mean." He winked, then headed out the front door.

"If I ever start acting like my sister, just kill me."

"She's not so bad." Faith shrugged. "I've always wanted a sister."

"Your mom's having a baby. Maybe you'll get one."

She squished her lips into a twisted circle. "Maybe. But it's going to be so much younger than me. It's like it's too late, you know?"

"I guess. But I'd sure rather have a baby brother or sister than a teenage airhead who thinks she's all that or a high school brother who's never even around."

I led the way to the kitchen. My breakfast sugar was wearing off. It was time for cookie baking and a lot of dough eating.

14

Faith

Faith woke in the bedroom that had been her grandmother's. Most of the pictures had been removed, but the quilt was the same one she'd seen folded each night and laid out again each evening when she'd lived here in the summer of 1987.

There'd been a few nights, though she never would have told anyone, not even Heather, that she climbed into this bed and slept next to her grandmother. There was a warmth that she hadn't experienced with her own parents, who seemed to grow more distant as she got older.

Crouton raised his head from where it rested on his crossed legs. He didn't need the ability to speak to make his message clear. The cat was not a fan of the new living arrangements. Well, he'd be even more out of shape when he discovered he'd be here alone most of the day.

Faith had given this project three months—a total of ninety-two days—and they were already on number two.

The air in the house was still stale from having been shut up without human activity for three months. Faith opened the back door, letting a cool breeze drift in before the temperature started to rise. The house still hadn't been updated with air conditioning, one of the many modern advances she wasn't sure she could go without.

Coffee. That was nonnegotiable. But that too would need to happen right away before the sun took over the day. She pulled a bag of her favorite ground beans from the box of food she'd brought from her place. The cream she'd brought in a cooler, along with a day's supply of Diet Coke, was already in the refrigerator.

She leaned against the yellow speckled Formica countertop and scanned the room for a coffee maker, but Mr. Coffee must have moved on too. Ten minutes later, she was clanking around with a percolator, the only java-creating device she was able to find. Her budget was tight, but coffee was essential.

With the grounds poured into the basket and water in the pot, she set the contraption on the burner and turned it up to high. It didn't take long for liquid to start sputtering around in the clear handle. Faith pulled her glasses onto the bridge of her nose and evaluated the color. See-through caffeine was not going to cut it today.

The pot shook and jiggled on the stove. Faith poured her cream into a CorningWare cup, then wrapped the handle of the percolator with a towel and filled her cup with coffee. Brown chunks floated to the top.

When she and Neil had been together, he'd made the coffee each morning. She should have known they were over when he bought her a Keurig and it wasn't even an occasion.

The coffee was worse than she'd imagined it could be. The flavor wavered between bitter and burnt, and if she wasn't careful to sip and sift with her teeth, she found herself having to chew. Maybe one of the community advancements in Deep Valley would turn out to be a Starbucks.

"This is an adventure. Nothing to fear but personal growth." She looked around for the cat but found she was talking to herself.

When had she ever been so alone? Faith left for college and lived in a dorm for two years, then a women's cooperative house for the next two. Not long after graduation, she'd married Neil. Then came the girls. She'd lived alone a total of zero days in her life, if she didn't count the time the girls spent with Neil in his apartment.

Last night, she'd come to a new place, moved herself in, and slept alone in a house that was far from familiar. It was a step, an accomplishment in independence. Maybe this would have made her father proud. Nothing she'd done during his life seemed to have met those standards.

Faith poured the remaining coffee down the drain, then searched Google on her phone for the nearest coffee shop. No matter what the reviews said, any coffee would be better than the swill she'd created that morning.

Less than six blocks away was a café, Merle's, the same place where she and Heather had shared a milkshake. The place where she'd joined Heather's family on another occasion to celebrate Brooke's birthday.

What better place to start learning about what the town remembered from 1987 than a place that was a regular stopping point that summer?

Walking in the door of Merle's was like peeling back the layers time had attached. She breathed in the scents of crisp-cooked bacon, rich maple syrup, and coffee.

From her memory, she couldn't spot a single change. A long counter stretched the left side of the rectangular room. At the end, an opening gave a view into the kitchen, where a man in grease-smudged white flipped sausages onto a plate. Along the wall were photographs of Deep Valley's logging history and a few heads from unlucky elk and deer.

A waitress approached the *Please Wait to be Seated* sign as she stuffed an order pad into her apron pocket. "Can I help you, honey?"

Faith blinked. It had been years since a stranger called her any kind of endearment. "A table would be great."

A gentle smile crept onto the woman's face. "Just you?"

"Yes. I'm alone." It must have been the familiarity of Merle's, but Faith had to hold tight to all her secrets before every step that took her to a place where she needed a table for one slipped out. She shrugged. "Just me."

"Well, honey, I'm sure that won't be for long."

Faith followed her to a small table by the front window, wondering what she'd meant by that.

"I'm Peggy." She dropped a menu onto the table. "If you need anything, give me a holler."

"Coffee would be a wonderful start."

"You've come to the right place. Merle only stocks the best. He's kind of a coffee connoisseur."

"Merle—the original Merle—still runs this place?"

Peggy nodded her head toward the kitchen. "That's the man right there. He's been flipping burgers since the days when my daddy brought me in here. Nothing much changes in the best places. There's no real need for it. I'll be right back with that java."

Peggy had to be in her mid-to-late fifties, at the very least, yet the math wasn't working for Faith. Did that mean the cook would be coming up on eighty? The job must be good for the soul, or he wouldn't be able to keep on going at it day after day.

Both Merle and Peggy would be good sources of information.

Scanning the room, she realized there were at least five tables of people who would likely remember the summer and fall of 1987. She pulled her notebook out of the hobo bag she hauled around with her, then found her favorite purple pen.

The opportunity to dig in deeper came with a cup of coffee. Peggy sat it in front of her, along with a miniature silver pitcher. "So, what brings you to Deep Valley?"

"My grandmother was from here, and so was my mom. I actually spent a summer here as a child. It was 1987." Faith let the information sit there, hoping it would open doors without her having to divulge too much too soon.

"That was the summer I married my high school sweetheart." Peggy looked off into the distance, as if seeing the man. "I can't think of a better time. Ted went on to heaven without me a few years ago. We never were able to have kids, so it's just me now, but I don't feel alone around here." She waved her arm through the air. "This community has kept me sane on more than one occasion."

The words were like a blanket of comfort, much like the one Faith had experienced on her last visit. What made one town so different from another?

"Well, I'm so glad you're here," Peggy continued. "How long will we have the pleasure?"

There was a hesitation that sat on Faith's chest, like verbalizing the plan to this stranger made it a commitment she couldn't take back. She inhaled a deep breath. "I'm here for the summer. I'm working on a project for work."

"What kind of work do you do?"

She should have anticipated the question. Wasn't this the point, to get out there and get the story, to make it public and remind the community—and the world—about Heather Crane? "I host a podcast."

Peggy dropped into the seat across from Faith as if they were old friends catching up on the years they'd missed together. "I love podcasts. What's it called? Maybe I've listened to it. My favorites are true crime. Is yours like that?"

Faith's mind whirled. Her usual answer wouldn't work anymore. "The focus, until now, has been on redemption after tragedy. It's called *What Happens Next*."

Peggy tapped her fingers on the table, her face lined with concentration. "It sounds familiar."

When Faith had first started drawing an audience, she'd been surprised. It seemed that most listeners were into the gore and shock, not really drawn to hope, but they had come, and their numbers continued to grow.

"Hey, Carl." Peggy waved at a round man sitting at the counter.

He turned their way, wiping strands of white hair back into place over his shiny head.

"This lady here does a podcast—What Was That?"

Faith's face fought through the confusion to paste on a smile. "It's *What Happens Next.*"

The smack of Carl's hands clapping together drew the attention of any customers who weren't already listening in. "That's a good one. The wife and I like to listen in the car. Whoo-hoo. What brings you to our neck of the woods? Are you doing a story here?"

Now every set of eyes looked directly at Faith.

She took a long drink of coffee that had cooled until it was just above lukewarm. "I am. But it's different than the usual."

Carl's seat squawked as he climbed down, revealing his short stature. He ambled over to the table and pushed Peggy aside with a nudge. Leaning forward, he spoke in a loud whisper. "Who's the subject?"

"Heather Crane."

The room dropped into complete silence.

15

Dora

Paul's pickup rumbled out of the driveway and down the lane. After a week of no contact, he'd shown up at the house solely for the purpose of checking the sprinkler system and mowing the lawn. That was Paul. Always the dutiful husband, even after he walked out and left his wife.

Dora had done her best to appear busy while he did his work, keeping her headphones in place and the podcast turned up. A few times, she'd had to rewind the show because her thoughts got carried away from the story, but that wasn't Faith's fault. Her program was fascinating. It was just hard to concentrate while the man you were supposed to spend your whole life with was tinkering around outside, only to return to some apartment he'd rented. Clearly, he was in the midst of a midlife crisis.

Now that he was gone, Dora plopped on the sofa. Her phone rang, startling her back up from her seat. "Hello?"

"Hey, Dora, this is Tammy."

Dora shook her head. Word must be getting around about the separation. She hadn't received a call from Tammy in at least a year. "Hello. How can I help you?"

"Something came up today, and, well, I don't want to be insensitive. Maybe you already know about this. I should mind my own business. That's what Jerry is always saying to me."

Prickles of fear accosted her arms and chest. She'd had this intense reaction to any unknown since the day her life had become a chronic nightmare. Her doctor's belief that it would get better with time was about as true as the saying "Time heals all wounds." Plain nonsense. "Tammy, could you let me in on what you're talking about?"

"Well, Jerry and I were at the diner this morning, having a cup of coffee with Joe, Archie, and Debbie. You know how the guys like to get together and chat all day, and they say we are the talkative ones. Really."

"And then what happened?" Dora's foot started tapping.

"That waitress down there, she was making time with a woman I'd never seen before. I was sitting with my back to them, so I couldn't see everything, but this gal, she was talking about doing a show about . . . I just can't."

"About what?"

"Heather. I'm real sorry. It must be horrible to have all that brought up again, but I thought you ought to know." Something clicked on the other line. Must be Tammy knocking her long fingernails against the phone.

Dora walked to the window and pulled the curtains a few inches apart. There was a car in Milly Ferdon's driveway. It had to be Faith. "Don't worry about it, Tammy. I appreciate you keeping me apprised of the town scuttlebutt. You have a nice day." She pulled the phone away from her face and found the disconnect button to touch on the screen.

Tammy was very wrong about one thing. Dora wasn't bothered at all if people brought up Heather. The truth was, none of her friends ever did. As if not saying her name would make the entire nightmare disappear. Heather was real. She'd been here, lived in this house. She still had a bedroom to come home to, and at least one family member waiting for her to find her way back.

Dora jumped away from the window, letting the curtains fall closed. Someone had come out Milly's front door, and for some reason, it sent Dora's heart running. She took long breaths, the kind that were supposed to relax the body and mind. They never worked. Again, she divided the curtain, but only just enough to see the house four down and across the street.

A tall woman with shoulder-length brown hair was coming her way with strides that would have her at the door in seconds rather than minutes. Though the hair was darker and the girl now a woman, there was no denying the gait that hadn't changed with time.

Dora stepped away, headed toward the kitchen. She wasn't ready. Maybe she could pretend she wasn't home, but she'd left the Buick in the driveway. She never did that. Why had she done it today?

The doorbell chimed once . . . twice.

She ran her hands over her hair, tucked her shirt into her jeans, and looked around for help, finding only her empty house.

"Heather was always so brave."

That's what people used to say about her little girl. It was true. Heather didn't back away from challenges. Most of the time it seemed like she was out looking for the next thing to conquer.

Dora rubbed her hands together until her palms grew hot, then walked to the front door. It took another burst of courage to unlatch the deadbolt and turn the knob.

Sunshine blasted into the dark living room. She blinked as her eyes adjusted, finding Faith halfway down the drive, having given up on Dora answering.

Their eyes met, and there was the child who'd spent day and night in this house all those summers ago. She was a stranger now, but that didn't stop Dora. She stepped out the door and met Faith, opening her arms and embracing her as if she could bring a tiny bit of Heather back with her return.

16

Faith

The way Brooke had described her mother led Faith to expect a woman broken under the burden of year after year of mourning. What she found in front of the house she'd once known so well was the same woman she'd left here all those years earlier. Dora Crane had more heart and love than any other mother Faith knew, including her own.

Her example stayed with Faith all these years, giving her a goal for her own role as mother, one she seldom met. Instead, she often found herself tucked away, eager to create her own life rather than live through her daughters. Maybe that was the burden of genetics. Faith's mom hadn't been a bad parent, just distant and quiet, like the many losses of life had erased part of her being.

Faith had been startled by the hug that happened before she could even introduce herself, but apparently her looks hadn't given out as much as she'd imagined.

"Oh, Faith. I can't believe you're really here. How are your folks and your grandmother? I sure miss having her down the road. Is she still planning to come back?"

Faith's hand slipped down to Mrs. Crane's hand and held it.

"Mom passed away a few years ago. My dad, he died about a year after we left Deep Valley." She didn't want to go into that time in her life. It was something she purposely skipped over any time the subject of her parents came up. "And Grandma, she's doing amazing. She's one of the toughest people I've ever known. She went to live in the retirement community, Sparrow's Nest, to be with her sister, but now that Great-Aunt Gerdy is gone, Grandma is thinking she might stay. She likes all the people taking care of her. She's held onto the house, just in case"—Faith's fingers fanned air quotes over the last three words—"but she's let different missionaries stay there over the years."

"Oh my goodness. It sounds like we have a lot to catch up on." Mrs. Crane glanced back at her door, still open, and took a breath. "Why don't you come on in? We can have some coffee. I may have some of Paul's cookies somewhere."

"Coffee would be great, but I could do without the treats." She patted her stomach.

Mrs. Crane gave her a quick up and down, then led the way inside.

A shiver ran over Faith's skin as she stepped into the past. The carpet was worn, a patch nearly bald at the entryway. Along the wall sat the wood-armed couch with the floral pattern, the same one she and Heather shared popcorn on while watching MTV. The only thing that appeared to be updated was the flat-screen television mounted beneath the wallpaper border.

In the kitchen, Mrs. Crane indicated a swiveling dark wood barstool. Faith sat, holding her hands tightly to disguise the shaking. She glanced down the hall. The reality that Heather wasn't going to come bounding out hit with more force than she'd felt at the first revelation that her friend had been gone all these years. It was all of a sudden deeply personal.

Heather had been ripped away. She deserved closure. So did

everyone who'd ever known her. The old longing for Heather returned even stronger than the first weeks after she and her parents had moved into the last house they'd ever shared. Back then, she'd felt the sting of rejection with each trip to the mailbox. Now, it was laced with guilt. Why hadn't Faith tried harder to stay in touch?

A proper Mr. Coffee started to gurgle as Mrs. Crane brought down cups from the cupboard. She set each one on a saucer, something Faith hadn't seen done in years.

"Cream and sugar?"

"Both, please." She suddenly regretted agreeing to coffee. She'd have a caffeine-induced heart attack if she didn't slow down. The coffee at the diner must have been double strength.

"You haven't changed." Mrs. Crane squinted. "Well, I mean, you have, but it's still you. It felt like you were gone too, having not seen you again. I tucked all your letters to Heather away, so she'd have them when she came home. It's strange, but I felt like they were important for her return. I honestly thought you must have known what happened but held out hope for Heather just like I did."

"I'm so very sorry. I didn't know about Heather until recently. If I had, I don't know what I would have done, but I'm sure I would have gotten in touch somehow. . . . They didn't tell me." The anger returned. How could they keep something like this from her? All those years of feeling she'd been rejected, when Faith had been the one who hadn't shown up.

Mrs. Crane poured coffee into both cups, then passed Faith a dish of sugar and a pint of half-and-half. She leaned against the stove, her hands wrapped around her own drink. "Brooke told me about your show. I've been listening. I really enjoy it."

"Thank you. Did she tell you she'd come to see me?"

Mrs. Crane's eyes widened. "No, but I knew she'd contacted you. She actually hunted you down?"

"It wasn't as James Bond as that, but she did come to my

house. Honestly, I'm glad she did. I'm sure you can see that Heather's case doesn't fit into my normal brand. When Brooke showed up, I wasn't planning on coming here. I can't even tell you why."

"Fear." She took a sip. "I've learned over the years that people don't want to get too close to a family that's experienced this kind of tragedy. It makes it too real, like it could happen to them. It's as ridiculous as being afraid of catching cancer, but feelings like fear have a lot of power."

Faith breathed deep into her abdomen. Fear was on top of her at that very moment. How was she supposed to ask the questions she needed answers to when this woman was still waiting, still hoping her daughter would be returned to her?

"Have you decided to report on Heather's story?"

"That's a hard question." Faith tapped a fingernail on the cup. "If I find enough information, I'm thinking I'll put out a separate show, like a special edition or something, but I'm not altogether sure it would help. It may bring up a lot of hard memories you'd rather keep buried." She regretted the last word while it was still halfway in her mouth.

"I've made a deal with Brooke. If you do a show on Heather, I will go to grief counseling. I don't think I need it, but it's important to Brooke. And having you draw attention to Heather's case is important to me. There's someone out there who has information. Every year, the chances of finding that person before they die gets smaller. I don't want to be dramatic, but this feels like my last hope."

Those words were like arrows, hitting Faith in the center of her heart. "I'll be here until the end of August, and I'll do everything I can. Heather was my dearest childhood friend, even if we only had that summer. And the way your family welcomed me, well, it's had a lasting effect on my life. I can't thank you enough for your love that came exactly when I needed it."

Mrs. Crane reached her hand across the counter and covered Faith's for a moment. "Faith, this means so much to me. It's like years of hopelessness have broken just by seeing you back in this house."

Faith swallowed. What was the point of renewed hope if it was destined to be broken again?

Mrs. Crane continued. "I have boxes of information, notes, and everything from the case. Detective Masters could fill in any of the blanks."

"Would you let me borrow your files?"

"Calling them files makes it all sound so organized. I'm afraid you're going to be disappointed on that count. You are, however, welcome to all of it. Anything I can do to help you, I'll do."

Faith sat on the living room floor in her grandmother's house. The ceiling fan hummed above as she made herself comfortable with a notebook, pen, and highlighter. Three cardboard boxes were stacked in front of her.

This was going to take a different level of organization than her typical episodes. There was so much information, along with the memories of numerous people. She'd need a timeline. Faith stood up, her legs already aching from moving the boxes and sitting on the floor. They'd need to adjust, because this was just the beginning of a long relationship with Mrs. Crane's case history.

Crouton weaved around her feet as she stepped into the kitchen and close to the basement door. She picked up the cat and stroked his fur. "Do you want to go down there with me? I sure would appreciate the company."

It was a long shot, but when Faith was a kid, her grandmother always had rolls of white butcher paper in the basement. She let Heather and Faith roll them out on the sidewalk one day. They'd traced each other, then used the outlines as life-sized fashion models.

Faith opened the door and felt the cold touch her skin. Leaning in, she snapped on the light. It didn't illuminate much, but it was better than only a phone flashlight app to guide the way.

The cat squirmed, pushing against Faith, then hopped down and ran away.

"Thanks a lot. Way to be a brave sidekick." The wood beneath her feet creaked with each step, until her feet landed on the cracked cement floor. As a child, the fear of this place came with a huge thrill factor. She and Heather had once sat down here in the dark, telling each other scary stories in a competition to see who'd last the longest. Heather won. After Heather's second story, Faith had found the stairs and jogged up to the safety of the kitchen.

She rubbed her hands together, resisting the detailed memories of those stories. A shiver shook her. It was just a basement. Though this was the only house she'd ever lived in that had one.

Grandma was predictable in a way that made her even more lovable. In the corner, near the shelf of empty Mason jars, was a roll of white paper. The little school supply box that held crayons sat next to it, as if preserving that summer.

Before the tears could come, Faith snagged the roll and left the basement. Never had a non-air-conditioned house felt so good.

She rolled out the paper, cutting off the end that held decades of dust. Then she used tacks from the bulletin board to connect the long section to the bare wall in the living room. About two feet in, she wrote the date of Heather's disappearance.

Faith took the lid off the first bankers box. A flyer sat on top, a picture of Heather from that summer. It was the one of the three of them—Heather, Faith, and Brooke—sitting on the curb eating popsicles, but Brooke and Faith had been cropped out. She could see three of her own fingers curved around the cement next to her friend.

With the tape she'd pulled earlier from the kitchen drawer, Faith attached the flyer right above the date she'd written.

Last seen September 17 at 5pm.

"Heather, where did you go?"

17

Heather

Mom came home every night, usually with a grocery bag on her hip. She'd unload the food, then get to work on dinner. Dad didn't do any cooking inside the house, but he'd gladly flip burgers on the grill. After Mom's first couple weeks as a working woman, I noticed barbeque showing up more and more often. She even stretched Dad's capabilities by introducing grilled corn on the cob and chicken to our menu.

Faith hated having dinner with her family. I didn't know why, but I could tell. She seemed to be avoiding her parents the way I'd avoided Nathan and his crew every summer until this one. I wondered if she was jealous about the baby coming, but I didn't ask her. Brooke was always telling me to mind my own business, and the last thing I wanted was to offend the one friend I had around for the summer.

I wanted to talk with Mom about it, but she was gone so much, and she worked for Faith's dad. I thought she might feel the need to tell him what I said the way grown-ups always blabber on about the things their kids say, as if privacy is only important after the age of eighteen.

I flopped down on the living room floor with an *Archie* comic book that Greg left lying around. If his friends came by, he'd deny it was his, so I knew I had nothing to worry about. Besides, he was in the backyard with Angela. I could have gagged when Spandau Ballet drifted in through the screen on the sliding door. He was probably trying to make a move on that girl. Gross. She was only an inch or two taller than me if you subtracted the tower of hair she managed to glue straight up from her forehead. Brooke thought this cheerleader that our brother had somehow bribed into coming over was glamourous. I thought she looked like a wannabe *Solid Gold* dancer.

The clock bonged two, and I was about to die of boredom. Another hour and I could watch reruns, but until then, there was nothing. My entertainment had become connected to my time with Faith. But she was gone for the whole day, visiting someone with her grandmother.

"Oh gag me!"

I turned to give Brooke my usual sneer. Everything to Brooke is dramatic. Everything.

"Would you just fix your hair and go outside? That boy is driving me crazy with that squeaky old bike."

I hopped up from the floor and stared out the window. "What boy?"

"He'll be back. He clearly has some kind of crush on you."

"You've gone insane."

"Nope. I'm sure he's the one who's cuckoo." She gave me a very rude up-and-down look. "When was the last time you shaved your legs?"

I shrugged. "Like, never."

"That's so embarrassing."

I rubbed the side of my calf. "Who cares if I have hair on my legs? Most of the year you can't even see them."

"You are so immature. Look." She pointed down the street. "That's the kid."

"Nathan? Not likely." Though he did seem determined to get Faith's attention. "You've watched too many of those summer-of-love movies."

Mrs. Ferdon's car pulled into her driveway. I looked at the clock. I was supposed to unload the dishwasher before Mom got home, but I'd been waiting, well, for the last minute to motivate me, I guess.

I nudged Brooke on the shoulder. "Want to come with me to see what Faith is up to?"

She rolled her eyes. "As if."

"As if what?" I cocked my hip and mimicked her expression. She turned and huffed back to our room.

Lifting my gaze to the popcorn ceiling, I uttered a quick prayer that God would not do to me whatever He'd done to my sister. I was less than three months away from fifth grade, the year of the dreaded body-change movies. The way I remembered it, Brooke had been human before she'd seen those movies. I wondered if I might be able to watch them in reverse.

I met Faith as she got out of the car, a shopping bag over one arm.

"Want to see what Grandma got me?" Her eyes were alive with excitement. I expected her to yank something cool out of the sack, like a snow cone maker. I may have been getting a little old for the Snoopy ones, but it had been a hot summer already, and we could really make use of a thing like that. Instead, she pulled out a neon tank top with a cover that was all cuts and holes. Great, now my best friend would be cool, and I would look like a little boy in my T-shirts and cutoffs.

"Nice."

"Faith, do you want me to take that stuff in so you and Heather can play?"

"Thanks, Grandma." She handed over the bag, then looked at me, mouthing the word *play*.

Before I could say something dumb, Nathan made another

circle of the neighborhood. He slowed. "Hey, girls, what are you doing today?"

Faith's chin dipped. "I don't know."

I could have gagged right there.

"I made some extra cash mowing Mr. Potter's lawn. Want to go with me to get ice cream? My treat."

"She doesn't have a bike."

I thought that would end it, but he dumped his in the yard instead. "We can walk."

"That sounds great." Faith blinked way too fast.

All the way to town, I made it my mission to be in the middle of our little group.

18

Faith

Faith stepped into the Deep Valley Police Department without an invitation or appointment. It wasn't that she wanted to surprise them, but her experience with law enforcement told her the less they knew about her ahead of time, the more likely she'd get someone to talk with her.

A man with hair so blond it was nearly white sat at a counter in the entryway, the space between Faith and him blocked by a clear divider, except where he'd pushed it aside.

She rolled her shoulders back and approached with an attitude she hoped would translate as confidence. "Good morning. I'd like to speak with Detective Masters as soon as possible, please."

He looked up, managed to wrinkle one eyebrow more than the other, and cleared his throat. "Did you say Masters?"

"Yes. Is he in?"

"I'm afraid not. Masters hasn't been here for some time. I assume you're not here for a current case."

"No." She shoved her hands in her pockets to control the nervous habit of picking her cuticles. "Can you tell me who is in charge of old cases?"

"Do you mean ones that have gone cold?"

"That's what I mean."

"Well, we don't have a whole lot of those. I think they get handed to whichever detective is available when new information surfaces. Is there a particular case you'd like information about?"

"Heather Crane. She disappeared thirty-six years ago."

He started typing. "I'm aware of the Crane case. What is your name?"

"Faith Byrne."

"And your connection to the case?" He watched her with a critical stare.

"Heather and I were friends. Best friends." No need to drop the podcast angle yet.

"This has been assigned to Detective Nobbles. I can give him your information if you'd like."

The name rang familiar, but she couldn't place it, like a memory floating in the fog of passing time. "Is he in now?"

The man typed a bit more into the computer. "Ma'am, giving him your information is the best I can do. Could you repeat your name?"

"No need." A man, tall and broad, stepped up behind the desk. "I remember Faith."

It came back like the swell of an ocean wave. Nathan Nobbles, the summer crush, the boy who seemed to show up wherever she and Heather were until they'd included him in their group. In 1987, Faith had thought he was the one for her, though she'd never once said that to Nathan. She'd barely admitted her crush to Heather. "Nathan."

"They call me Nate nowadays." He disappeared, then walked through the door at the side of the entryway. "I didn't think I'd ever see you again."

He was tall, so tall. But of course he was. He'd grown up too. Heather was the only one of them who'd been preserved by time. As he came closer, the same unease accosted Faith, just like it had all those years ago when they were children. *Puppy love*, her grandmother had called it. Maybe so, but shouldn't it be gone by now?

There was an awkwardness in the room that felt as if it was on display for the world. Should they hug like old friends or shake hands like new acquaintances? She leaned one shoulder in and took his hand, then wished the floor would dissolve and swallow her up with all her lack of grace.

It all came back in a wave of memories. His face lit up with a smile that was the exact same as she remembered. She'd written pages and pages about that smile in her first diary. Back then, she was naïve enough to believe she could someday marry Nathan Nobbles, and she'd done the work to prepare, writing Faith plus Nathan a hundred times in her schoolgirl cursive.

They both stepped back, silent for a beat too long.

"I can't believe it's really you." He shook his head. "I've thought about you over the years. That summer sticks in my mind. I think it does for a lot of us who were kids then, because of the way it ended. We were innocent and afraid of nothing, then Heather was gone. Not a kid in this town didn't find themselves suddenly under new rules and curfews. It changed Deep Valley."

Faith had raised her own girls with careful watchfulness. Times had changed since 1987, when it felt like children were safe to explore the world. Her fears of abductions, injuries, and assaults were alive and well without the knowledge of Heather's disappearance. What if she'd known? How much more would she have worried for her children's safety?

"No one told me."

"About Heather?"

She nodded. "I'm still stunned and confused. It's like my heart is broken by a wound that almost everyone else has had years to deal with."

"It's Heather that brought you to town?"

"Brooke contacted me. She wants me to bring attention to the case on my podcast."

He scratched behind his left ear, giving her a view of his ringless finger. "You're one of those true crime people?" The words seemed to deflate him.

"No, well, not really. My show is about triumph after traumas and tragedies. It's more about the human ability to go on."

"You may not be looking at the right case then. I'm sorry to say there's nothing heartwarming about the fallout of Heather's disappearance."

"I know. It's not a good fit, but I'm here for the summer, and I want to do whatever I can to help the Cranes get the closure they're needing. Maybe it's not too late for a hopeful ending."

The door swung open, and a woman in a police uniform blocked it with her foot. "Nate, we got the warrant. You ready to go?"

He looked back and gave her a thumbs-up, then returned his gaze to Faith. "Look, I'll do what I can to help you, especially since the family is on board, but I've got to go now. Could we have lunch tomorrow? That would give me a chance to get some information together."

"Sure. Where?" It felt like her old fantasies of him asking her out on a date.

"Remember that old in-and-out where we'd get ice cream?"

She nodded.

"It's a barbeque restaurant now. It still looks close to the same from the outside. They make the best brisket in Oregon. How about there at noon?"

"Perfect."

He set his large hand on her shoulder. "It's so nice to see you again." Then he turned and left the room, her heart beating like the silly girl she'd been that summer.

Faith had never really cared for barbeque. Burgers on the grill were one thing, but the smoky flavor that came from a day in the smoker wasn't her ideal meal. The inside of the little business that had at one time been a house, then an ice cream and burger stand, was transformed. There was a rustic farmhouse look to the place, and old metal street signs hung from the walls, perfect for the kind of food they served.

Looking around, she could hardly believe this was the same place they'd loved as kids. She'd eaten so much ice cream that summer. Oddly, that had marked the beginning of her concerns about her weight and her appearance. She'd changed over that summer from a little girl to a girl with interests outside of toys and make-believe. That hadn't come without growing pains.

"Hey there."

She hadn't heard him arrive, so lost in her memories.

"Sorry I'm late."

Faith glanced at her watch. "No worries."

He took the seat across from her. "This is weird."

"What?"

"Being here, with you, after all this time."

Weirder than she could put words to. She nodded but looked away, not able to stare at his face while remembering the depth of that summer crush. "And here you are, a cop. There's so much here in Deep Valley that I wasn't expecting." She cleared her throat, then took a sip of water. "Were you able to bring me any information on the case?"

"Of course. Yes. Let me run up there and order real quick, then I'll go through it with you." He asked what she wanted, then went up to the counter.

She shouldn't let him buy her food. There was an intimacy in it she couldn't afford right now. Summer crushes were one thing at ten, but a whole other game at forty-six.

Nathan—no, Nate—came back with a tray of veggies and

ranch dressing. He set it between them, picked up a carrot stick, twirled it in the dip, and took a bite with a loud crunch. From the messenger bag he'd carried in, Nate pulled a file, much smaller than what she'd expected to see. "You need to remember, this was 1987. Times have changed, and the way we investigate is not like it once was." He flipped it open. "There was a report issued at 9:37 the evening of September 17, 1987. A woman called to say her daughter hadn't come home." He looked up. "That was Mrs. Crane."

Faith nodded, the celery she'd swallowed forming a fibrous lump in her throat. "It would have been dark then. We were never out that late, at least not that our parents knew of, and if we were, the three of us were together. Did you know anything about it?"

He shook his head. "It would have been very dark. I've wondered what she was doing for years." He wound his fingers into a paper napkin. "An officer arrived at the house around 10:30."

"Almost an hour later?"

"You've got to understand, nothing like this had ever happened around here before. It was probably assumed that Heather was at a friend's house and lost track of time."

Faith thought about that year. After that summer, they'd moved to a town called Goshen. Even though she hadn't made a single friend the year they lived there, her parents would never have called the police by 9:37 if she wasn't home. It was just assumed that everything would be all right.

"When the officer arrived, he found Mrs. Crane and her daughter, Brooke. The son and husband were out looking for the girl . . . Heather. Mrs. Crane had called everyone she could think of, and no one had seen Heather that night." He tapped the page. "Here's something interesting. It says Heather had been taking care of Mr. Potter's cat while he was away to scout good hunting locations. Do you remember that old guy?"

She searched her mind but couldn't come up with a Mr.

Potter. "He must have been in the neighborhood if she was taking care of his cat."

"He was. I used to mow his lawn. He'd always seemed like a nice guy, but after Heather's disappearance, I was no longer allowed to work for him. Rumors in a small town travel fast. People around here had him tried and convicted before the week was out."

"Was there evidence?"

Before he could answer, a girl wearing a red-and-white check-ered apron approached the table with a tray. She unloaded a gigantic salad, two sodas, and a plate piled with meat.

He wiggled a finger at her plate. "You are the first person I've ever been here with who ordered a salad."

"So this is where you're taking the girls these days. Seems like nothing has changed."

He forked a chunk of meat, plunked it into his mouth, and let out a satisfied sound. "You are missing out. And no, this is not where I bring dates, if that's what you mean."

She should stop now, stay away from personal subjects. "Where does the local detective take dates?" Faith pinched her-self on the outside of her knee. Her mouth was making its own rules today.

"I'm not much of a dater. I've only been on a handful in the last five years, and each one was a new disaster."

"Seriously? I always imagined you to be a family guy." She sipped her diet drink.

"I was—or I wanted to be. My wife had cancer. She's been gone for a number of years." He shrugged. "It's hard to start over, you know."

She did know. Faith was lucky. She had her girls. Even if she wasn't Neil's biggest fan, she was still glad he was alive. "I'm so sorry."

"Thanks. I'm okay now. It's been a rough ride." His smile

was weak, maybe still a little fragile. "What about you? Are you married?"

She flashed a bare hand. "Not anymore. In fact, my ex, along with my two daughters, are in Hawaii this summer. He's getting married while he's there."

"Ouch. I'm sorry."

"Don't be. I got two wonderful children out of the marriage. They're worth all the heartache. Any kids for you?"

"No. By the time we got around to having a family, it was too late. Patty was diagnosed, and that was the end of those dreams." He stabbed a chunk of brisket and held it out to her. "Give this a try."

The action felt too friendly, yet very comfortable. She bit the meat off the fork, her gaze staying connected with his. "It's good."

"I told you." He broke the connection. "So, the thing with Mr. Potter."

Faith swallowed, the meat suddenly hard in her throat.

"They served a search warrant for his property. Inside the house, they found a plaid button-up shirt that belonged to Heather. Mr. Potter contended that she must have forgotten it when she was taking care of his cat. Brooke said it was the shirt Heather had been wearing the last time she saw her. But here's the really weird thing. Mr. Potter reported his pickup stolen three days later. I assume he was under surveillance, but I don't have anything in the report that confirms that. The truck apparently was taken from right there in front of his house in the middle of the night."

All desire to eat faded. "That seems damning. Did they find anything else?"

"Not that I can see in the report. Without being there firsthand, it's hard to determine what the officers were thinking. There was never enough evidence that they felt comfortable making an arrest."

"But the truck. What if he used it to take her somewhere or get rid of a body?"

"I wish I could tell you more. It seems like something is missing. But we know she wasn't in the house. It was thoroughly checked."

"What about Detective Masters? Can we talk to him, see if he remembers anything?"

"I checked into that. He's not in great health. His daughter was not happy that I called. She doesn't want him upset."

"Do you think she'd let me talk to him?"

He wiped barbeque sauce from the corner of his mouth. "It wouldn't hurt for you to ask."

19

Dora

The high growl of a pressure washer woke Dora before she was done sleeping. Who would be so inconsiderate? This was a decent neighborhood, for the most part. Wrapping a light robe around her shoulders, Dora went to the window to figure out who was starting their summer maintenance projects before most people had sat down for coffee.

No matter what the angle, the perpetrator was out of sight, somewhere down the road in the direction of the devil's house.

Dora threw on an outfit and brushed her fingers through her hair. If it was the Potter place, she wanted to know about it. Mel Potter had known what happened to Heather. There was no doubt in her mind. The least he could have done was leave a letter before his death, given her the resolution she needed. But not Potter. That old villain chose to go to his maker with his secrets fully intact.

The house had been inherited by Potter's son, the newer Mr. Potter, who was the image of his father in the eighties, an aging man with little hair left and white whiskers around his jawline. She wasn't a fan of him either. Every attempt Dora had made to get a look inside the house was met with threats of legal action. Even with his father long buried, the guy couldn't see fit to let Dora have a chance at the same kind of peace.

Only one house separated her house from the Potter place. One small barrier, not enough to allow her a single night without the sickening feeling that she was laying her head down only feet from where a monster had lived.

Paul wanted to move. He'd been trying to get her to agree since the first anniversary of Heather's last days with them. But how could she? What if Heather had amnesia? What if her memories started to return, and the only way to bring her fully back to them was to let her come home to the same house she'd lived in since she'd been a newborn? Maybe the possibilities were small, but they were there. Paul couldn't step away from statistics long enough to embrace hope.

Leaning up against the garage door of Mel Potter's old house was a *For Sale* sign yet to be planted in the front yard. It seemed the last renters, a couple who almost let her in despite their landlord's strict ruling against it, must have already moved out. How had she missed that?

Dora used to be up-to-date on all the neighborhood happenings. She was the first to bring cookies to new homeowners, the one who was called to provide meals when others were unwell, to take care of a child when his or her mother was in the hospital giving birth to a new baby. Somehow she'd become the scary old woman no one bothered. She couldn't remember the last time someone had called out to her and waved. Her front porch didn't even have a chair or bench to sit on anymore. Long gone was the welcome mat.

With her arms folded across her chest, Dora stood glaring at the house she despised.

"Mrs. Crane." There wasn't an ounce of love in the voice that came from behind her.

Dora turned. "Mr. Potter."

"I've told you a hundred times that you're welcome to call me John."

"And you can still call me Mrs. Crane."

He tapped the edge of an envelope on his palm. "As you can see, we're getting ready to sell the house. I'm sure you'll be as happy to see us go as we will to be done with this misunderstanding."

"My daughter is not a misunderstanding, and if you had any decency in your body, you'd let the police search the premises."

"I'm sure you remember that they did search the house, and they found nothing but the shirt that your daughter could have easily left behind when she was feeding that cat. My dad was cooperative. He did all he could do to help. You are welcome to take up your desire for another search with the new owners, but until then, I have a letter for you from our attorney." He handed the envelope over.

Human reaction when something is held out to a person is to take it. That instinct could be unkind. Dora pulled a single sheet of paper out. It was a letter, very formal in appearance, from an attorney's office warning against interfering with the sale of that man's house. Apparently, another copy was being sent to her children, though they would never think to get in the way. That was more than likely another attempt at controlling Dora from letting any potential buyer know that the house they were considering could very well have been the home of a snake.

"Mrs. Crane, I understand what you went through. If I thought for even a second that my dad was involved, I'd let you tear the place down searching for clues, but he wasn't. There's no evidence to support the theory that he ever knew what happened to your daughter."

Dora stepped back, fury tightening her muscles. "Don't you ever tell me you understand what I'm going through. You don't know the half of it. Did your little girl get ripped away from you? Have you had to live for decades without your child, without knowing if she's out there somewhere, suffering?"

His face paled.

"I didn't think so." Dora crumpled up the letter, spit on it, and threw it at the man's feet.

The hum of the power washer stilled.

All around her, neighbors had come out of their homes, some still in pajamas, all gawking at her. Once again, the crazy woman with the missing kid was harassing the son of the suspect. The pounding of her heart grew powerful, hitting her ears like kettledrums. She tried to breathe, tried to get air deep into her lungs, but her body was fighting against her, clamping her chest tight. Darkness came from the sides of her vision, pressing in, pushing out the brightness of the summer day. Beneath her feet, the world tipped one way then the other.

"Mrs. Crane?" The voice was familiar, distant. "Mrs. Crane? Are you okay?"

Someone put something soft under her head. Another person rubbed her ankle. Dora opened her mouth to respond but could only manage one word. "Heather."

"Call 9-1-1. We need an ambulance."

I wonder who that's for.

20

Heather

"I can't be seen riding this little kid bike, Mom. Don't you understand? It's, like, so embarrassing." Brooke used the word *like* as if all communication was dependent on its inclusion. "No one my age has a banana seat anymore."

"No one? You're telling me there is not a single fourteen-year-old girl on this planet who rides a bike with a banana seat?" Mom rubbed a kitchen towel along the ridged lid of her favorite orange Tupperware bowl.

"You don't understand. I will, like, die for sure if I have to ride that thing around." Brooke crossed her arms on the counter and flopped her head down, her boyband hair too stiff with hairspray to move. There had to be a use for that stuff down in California, where they had all those earthquakes. Maybe it could be used to hold their pictures to the walls.

Mom put the lid into the cupboard. "I think I understand you quite well. What I'm hearing is a girl whose priorities have gotten off track." She turned to me. Apparently my trying to be invisible so I could watch Mom school my sister wasn't working. "Heather, do you think Faith would want

Brooke's bike? I know she doesn't have one. Maybe she'd appreciate it."

"Mom." Brooke stood up, her mouth hanging open.

"What, Brooke? You can't be seen with it, so I'm finding somewhere for it to be where you won't have to."

Brooke twirled around and stomped out of the room. A few seconds later, the door slammed.

"What's wrong with her?" I opened the fridge in search of something, I wasn't quite sure what yet.

"It's only a stage. I'd be careful what I said if I were you. You're only a few years behind her."

I moved a box of Velveeta out of the way to see if anything yummy was hiding behind it. "No way. I'm never going to be so stuck-up."

Mom actually laughed. "Okay, kid, get out of the refrigerator. You're letting all the cold air out."

"But I'm hungry."

"Dinner is in an hour. You won't starve before that."

I wanted to point out that it was meatloaf night, and I needed some nourishment so I could eat as little dinner as possible, but I knew better. Last time I complained about meatloaf, Mom reheated it for three nights and served it to me while everyone else had fried chicken, spaghetti, and pizza. The woman was an evil genius. "Can I take the bike over to Faith?"

"Sure, but be back in time for dinner." She tipped her head forward, giving me that Mom look that said she knew exactly what I was thinking, so don't bother. "You got it?"

"Yes, Mom. I'll be back before dinner."

Outside, I pushed the garage door open and detangled Brooke's bike from the rest of them, only scraping my shin on the metal pedals one time. I ran with it beside me across the street and down the road.

Mr. Potter was outside, watering the azalea bushes. That always made me sad. Mrs. Potter had loved to be out in the yard. She always said she was tinkering, but whatever it was she was doing, they'd had the most colorful house on the block. After she died, Mr. Potter let the weeds crowd in and neglected to water her many kinds of flowers. By the time he was able to get himself moving again, only the azaleas were left to tend.

I lifted a hand and he waved back, then motioned me over. My gaze bounced to Faith's door and back to Mr. Potter. There wasn't a lot of time before dinner, but my parents would have a fit if I didn't respect my elders.

I let the bike flop over onto Faith's yard, then jogged a few houses down and across the street, only remembering to look both ways when I was in the middle. "Hello, Mr. Potter."

"I'm glad I saw you. I've been thinking about getting my old bones away from the house for a couple of days. My sister is recovering from a broken ankle, and I thought I'd head out to Idaho and visit with her while she's down and out. Do you think you could mind the cat? Whiskers requires a lot of attention."

I shrugged. "Sure. That's no problem."

"I'd pay you, of course."

That sounded real good, but again, I heard my mother's voice in my ear. "It's okay. I don't mind doing it."

"Nonsense. You're doing a job, so you should be paid."

"Thank you." It seemed disrespectful to refuse the money twice.

"Come on in. I'll show you where everything is."

Another glance at the bike. No chance we'd have time for a ride before dinner now. "Okay."

Inside, the house was cool, one of the only places around that had air conditioning. It smelled odd, like the hospital where we'd gone to visit my grandmother before she'd died.

He led me to the back of the house, where the kitchen was. A cat tree sat on the linoleum floor. "This is where you'll find him most of the time."

Whiskers lounged on the top level, his tail swinging back and forth over the edge.

"He gets fed twice a day, but only one scoop. The vet says he's fat, so she put him on a diet. He'll squawk at you for more, but don't give in." Mr. Potter smiled. It was such a rare sight, I couldn't help but stare.

21

Faith

Faith could hear the ambulance long before the flashing lights made an appearance. Stroking Mrs. Crane's hand, she wished they'd get over here and help her before it was too late.

The EMTs who emerged looked like they were only a few years older than Harlow. Was that another sign that she was aging faster than she realized?

The woman, her hair pulled back in a tight ponytail, knelt beside Faith. "Ma'am, my name is Jessica. Can you hear me?"

Mrs. Crane moaned.

"Excellent." She ran through a series of questions, not able to get much in the way of answers. "Do you know this woman?" she asked Faith.

The answer was complicated. She had kind of known her, at one point, in the weird way any kid knows their friend's parents. "Yes."

She tipped her head toward her partner. "Can you give him any information you have for her?"

Faith rattled off her approximate age, her name, and the name of her family members, but couldn't help with medical history. "I'll contact her daughter. Brooke will be able to give you the rest."

"Have her meet us at Good Samaritan."

Faith nodded, already scrolling through her phone contacts. Brooke's phone went to voicemail. She looked around to the other neighbors standing nearby. "Could someone go see if her husband is home?"

A woman with a baby on her hip leaned close. "I think Paul moved out."

Faith's heart sank. She knew that kind of loss all too well. "Are you a friend of Mrs. Crane's?"

"Not really. She doesn't come out much. I'm not sure anyone in the neighborhood knows her all that well."

Faith rubbed at tension along her collarbone. This wasn't the same place it had been when Mrs. Crane knew everyone. She was like the center of a large family made up of people who just happened to live near one another. How had she become so isolated?

They lifted the stretcher that now held Heather's mother.

"Can I go with her?"

Jessica looked around. "If there aren't any family members here, I don't see why not."

As the EMTs prepared to leave for the hospital, Faith tapped out a text to Brooke.

Please call me as soon as you see this.

She read it three times, assuring herself that it conveyed urgency without causing panic, then hit send.

They arrived at the hospital emergency department in only minutes, the benefit of a smaller town. With a great deal of skill and more than a little strength, the EMTs unloaded the stretcher. Jessica's partner was already rambling off information to a man in scrubs before Faith could climb down from the ambulance.

"You're going to have to stay in the waiting room now. They only let family members into the treatment area." Jessica patted Faith's shoulder.

"Thanks." Faith stood, facing the hospital doors. As she reached them, her phone sang out a pop song Ava had installed as a ringtone.

"Hey, Brooke."

"Is everything okay? Did you find something?"

The questions were at first confusing, then Faith remembered why she was here to begin with. It was her job to look into Heather's disappearance, but seeing Mrs. Crane, she wondered if this whole case should be pushed back into the shadows. If Faith uncovered anything, it wasn't likely to be good. "It's not about Heather. Your mom, she collapsed outside Mr. Potter's old house."

"What was she doing over there? Do you know they've threatened legal action if she doesn't stay away from that house?" A sound like something between a cry and wheeze came through. "What happened? Is she okay?"

"I don't know. I came with her to the hospital, but I'm not family. One of the neighbors said your dad had moved out. I didn't know how to get ahold of him."

Brooke's voice dipped. "I'll call him. Can you wait there until we arrive? I don't want Mom to be alone if something happens."

"Absolutely." Faith hadn't even considered leaving.

The phone call ended.

As Faith sat in the waiting room, a place that reeked of sorrow and fear, even with the carefully designed surroundings of muted colors and comfortable couches, she realized how much her life had been impacted by Heather's mother. She'd been an example to Faith that summer, a mom who connected with her children on a deep level, who did what she had to support the family financially but didn't allow her work to interfere with her relationships.

Faith grabbed hold of that memory and did her best to emulate what she'd seen in Mrs. Crane as she raised her own daughters. Yet, here they both were, left by the men who were supposed to love them and stand by them.

Digging her fingernails into the seam of her jeans, Faith wished she'd reached out to the Cranes. Maybe she'd instinctively known there was something wrong, some piece of a story that would break her heart if she looked back at the place and people of the summer that had formed so much of who she was. As if looking would break the beautiful memory into a thousand useless shards.

Time ticked away with no one coming back to give her an update. Faith repeated to herself that this was only because she wasn't a relative, not that there was anything seriously wrong, but the cold of the air conditioner along with the television playing without volume left her edgy and uncertain.

Finally, the doors opened, and Brooke jogged in with her father. Mr. Crane had aged more than she'd imagined he would. His thick brown curls had nearly all washed down the drain. What remained was fine and more salt than pepper. Above sunken eyes, his brows were taking over, and long wrinkles curved down from the outer corners.

They went straight for the intake desk, leaving Faith still alone and cold, feeling like an outsider who once had a place in this family. She couldn't hear what they were saying, but when Brooke and her dad turned to each other, it didn't feel good. Brooke followed a nurse through two large doors labeled *Personnel Only*.

Mr. Crane ducked his head and walked her way, not seeming to see her there. Would he recognize Faith after all these years? Did she even want him to?

From what she'd gathered, he wanted to move on, but Mrs. Crane was the one who couldn't do that. Was that why he'd left her? He could see Faith as another person indulging Mrs.

Crane's need to see a possibility for her daughter to come home.

Mr. Crane took a seat in the corner, holding his head in his hands.

Was there really any chance that Heather could come home? There'd been a few cases where kidnapped girls had come back years later, but thirty-six years? At what point was a mother supposed to start living again?

"How've you been?"

The question shook her out of her thoughts. Faith scanned the room. He had to be talking to her. No one else was around.

"Cat got your tongue?"

She swallowed, then caught the mischievous look.

"You always were the quiet one in that duo."

"I suppose so." Faith moved closer, taking a seat across from him.

"My Heather, she was nonstop. I remember wondering if you were always quiet or if Heather wasn't giving you a chance to get a word in."

She couldn't help the smile. That was the truest recollection of Heather she'd heard since arriving in this town. "I'm not sure I would have said anything even if Heather didn't use all the words. I actually appreciated that about her. I never felt like I was forced into conversation. She could carry it for both of us."

"She sure was a spunk, wasn't she?"

The *was* in his words stood out. No matter what happened to Heather, the girl with the endless rambling and never-ending excitement for adventure would never return. She was a memory that brought comfort and brokenness. She was everything Faith had wanted to be but was too scared to attempt.

A tear tickled the corner of her eye. How could a loss so long in the making still have power? "I miss her."

He rubbed his hands together. "So do I." His eyes met hers. "I want you to know that I am glad you're here. Seeing you brings a bit of Heather back to me. The last memories of her were all with you. I've been praying that you can help get Dora to accept this and move forward."

"I don't know that I have that kind of influence."

"You have more than you know. Did Brooke tell you that Dora agreed to pack up Heather's room at the end of the summer?"

"No." An image of Heather's things still where she'd left them caused physical pain in Faith's chest.

"She said she'd do it because you were coming, and you'd get people talking again, maybe find out what happened to our girl."

Faith let out a long breath. "I'm just a podcaster. At one time, I was an investigative reporter, but that's still not a detective. I can't guarantee anything."

"All these years we've depended on the police for closure. I give you just as great a chance at solving Heather's case as any of them at the station. You knew her. To them, she's just a cold case."

"Not everyone. Nate Nobbles, do you remember him?"

"He hung around with you two quite a bit that summer, didn't he? I remember Brooke going on and on about how Heather needed to spend more time caring about her appearance if she was going to get that boy to notice her." Suddenly, his cheeks went slack. "Do you think he knows something?"

"He's a detective. He's been given Heather's case."

Mr. Crane shook his head. "I never keep up on that stuff. That's Dora's area."

"I think he's a good guy. He should be an asset as we dig into what happened."

The nod of his head was slow but definite. "How can I help?"

"If you're up for it, you can tell me what you remember

from that night." Faith reached for her purse, then realized she didn't have it with her. For all she knew, her front door was wide open and Crouton was out terrorizing the neighborhood birds. She pulled out her phone. "Do you mind if I record this?"

"Nah. I don't have anything to hide."

She swiped the phone to life, then selected the voice recording app. "Okay. If you could tell me what you remember from the night Heather disappeared."

"I remember everything. You don't forget a night like that no matter how hard you try." He scratched at a worn spot on his jeans. "Dora had been working . . . for your dad, in fact. It was new to us, she'd always been around taking care of whatever needed caring for. I took advantage. I know that now. I didn't give her the space to go after her dreams."

He was off topic, going down another road he seemingly needed to explore. "Dora had so much inside of her when we met. She was brilliant and so talented. She was an artist then. I never meant to get in her way, but I think I took advantage of the fact that she would always put us first. I honestly can't remember a time when I took all three of the kids out so she would have time to paint. Slowly, her hobby faded into the background, and then when Heather left us, the rest of Dora went with her."

He wiped away a stray tear. "I'm sorry. That's not what you asked." Mr. Crane pulled a napkin from his pocket and blew his nose, then tossed it into the wastepaper basket. "The last day. It was still quite warm, an Indian summer for sure. Dora was gone late that night. She was giving her notice to your dad. She'd really struggled with the job the last few weeks. I assumed it was because school was getting started and Dora was used to being the class mom and all-around volunteering wonder woman. I didn't give her reasoning enough thought. I was glad that she'd be home again, and dinner would have a bit more variety." His laugh lacked humor.

"Heather was taking care of Mr. Potter's cat that week. I have a hard time remembering, but I think he wasn't supposed to be back until Saturday, and this was a Thursday. She'd go over there and give the animal some attention, feed it, and make sure the water was fresh and clean. It's something she'd done a few other times that summer. Do you remember that?"

"I do now." Faith closed her eyes for a moment, letting the memory surface. "We felt like we were so grown up, being in Mr. Potter's house on our own. The cat was super friendly, and we couldn't give him enough attention. We'd use the money Mr. Potter paid her to get ice cream."

The sadness that stained his eyes had a depth she was afraid to look into. "Did anything . . . wrong ever happen? You know, with Potter?"

She knew exactly what he was asking. It was a question she'd asked herself a hundred times since she'd had lunch with Nate. "I don't know if it would be better if it had, but no, I can't think of anything odd. We didn't have a lot of contact with him. It was only when he'd ask her to look after the cat, and then he'd pay Heather when he returned. If she was uncomfortable with him, she didn't share it with me."

He exhaled. "I'd never had a thing against the guy until he came up as a suspect. The man had lost his wife a few years earlier. I guess that could change a guy."

"Dad." Brooke reemerged and took his hand. "Are you okay?"

Mr. Crane straightened, his strength seeming to return. "Aw, I'm fine. How's Mom doing?"

"The doctor is running a few more tests, but they said it wasn't anything like a heart attack or a stroke. They said you could come back with me now, if you want. Mom was okay with it." Brooke's face told the story her words were leaving out. She needed her dad with her.

Faith stopped the recording. "We can get back to this another time. I think Mrs. Crane and Brooke could really use you now."

He stood, and Faith followed his example.

"Thanks for being here and making sure Dora got to the hospital. We owe you a little more each day."

"Not at all." This wasn't the time to let loose all the things that summer with their family had given her.

Mr. Crane reached out and pulled her to him. Before she could stop them, her own tears were flowing.

22

Dora

She could hear them in the kitchen, talking in voices they thought were so sly. Paul and Brooke spoke of her care as if she'd been put on hospice. It was only an *event*. That's what the doctor called it. A result of untreated high blood pressure and a great deal of stress, topped with a touch of dehydration. Their pity only made her feel more pathetic, an old bird with little to do but lose her feathers one at a time until she could no longer fly.

Dora sipped the ridiculous chamomile tea Brooke had made for her. For goodness sakes, the temperature was in the eighties. Who in their right mind made an old woman drink hot tea on a day like this? She'd be better off taking care of herself, and that's exactly what she would tell them if they'd stop their mumbling in the other room and include her.

Pounding reverberated through the window screen. Potter's son would be busy with all the repairs and beautification so he could get every cent possible out of the old man's house. People like that had a lot of nerve, moving on in the world as if nothing important had really happened here.

Paul shuffled into the room. His body was giving in to age, even if his mind was determined to keep going. "Brooke and I talked. We feel it's best for her to head home and take care of her family. I'll be staying in my room for a couple days until you're back on your feet."

"Nonsense." Dora stood, maybe a bit too quickly as the room did a small wave before leveling itself. "You do not have a room here. I'd prefer not to discuss this in front of our daughter, but since the two of you felt it necessary to chat about my well-being without me, I guess it's all out in the open now. Paul, you moved out of this home. You decided you could no longer live with me. I will not take your sympathy. You made the decision to move on, so be about that."

"You're being ridiculous. It's not like we're getting a divorce."

"Oh, isn't it? I'm not so sure about that." She eased back down, feeling the pounding of her heart taking over her body again.

"You are out of your mind. Do you know that?" The vein in the side of his neck started to bulge the way it always did when he got angry. "All I'm trying to do is get you to see what you're doing to this family. We can't live in the past forever."

"Oh, so it's the give-up-on-Heather conversation again?"

"Do you think this is what she'd want? Do you really feel like she'd be okay with how we've been living? It would break her heart." Tears were in his eyes, but she couldn't let herself care about that.

"I want you to leave. I don't need either one of you here." Dora focused her gaze on the coffee table. "I need to rest. Please, go."

"Mom, I could stay. It's really not a problem."

"Brooke, I'm sure your intentions are good, but you are old enough to understand that sometimes people need to be alone. Please, go with your father. I have my new phone right here. I can call you if I need you." That wasn't altogether true. Dora was still confused about half the time she tried to use it, but she could listen to the podcasts, and that felt like a victory.

"I'll be back in the morning." Paul walked right out the door.

"Don't bother." She threw the words out behind him, but he'd never hear them. "Brooke, you go on too. I need to rest." The way her voice took on that feeble note scared her. She should want to do better, try to be there for her remaining daughter as well as her son and grandkids. "Charity showed me how to color on my new phone. I think I'll give that a try."

"Okay, Mom." Brooke leaned over, dropping a kiss on Dora's head. It was an oddly personal offering. "I'll check back in later."

Dora laid her head back on a pillow and listened for the car to leave, before remembering Paul had just replaced his truck with that overpriced hybrid. The thing was sneakier than a rodent.

Two and a half months, and then she'd have to pack up Heather's room. Why had she agreed to this?

With a grunt that hadn't been there a year earlier, Dora got herself up. She took another sip from the glass of water Brooke had set on the coffee table and walked down the hall until she came to the last door.

This door was never opened. She considered buying a lock for it at one point, fearing Paul would get rid of everything and she'd forget Heather, forget all the tiny little things that had made her child laugh. Her hand rested on the knob for a long time until she found the strength to twist it and push her way into the past.

The room had changed quite a bit since that night. She always forgot about that until she opened the door. Brooke hadn't been able to sleep there. Eventually, Greg let her have his bed, and he moved to the couch. Then, as if life went into fast-forward, he was off to college, and he'd never truly lived at home since.

Over time, Brooke had moved her things from here to her

new room. The carpet still showed where her bed had been and where her dresser had sat.

Dora closed her eyes and saw it all the way it had been when her life was complete. Brooke would be flopped on her stomach, the Walkman headphones shooting muffled lyrics into the room. Heather was never into music like her sister. When she wasn't outside, she liked playing board games and creating art. She'd sit in here for hours doing paint by numbers. Dora had planned to teach her how to properly paint but hadn't found the time. And now she never would.

With her wrinkled hands, she picked up the pillow and held it to her nose. The scent of Heather was long gone, replaced with the gentle tickle of dust that invaded even a walled off section of time. She wasn't out of her mind. Dora knew Heather wasn't coming home. Even five years ago, that might not have been true. She'd been bolstered by the return of Jaycee Dugard, obsessed by all the twists and turns of that story. It gave her hope when Jaycee was discovered after eighteen years.

How could she pack up the memory of Heather when there was always that niggle of hope, that chance that one day she could be the mother with the miraculous reunion?

23

Faith

A quick look at the app showed not a single Uber driver in Deep Valley. They barely had a bus system. Faith walked from the hospital into town, where she picked up a few groceries. From there, she'd planned to walk the mile or so back to the house with the brown paper bag on her hip.

As she left the store, the summer heat hit her like a slap across the face. At nearly noon, her stomach was growling, her mouth was dry, and the groceries seemed to have gained weight somewhere between the cash register and the door. Waves of heat wove up from the asphalt, but through them, she spotted a familiar face in the parking lot.

Nate waved her over, clearly finishing a conversation with a man who didn't look to have enjoyed the interaction. "Can I carry that bag to your car, ma'am?" He dipped forward in a truly dorky and endearing way.

"No car. I walked."

"Then allow me to give you a ride." A sudden feeling of unease rose up, a dream coming back to her from the night before.

Heather, Nate, and Faith had been sitting on the top of the cliff over the swimming hole, but it was much higher, stretching up and away from the water. He'd put his hand over hers, and Heather tried to stop him, so Nate had shoved her off the edge. For a minute, she could hear Heather's screams as she plummeted toward the river below, but Nate's expression stayed consistent, his smile and eyes focused on her as if Heather's plight was nothing to him.

"You okay?" Nate unlocked the passenger door of his dark sedan and held it open.

Faith hesitated. There were times when being completely irrational and siding with a person's gut feeling saved lives. Yet, she couldn't deny her growing mistrust of all men, no matter their intentions. "I'm fine. My imagination has been crazy since coming back here."

His head bobbed in agreement.

Back were her feelings of security, another unfounded feeling. She slid into the seat and buckled. A photo of a beautiful woman was taped to the dash, its edges worn with much handling. "Is that her . . . your wife?"

"Yes. I still like to have a bit of her with me." He sighed. "It's probably time to take it down."

"I don't see why you would. If it makes you happy to have her picture there, it's not hurting anyone." Faith tugged at her seatbelt.

He pulled out of the lot, dropping the visor to shield his eyes from the sun. "Did you know that you were my first real crush?"

A chill prickled her skin. Maybe the air conditioning picking up. "I was never really sure. You spent a lot of time with me and Heather that summer. I always wondered what you could see in a couple of girls."

"It was an odd summer. I wasn't fitting in with the guys I'd hung out with anymore. And then I met you. You were all I could think about back then. I was always trying to find a way to get you alone, but the two of you were stitched together."

That kind of transparency was tricky. It usually came with the expectation that the other person would share it too. Faith scrambled for words to fill the space between them. "We've talked about what's in the case file, but I'd like to hear what you remember from the day of Heather's disappearance."

The breath he blew out lifted the wisps of hair hanging across his forehead. "I didn't know anything had happened until Monday at school. By then, it was the fourth day, and people were starting to think she wasn't coming back. School started not long after you left. Heather and I slid back into our groups of friends. We'd only been in school for a week when it happened. It was also the week my grandpa died. I'm pretty sure we weren't even in town that Friday or I would have known earlier. We took off to be with my grandma at some point in the night or the next morning. When I found out on Monday, I snuck off to the gym. It was dark in there, not a P.E. period. I hunkered down behind the bleachers and wept like a child. I guess I really was a child back then, though I felt like I knew everything."

"I've never felt like that."

He turned to her for a moment, then switched his gaze back to the road. "Not even in your teens?"

Faith's teen years had been a mess. While her classmates were spinning in an excited whirlwind of future possibilities, she was still coming to terms with the losses that had left her and her mother alone and, for the first time, without financial stability. Moving back to Grandma's house was the obvious solution, Faith had known that even then, but Mom wouldn't hear of it. Her pride kept them on the edge of eviction. "Nope. Not even then."

Heather's house loomed in front of them, no cars at the front curb, no one out watering the flowers or mowing the yard. There seemed to be a cloud over the home even on the sunniest days.

Nate pulled up in front of Faith's temporary home. He pushed the visor up and stared along with her into the past. "They brought counselors and all the local pastors in to support the students, but I didn't say a word to any of them."

"Why?"

He absently rubbed his thumb along the corner of the photograph. "I'm not sure now. There was a lot of anger. It might have been fear or even pain, but at that age I wasn't able to handle all the feelings, so it came out in rage."

She shifted closer to the door, but he spoke again. "You know, I found out years later that my parents had known since that first call, but they actually let me go to school and find out there. It was a crazy time for our family, but still." A little of that anger was visible in his eyes now.

"That's horrible." How was it that she could actually feel guilty because she thought she'd had a hard time when she now knew the hurt he'd endured?

"No one knew the right thing to do back then. I can understand that they were in shock too, but it's not really an excuse."

The curtains moved, and Crouton's face smashed against the windowpane.

"Looks like we're being watched."

"Oh my goodness, I ran out to see about Mrs. Crane this morning, and I hadn't fed Crouton yet. He's got to be starving, and he holds a nasty grudge." She popped the door open, then looked back at him. "Would you like to come in? I could make coffee."

"Well."

"Just so we could finish up our talk about what you remember. I need it for the show." A flush heated the skin on her neck and made Faith want to climb under the car to hide. After all these years, and she reacted to this man like she had when they were kids.

"I'm going to have to take you up on that coffee another

time. I've got a case I'm in the middle of, and I'd like to get a few details pounded in before the end of the day." He nodded his head in a way that felt like a dismissal. "We'll stay in touch."

She closed the car door and he drove off before she'd moved from her spot on the sidewalk.

Faith jotted a few notes from her quick conversation with Nate. She'd sketched out a plan for the first episode of what she'd decided would be a special series. In that, she'd share the perspectives from first knowledge of the disappearance.

What she needed to move forward was any information Detective Masters could share from the initial investigation. She wanted more than a report. If only Faith could get his gut feelings from that night, the regrets and concerns that didn't make their way into the paperwork.

Faith flipped her notebook open to the section where she compiled contact information. Sheila Masters Blane was the daughter who cared for Detective Masters. She punched the number into her cell and waited.

"Hello?"

"Is this Sheila?"

"It is, but I don't have a car warranty, so don't bother to tell me that mine is expired."

Faith immediately liked her. "I'm not a solicitor. My name is Faith Byrne. I lived here the summer of 1987." She caught herself before mentioning the podcast. The show might not work to her advantage with Sheila.

"You're calling about Dad and the Crane case?" Her voice had gone flat.

"I am."

"Why? What's the point of bringing all this up after so many years? He's an old man. His health is very fragile."

"I understand. My dad has been gone for some time now." She paused. What could she say to make Sheila care about a case this cold that didn't seem to have any hope of closure? "Heather was a friend of mine, probably the best friend I ever had growing up. Her family needs to have closure in one way or another."

"And you think you can do that? Are you a cop?"

"No." Faith stretched the tension out of her neck. "I'm, well, I used to be an investigative reporter."

"And now you are a what?"

"I have a podcast." She dipped her head, waiting for the response.

"You're one of those true crime junkies?"

"No. It's not like that at all. My show is about stories of hope and triumph that come out of tragedy."

"And you think you can make a story out of the Crane's situation. You know, Brooke and I were good friends in high school until Heather disappeared."

"What happened then?"

"She wasn't the same anymore. Didn't want to go out or have fun, and I was a self-centered teen who couldn't put myself in her shoes." The regret dripped from the words.

"I'd like to bring attention back to Heather's case while there are still people around who might be able to give us some answers to what happened to Heather. You could be a part of that."

Faith let the silence sit between them, fighting her natural instinct to try with words to win the battle.

"What do you need from Dad?"

A breath released from Faith, deflating the tension from her body. "Could I come by and have a conversation with him? If it's too much, we'll end it."

"Okay. He's usually best in the morning. Could you come by tomorrow around nine?"

"Absolutely." Faith jotted down the address and thanked Sheila, then hung up before she could change her mind.

The phone buzzed in her hand. Harlow. "Hello, honey. How's the trip going?"

No response.

"Harlow? Can you hear me?" Faith jumped to her feet, as if she were heading to her daughter to fix something.

"Oh, hi, Mom. I wasn't in a good place for reception. How are you?"

"Good. But I want to hear about you. How's Hawaii?" They exchanged texts every day, but listening to her daughter's voice was healing.

"It's warm, like, all the time."

"You say that like it's a bad thing." A tiny niggle of guilt crawled over her. Would it really make her happy to have her child unhappy? What had this divorce and subsequent competition with Neil done to her? "You have the wedding this weekend, right?" The chirpier tweet of her voice sounded like it came from an old-fashioned cartoon character.

"Yeah. I think that's the thing. Mom?"

"What? Are you okay?" The guilt flared hotter.

"I feel bad. I know you said we could come here and all, but you're alone. I didn't even think about how you'd be by yourself while Dad is . . . starting over." The sorrow in that voice, it was something a mother couldn't handle.

"Oh, sweetie, you don't need to worry about me. I haven't even given your father's wedding a thought." *Except every moment I'm not working.* "I'm having a wonderful summer reliving memories and reconnecting with people I haven't seen in decades. I'm fine, okay?"

"Really?"

"Absolutely."

"Are you reconnecting with anyone in particular?"

She should have expected this, but hearing it from her own child felt wrong. Harlow was clearly asking about men. Had she reconnected with a man in a way that could become a relationship? Of course not. She was a mom. A mom in her forties with a job and a house and . . . well, that was all, but she wasn't ready for dating. Even thinking about it seemed inappropriate. "Nothing like that. Just old friends."

"Okay." She sounded disappointed.

From somewhere distant, Ava's voice called for her sister.

"You hug your grandparents for me and wish Wendy luck." Hopefully, Harlow hadn't caught the snarkiness that went along with that wish. Maybe someday she could think it and actually mean it, but that certainly was not today.

24

Heather

With two bikes, Faith and I could go anywhere, and we did. Nathan insisted on joining us more often than I wanted. It's not like I had a problem with being friends with boys or anything, but I had a feeling his interest in Faith was a bit more than as a buddy.

One afternoon, we took off on an adventure and found ourselves in the partially built neighborhood that Faith's dad was building. Neither of us had known or cared where this was, but when we stumbled across it, we were amazed. Houses lined new streets, all in different stages of completion. The air was filled with the smells of wood and the pounding of hammers and the whirling of saws. There was excitement all around us as a whole new section of town came into being.

"What are they going to do with all these houses?" I asked to no one really.

Nathan pulled his bike up next to mine and flipped his kickstand down. "There's a computer company moving this way. I heard my folks talking about it. Dad's hoping to get a job there since the mills have been down so much. I guess a lot of people will be moving here for the jobs."

I rolled my eyes. "People moving to Deep Valley for jobs? That will be the day."

"No, he's right." Of course Faith would agree with him. "That's what my dad says too. The computer place will need a thousand people to work there."

Climbing off my bike, I tipped it onto the curb. "There's only three thousand people in Deep Valley. I think that includes the kids."

"Times are changing." Nathan put his hands on his hips and nodded.

"You look like an old man when you do that," I told him.

His arms dropped to his side. The least I could do was to keep his ego in check if he was going to be hanging out with us all summer.

"I wonder what it's like here after the workers go home." I could imagine climbing around in the half-built houses, pretending Faith lived on one side and Nathan on the other. We could imagine we were getting together for some sort of fancy dinner party.

The possibilities seemed to have Faith in her own trance, but Nathan was a planner and a doer. Okay, he was a lot like me, and that might have been part of the reason I sometimes found him a touch annoying.

"I know what we can do." His eyebrows set themselves up like rising umbrellas over his dark eyes. "What time do your parents get home from here?"

"My mom is back by five fifteen, on the dot," I said.

"Dad usually comes in around six. We have a late dinner—when I don't eat at the Cranes'." Faith flashed me a conspiratorial smile.

"What if we had a very late dinner here in one of the houses? It would be like they do in the big cities." Nathan rubbed his palms together, probably thinking more about food than the adventure.

"What do you know about big cities? You've lived here since you were born." I was doing a solid job of checking his ego. "Anyway, my mom will never let me come here that late."

Faith shrugged. "I'm sure I could get out."

No way would I let them do this without me. "I guess I could tell my parents that I'm eating with Faith. I mean, it would be true." My parents expected me to push the boundaries. It was kind of my thing. I think my dad even respected me for it a bit, but I wasn't a liar. Even when a fib could get me out of trouble, I told the truth and took the punishment. At least, I had up until this point.

We were at the edge of the development. Somewhere farther along were the trailers my mom talked about. They'd been brought in to make offices during construction. If we stayed on this end, no one would ever know. "Let's do it. Brooke is going camping with a friend this weekend. On Thursday night she'll be a mess of packing and demand all of my mother's attention."

"Thursday," said Nathan, like he was making a pact.

Again, Faith shrugged. "Sounds good to me."

25

Dora

Dora felt like her teenaged self as she dressed in the darkest clothes in her closet. Handymen were still in and out of the Potter house all day, but it was always quiet at night. She'd taken midnight strolls the last two days just to be sure. Tonight, she was going out for more than a walk.

Frog noises from the creek down the road filled the night, obscuring her ability to hear if anyone else was out there but hiding her own sounds as well. She looked around, the picture of a casual neighbor, outside to enjoy a chilly walk after a hot summer day. All except for the metal detector she had slung along her side.

When she reached Potter's place, Dora scanned the area, not a light on in any house. The streetlamp was closer to her place, leaving the house of horror in a convenient shadow. As if she'd just thought of it, she turned, skimming along the side yard to the gate that led to the back. She hadn't been in the Potter backyard since Mrs. Potter was alive. That poor woman. Imagine her looking down from heaven and seeing all the trouble her husband caused. Even after death that must have been heartbreaking.

The gate opened with ease. It must have been one of the repairs, as Dora had never had that kind of luck with her own. The soil here sunk beneath her feet. She clicked on the key ring–sized flashlight and discovered new grass in its infancy. What were the chances she'd find any clues after all this time, and with the tilling that must have gone before the planting?

With the light switched off, she made her way along the edge of the house, avoiding the sensor that was barely visible in the moonlight. The last thing she needed was a motion-controlled floodlight to announce her presence. When she was directly under it, she reached high and turned the switch. Only a fool like Potter's son would install a light low enough for a woman Dora's height to switch it off.

The sliding glass door was tucked under an awning, which covered it in darkness. She felt for the handle, found it, and pulled. The lock was not engaged, but it only moved a couple inches before running up against something in the track.

If she couldn't get inside, she'd start with the backyard. At her touch, the metal detector—a purchase she'd made from her new smartphone, thank you very much—came to life. Unfortunately, it animated with a loud beep and a flash of colorful lights, all amplified by the silence of the night.

Dora sandwiched the device between herself and the siding, then found the volume control and notched it down. It had a hole for a headphone cord, but she was afraid she wouldn't hear someone coming. With one hand shielding the readout, Dora began to search the yard for signs of metal. Heather's bike was somewhere, and if she found it here, it would prove Potter was involved.

It might be too late to make that old monster pay for whatever had happened to Heather, but she'd be sure everyone knew he'd been the one behind it. A faint beep called her attention. The lights were flashing like an eighties school dance.

Dora set the machine aside and started to dig with her

hand. With the ground freshly turned up, it was easy. Three inches down, her finger caught on metal. When she got it out of the damp earth, what she had was only a pocketknife that had seen its day many years past.

An hour stretched by, with the device hitting on spot after spot. Finally, she came across something bigger. Dirt put pressure under her fingernails, made the skin on her hands sore and raw. It was sharp, like the jaws of a tiny trap. When Dora freed the treasure, she held it up in the moonlight, poking clods of dirt from within its openings. She held a pedal, like the ones Heather had on her bicycle.

Dora collapsed onto the cool dirt, holding the piece to her chest. Maybe, after all these years, she'd finally found something.

Lights flooded the backyard, sweeping over her like a hot wind.

"Ma'am. We're the police. Please show us your hands."

Dora rolled to her bottom, raising her hands in the air, the pedal still clenched in one.

"I'm going to need you to drop whatever is in your right hand."

She held tighter. "I can't do that."

"Ma'am, that was not a request. Drop your weapon." The voice was as stern as her father's when he'd been really fired up.

She wanted to obey, but her fingers would not release the pedal. "It's a bike pedal. My daughter's."

"Okay. Please put it down. We can have a good talk about all this after you do."

Dora let her arm fall to the carpet of newly sprouted grass, the treasure now a weight too heavy for her to hold.

26

Faith

Faith rolled over in bed, exhaustion still hanging onto her. Something was living in the attic, and it was the kind of something that liked to be awake all hours of the night. She'd gotten out of bed two times in the dark of the night just to check the pull-down stairs, making sure they hadn't been opened. Harlow and Ava had always wanted a dog. If they were here now, this would be a good time to ask again.

She scanned the nightstand for the clock, her eyes blurry. A burst of panic woke her up with a jolt. If she was going to get to Detective Masters' house in time, she'd have to be in the car in less than fifteen minutes.

Crouton hopped onto the bed and meowed.

"I know. Feed you first. It was one time, not a habit."

Another point for dogs: They didn't hold a grudge like a cat.

Faith threw on an outfit that would look professional but keep her from overheating. She ran a brush through her hair and pulled it into a non-messy bun. A few swipes of makeup, and she gave herself the it-will-do nod.

Popping into the kitchen, she stared longingly at her new coffee maker. How could she keep doing this to herself? Was it so hard to prep the coffee maker before bed, the way Neil had always done it?

She fed the cat, grabbed her notebook and bag, then headed outside. It seemed to be heating up earlier each day, with the sun already warming the side of her car. Across the street, dirt littered the sidewalk in front of the Potter house. Whoever was hired to do the yardwork was making a horrible mess.

For the entire drive, Faith's eye darted from the road to the clock on the dash. She pulled into the driveway with exactly one minute to spare.

The front door opened as Faith climbed out of the car.

"Good morning. You must be Faith." The woman seemed younger than Faith had expected, even knowing she was at least two years older than herself. Sheila's hair was a silky blond, with large flowing curls tied back in a loose band near the base of her neck. She dressed in clothes that would impress the kind of people who lived in the nicer areas of Deep Valley. She walked down the driveway with her heels clicking along the cement. "Dad is in good spirits today. You're very fortunate." She tipped her head in a way that indicated they were in on something together. "Come on in. Would you like some coffee?"

Faith had fantasized about an offer like that throughout the drive. "I would love some. Thank you." The formality made this feel more like a job interview, with Sheila being the boss's secretary.

Inside, the house was painted in soft yellows. Everything here had a place. It was the kind of home that would be the feature spread in a décor magazine, if it were larger. A man leaned back in a recliner, a lidded water bottle beside him, a light blanket over his legs.

Sheila led her to a chair near the recliner. "Daddy. Ms. Byrne is here to talk with you about that little girl who went missing all those years ago. Do you remember?"

"I'm not dead. Of course I remember Heather Crane. If I forget something like that, well, you can go ahead and pull the plug."

"Daddy." Sheila twirled around and clicked off toward the kitchen. "You're so silly."

When she was out of view, he leaned toward Faith. "I raised that girl, and now, just because I got a bum ticker, she thinks she can treat me like I'm the child. I've wiped her hind end."

Faith held back a grin, not sure how much the man was kidding. It would be a difficult situation for her too. She wouldn't last ten minutes with Miss Perky as her caregiver. "Thank you so much for being willing to talk with me. I don't want to take up too much of your time."

"Honey, I got time. It's all I got. If you're not sitting here yakking with me, I'll be watching the television until she makes me turn it off for my naptime. What do I need with all this sleeping? You'd think a person could do what they want when they get this old."

"I'm sure she means well."

He grunted. "Maybe so, but I think she should get a pet or something else to look after."

"Detective Masters, do you mind if I record our conversation?"

"Not a problem. It's not like anyone could come after a man like me for sharing too much information. What can I tell you about the Crane case?"

"When did you first hear that a girl was missing?"

He rubbed his hand across his smooth cheek. "I was home that night. School had started back up. I kind of think it might have been around the first weekend after the start of school. Sheila and her brother, they're twins, they were teens. I thought for sure I wouldn't make it through their school days without the embarrassment of being called down to the station to bail out one of my own. But that night, the call was about another kid. The mom was worried. Her ten-year-old wasn't home. The sun had gone down. The officer who took the call didn't make much of it. He figured she was out with a friend and didn't get home on time. The days were getting shorter and all. The officer gave me a call because he was worried the mom was going to come unglued."

Faith's stomach roiled. What would she do if Ava or Harlow didn't come home on time? They were getting to an age where that was bound to happen. But when they were ten, she would have panicked.

"I took my time getting out of the house. I'm kind of embarrassed about that now. Nothing like a kid disappearing had ever happened around here, and I didn't expect it ever would. When I go to the Cranes' house—" He started to cough, hard, bending over at the middle.

Faith reached for the water and handed it to him.

He sipped but continued to convulse.

"Daddy?" Sheila set Faith's coffee on the table beside her. She took a napkin from her pocket and held it by her father's mouth.

He started to calm and took another sip. "I'm okay." He hacked again. "No need to call the undertaker."

"I wish you wouldn't joke like that." Sheila stood, brushing at her skirt as if there was a single bit of lint in this house that could have attached itself to her.

Detective Masters waved her away. He blew out a breath. "Yeah. So, I got to the house and only the mom and older sister were there. The dad and son were out looking. We alerted all the men on duty to be on the lookout for a kid on a bike. They weren't a rich family. I didn't figure anyone had taken her for ransom or anything, and we didn't have anyone in town who we were concerned about for other reasons. Back then, we gave folks the benefit of the doubt, assuming they were decent people until we knew otherwise. Times have changed.

"I tell you, I was starting to get worried by the time eleven rolled around. I spent that night in the Cranes' kitchen, sending out orders from there. We had state police watching for her, I called all the families Mrs. Crane had already contacted, having parents wake their kids up if they were willing. Most were, but none of Heather's friends had seen or heard from her."

Faith pushed a lock of hair away from her eyes. "What about Nathan Nobbles? He was a good friend of Heather's. Did you or his parents talk to him that night?"

Detective Masters closed his eyes, laying his head back on the headrest. He stayed like that so long, Faith wondered if he'd dozed off. "I don't remember talking with Nate myself. I believe his mother woke him and asked if he'd seen her. She told me he hadn't."

The coffee Faith had been sipping turned to acid in her stomach. It sounded an awful lot like Nate had known about Heather going missing that very night, not on Monday at school.

Masters started up with another coughing spasm.

His daughter rushed into the room. "I think that's enough for today."

There was so much more Faith wanted, but the man's face had grown ashen, and dark circles were appearing under his eyes. Sheila wasn't being overprotective. He needed to rest.

Faith lay her hand on Detective Masters' shoulder, the bones oddly evident for such a large man.

He looked up at her, wiping his mouth with a tissue.

"Would it be all right if I came back to talk again another day?"

He nodded, but his eyes had already closed.

Faith switched off the recording app and pushed her phone into her pocket. She thanked Sheila for the time and the coffee, then let herself out.

Neighborhood kids were gathered around a portable basketball hoop. Three girls sat on the curb, each with a popsicle in her hand.

Faith fought the urge to stare, wondering if they'd be friends forever or if they'd be pulled apart by circumstances. Life felt cruel at the moment, an endless series of pieces being torn from beating hearts.

She climbed into her car, leaving the door open as she started the engine and let the air conditioning push out the heat. A sweltering day like this one promised to be perfect for a trip to the mountains and a look around Mr. Potter's cabin.

27

Heather

We actually did it. We pulled off our first true deception, at least for me, and it gave me a thrill and a stomachache all at once. Nathan insisted he did stuff like this all the time. I didn't believe him for a minute.

The three of us met up at the edge of the development. We stashed all three bikes behind a giant mountain of gravel, then started to wander through the partially finished houses. It was silent here, all the sounds of progress having gone quiet for the day. We wandered through a row of houses with see-through walls, all boards with no dressing, and we tried to guess the final layout.

It was Faith who found the one we would claim as ours. It was two stories, with a skeleton of a staircase leading to the top. I think we were all a little worried when we climbed those steps, but the view from the upper level was worth the uncertainty.

"I can see downtown from up here. Look." Nathan pointed to somewhere behind my back.

Shifting, I saw the top of the courthouse in the distance. "Those roofs over there"—I pointed to a place between the courthouse and where we were—"I bet that's our neighborhood. It sure seems closer when you look at it from up here. I wonder if we screamed, would they hear us?"

Faith shrugged. "We couldn't hear the pounding from down there, so probably not."

Nathan stood and walked to the edge of the plywood, where a spot had been created to hold a window. "Hey, Faith? Do you think your family will move into one of these places when they're done?"

"I sure hope so. Dad said we were done moving around after this project. He promised that the next house is the one we stay in."

"So." Nathan turned to us. "We could be standing in your bedroom right now."

"Oh, gag." Faith pretended to stick her finger down her throat. "I doubt it would be this one. There's just the three of us."

"But your mom is having a baby," I said.

"I guess." Faith never wanted to talk about the baby, so I rarely brought it up, but it seemed strange that she wouldn't be excited. "What did you guys bring to eat? I'm starving." She pulled three oranges out of her backpack and set them on the floor between us.

Nathan returned, creating a triangle again. He placed five pepperoni sticks on the floor.

"I wasn't able to bring any dinner food, but I got these." From my pocket I presented six Oreos.

"I think this is a very nice dinner." Faith crossed her legs and folded her hands, her back as straight as an arrow. "We have a fruit, a meat, and a dessert."

"And no vegetables. This is my kind of meal." Nathan leaned forward to grab a pepperoni stick, but Faith slapped his hand.

"Not so fast. This is a proper dinner, so we will start it with a proper blessing. Nathan, you may do the honors."

I giggled as Nathan squirmed in his place on the floor. "Okay, but we don't really do that at our house. I'm not sure what I'm supposed to say."

My shoulders shook with laughter. "It's not hard. You thank God for the food we have, ask Him to provide for us, and thank Him for His forgiveness that we don't deserve."

Nathan looked more confused than before. How could someone our age not know how to pray? It seemed like the kind of thing you learn as you grow up, like how to talk and walk and irritate your siblings.

"Heather, why don't you do it this time so Nathan can hear it? He'll do the next one."

I was a little stunned about that. We were going to do this again? And how do you thank God for the food you swiped from your parents to take to a place you lied about? "I'd rather not."

Faith finally took the responsibility and said our prayer over the odd dinner. I wondered for a minute about the story of the loaves and fishes. This seemed like that kind of meal, but what we had was all we were going to get.

We talked about all kinds of things that night—our hopes for the future, our questions about what the new school year would bring. We were all nervous about fifth grade and the move to the middle school. Hearing it from Nathan and Faith made me feel a whole lot better. Maybe it was like Mom always said: Everyone is going through the same thing.

28

Dora

Dora decided to not make a phone call until morning came. That gave her time to decide who to contact. Paul and Brooke were out of the question.

At one time, Dora had many friends she could call at any time under any circumstances. Tragedy took a toll on those relationships. The other moms she'd raised her children alongside could only handle so much of Dora's reality. She didn't fault them for growing distant. If it were turned around, Dora may have done the same thing.

But what about now? With the kids grown, why hadn't any of those friendships returned? Could they be revived? Or was she destined to spend the rest of her life alone, without community, family gatherings, her husband?

Something had to change, and maybe the discovery she'd made in the yard was the beginning of that resolution. They'd taken her treasure when she'd been placed under arrest. But they had it, and with Faith's help, the officials would be forced to take this evidence seriously.

Faith. That's who she could call. It was embarrassing enough to be a seventy-something woman detained at the pokey. She didn't need anyone who actually lived in Deep Valley knowing about it.

"Hello?" Dora called out her kindest grandmotherly voice.

An officer, a woman who couldn't be older than twenty-five, came to the front of the giant hamster-cage room. "Did you need something?"

"Yes, dear. I'd like to go ahead and call someone to come get me."

The officer's eyebrows raised. "I'm afraid you'll need to be arraigned first. Mr. Potter has filed charges against you, and he seems determined to see this thing through."

"Well, he has a lot of nerve. I found that pedal, you know. That's proof. His lousy father did something to my little girl. I can't believe this."

"You're still welcome to make a call. I'm sure the judge will let you go without too much trouble." She tipped her head. "This is a hard situation." She unlocked the door and led Dora to a phone.

"Can I file charges against that Potter kid? He was hiding evidence. That's clear, isn't it?"

"I'm sorry. I don't know anything about that." She clasped her hands together and stepped away from the telephone.

Dora picked up the receiver, then stopped, her finger over the buttons. "I don't know the number without my cell. Can you get it for me?"

"I'm sorry. I can't do that."

Dora's mouth twisted. Faith had mentioned Nathan Nobbles being the detective who was now in charge of Heather's case. "I need Detective Nobbles. It's an emergency."

"Ma'am, he works in a different building."

"Give me that number then. Or I guess I could just dial 9-1-1." She angled her chin in challenge.

"That won't be necessary." The officer punched numbers into the phone.

It rang seven times before it was picked up. "Nobbles."

"Nathan?"

"Yes. That's me. How can I help you?"

"Oh, Nathan, you sound so grown up. This is Mrs. Crane, Heather's mom. I've had a little bit of trouble that has me in a legal predicament. Do you think you could get Faith to meet me at the courthouse? They want me to chat with the judge."

He was quiet so long she thought he may have hung up on her. "Of course. I'll get the message to Faith, and I'll join you all, if you don't mind."

"I think that would be wise. Thank you, dear." She hung up the phone and swung her gaze back to the officer. "Lock me back up, please. I'm a horrible threat to the community."

Another officer led Dora into the courtroom, her hands cuffed as if she were going to break loose and go all *Die Hard* on the building. Nathan and Faith were both there. They sat together in the row behind one of the tables, but a flicker of shame kept Dora from making eye contact.

When Dora's turn arrived, she was given a seat on what seemed like a stage, because none of this could be real.

The judge spoke directly to her. "Mrs. Crane, I'm beside myself with this one. You've been brought in for trespassing and attempting a theft of property from one of your neighbors."

"Your Honor, that is no neighbor. Mr. Potter did something to my daughter."

"I understand the circumstances of this case. But I need to have your word that you will stay away from Mr. Potter and his property."

"But, Your Honor—"

"No. If you don't agree to this, you will remain a guest of the Deep Valley Police Department."

Dora hung her head. She looked back at Faith and Nathan,

grateful not to find that Paul or Brooke had joined them. "I understand."

"And you agree?"

"I do."

"Excellent. We'll get you out of here soon. Do you need the court to appoint you an attorney?"

"No thank you, Your Honor." It didn't need to be brought up that she'd had a few of these little run-ins in the past and had found a nice lawyer she'd use again.

"Okay. Check with the office, and we'll get you on the schedule. And no more midnight treasure hunts. I understand the Potters' yard looks like a minefield." She banged the gavel, and Dora was dismissed.

29

Faith

Somehow, sitting in the courtroom while Dora Crane stood cuffed in front of a judge squeezed Faith's heart tighter than her own mother's funeral.

The phone call from Nate had caught her as she was about to drive out of town on her next search for truth. Up until Neil walked out, Faith's life had been like a row of dominos, even keel with no surprises, and she'd hated that. Now a mundane day might do her good.

Nathan was invaluable with his knowledge of the situation. He talked Faith through the procedures and explained what would happen next and how Mrs. Crane's life would be impacted by the judge's order. It was an hour before they led her out and Mrs. Crane was once again free.

"I'm so sorry, Faith. I didn't know who else to call." She seemed tired, as if age was tackling her exponentially.

"Don't worry about that. I'm glad you thought of Nate." She looked over at him, standing beside them like a boy embarrassed to be introduced to his girlfriend's mother.

"Thank you both. Nathan, what will happen to the pedal? Can

I get it back? Are you running tests on it?" Her fist clenched and unclenched in a rhythm. "It's proof, isn't it?"

"My boss has decided I'm not to be involved. When they let me have Heather's case, they didn't realize she and I had been friends." He avoided direct eye contact. "I'm not sure what's going to happen with the pedal. It was dug up without permission or a warrant. That alone makes it inadmissible. Besides that, there'd need to be some proof that it was one that belonged to Heather."

Mrs. Crane looked at Faith. "I've listened to all of your shows. I know there are ways they can do all sorts of testing. Can't they figure it out? I have pictures of Heather and the two of you on your bikes. You'd be able to see if it's a match, right?"

"Did you get a photo of the pedal before the police showed up?" Faith's hands itched to get ahold of Mrs. Crane's phone and see this evidence for herself.

She shook her head. "I'd only just dug it up when all the lights came on. How did they know I was there?"

Nate dipped his head, scratched at the thinning patch. "Potter had a security camera installed. He saw you digging around and called the police."

Dora stood taller. "I don't care. If they want to blast that video all over the television, that's fine with me. I want to know what happened to my daughter. What mother wouldn't?"

"But they have solid proof that you were trespassing and that you dug all those holes." Faith reached a hand toward Mrs. Crane. "I'm worried about what's going to happen when you go back to court."

Nate pulled his phone from his pocket and glanced at it. "I've got to run." He turned to Mrs. Crane. "Please, for the sake of the case and your freedom, stay away from the Potter house."

"I'll make sure of it," Faith said. "Let's get you home. A jail cell is not a good place for you to be recovering from last week's incident."

Nate's eyebrows furrowed. "What happened last week?"

A blush worked up Mrs. Crane's face.

"She collapsed right out front of the same house."

The look he gave Faith was one of complete shock. She couldn't blame him. She'd been in town for a couple of weeks, and it seemed as though she hadn't had one day of boredom since. To think, she'd been worried what she'd do with Harlow and Ava gone for the summer.

Nate gave his phone another look, then waved as he jogged off toward his car.

"That boy grew into a very handsome man." Mrs. Crane looked straight into Faith's eyes. "I think I remember him having a crush on you that summer. I don't think it ever went away."

"It's nothing like that. We both want to find out what happened to your daughter."

Mrs. Crane bit at her bottom lip and looked out into the distance. "You know, everyone around here has been telling me to bury Heather, even if I have nothing to bury. My family wants me to grieve for her, to move on without always waiting for her to come running in the door." She stepped toward a wooden bench with a memorial plaque along the back and sat. "But finding that pedal . . . there really isn't any hope of bringing my baby back alive, is there?"

Faith took her hand, covering it with her other one. It felt cold, as if Mrs. Crane's body were going into shock. Hope was life-giving, wasn't it? Could she survive without hope? "I don't know." Grief seemed to pour from the sky, spreading over them, weighing them down. "I know you made that deal with Brooke about the grief support group. Why not give it a try? Sharing the burden with others could be what you need."

Mrs. Crane shook her head. "I couldn't go in there alone, and I can't go with Paul or Brooke. It's been too long. I'm too late."

"I don't believe that. Nate mentioned the group too. He went for a while after his wife died. He actually suggested I give it a try." She hadn't meant to share that last part. Going to a grief support group when her life was levels easier than those who had lost a child or a spouse to death, it felt presumptuous. Self-centered.

"If you'd go, I could go along with you." The quiet words held power. If Mrs. Crane were to take a step toward healing, she'd need Faith to walk it with her. How could anyone say no to that?

Faith squeezed her hand. "We'll go together."

They leaned into each other and stayed there like a statue formed on a bench for a long time, watching people thread in and out of the courthouse. Everyone had a story, and maybe everyone needed a little help toward healing.

Wednesday came too quickly. Faith spent the day going over her notes and typing up her script for the trailer she planned to record the next day. It would take at least one segment to set the scene and connect her listeners to the case she was presenting. And since she had weeks of her regular episodes prepped and ready in the queue, she had time before new material needed to release.

People thought podcasting was easy. They assumed she turned on the mic and just told a story, but there was so much more to the process. They'd be shocked if they knew each episode represented at least thirty hours of work.

With one hour until she and Mrs. Crane were to leave for the meeting, Faith was filling her time, trying to keep her thoughts away from what was to come.

Crouton hopped onto the table Faith had set up like an office. He pawed at her hands as she typed.

"Stop, please." Faith shook his furry foot off.

With no regard for her needs, the cat stepped over her arm and plopped himself down on the keys, sending a string of letters across the screen.

"I think what you're trying to tell me is you aren't getting enough attention."

Crouton rubbed his head against her right wrist.

She picked him up and held him against her chest, stroking his fur in the long motions he'd trained her to use.

His beautiful purr rumbled against her. "I'm sorry. You feel neglected."

Something crashed overhead. The cat leapt from her arm, leaving a scratch across her collarbone.

Faith jumped up, her heart on horror-movie speed. Enough already. She had to know what was going on in the attic. Taking her keys from the rack, she unhooked her pepper spray and set it to fire. With one hand, she grabbed the hanging knob and pulled the attic stairs down. They squawked like a dying chicken. Whatever was up there had full warning of her plan. She turned on the flashlight app on her phone and tucked it under her chin, leaving one hand for the feeble railing.

The steps seemed to bow with her weight. Her death would make it into the top ten funniest ways to die. Her head made it through the opening before the light could display the surroundings. Something hissed. On instinct, she pressed the trigger and filled the space with caustic fumes.

Stabbing pain in her calf shot her through the opening where she landed hard on a rafter. She caught sight of Crouton running away as her eyes began to blur with tears.

At some point, she'd lost her phone and the pepper spray. Nearly blinded, Faith swept her hands around finding the phone upside down in a mound of fiberglass insulation. She shoved it in her back pocket, the light useless now, and rubbed at the waterfall that had once been her eyes.

Immediately, she recognized her mistake as itching joined the burning. Whatever was in the attic wasn't worth this. With her weeping eyes shut tight, Faith felt her way down the steps and to the kitchen. She located the cold water handle and turned it, then plunged her face into the cascade of water. There had never been a better feeling.

Five minutes into this blessed relief, her back started to twinge, unhappy about the position. Faith eased herself back to standing, dabbed her wet skin with a kitchen towel and blinked the world into semi-focus. That wasn't even a direct shot. She'd be more careful with pepper spray in the future. The thought of hitting someone full force by mistake now hit a bit too close to home. Be sure before hitting the trigger.

Someone knocked at the front door.

Faith squinted at her watch. She still had twenty minutes before she needed to pick up Mrs. Crane for the meeting. Whoever was on the other side could come again another time.

They knocked again, this time with more vigor than the last.

"Okay. I'm coming." She dabbed again at her eyes and nose, then swung the door open.

Mrs. Crane stood there, her purse clasped in both hands. "I'm sorry to be early. I was afraid I'd change my mind if I didn't get out of the house when I did." Her head leaned forward. "What in the world happened? Are you okay?" She pushed her way through the door.

"It's nothing. I accidentally activated my pepper spray." She shook her head. "I feel like a fool." She wanted to say *idiot*, but years of teaching her children not to say that word was ingrained in her vocabulary. "I'll be fine in a minute."

Mrs. Crane touched the skin beneath Faith's right eye. "You have a rash here."

"Fiberglass." Oh, yes, she was a responsible adult.

"Let me get you an ice pack." She moved on into the kitchen as if this were her home, returning a moment later with a frozen bag of lima beans. "This was the only suitable thing I could find in there."

"I like lima beans. My kids won't touch them, so I thought I'd enjoy them this summer without anyone to complain."

"Well, you can enjoy this bag on your face." Mrs. Crane placed it over Faith's right eye. "Do you think we'll have to miss the meeting?" A note of hope rang in her words.

"I'll be fine in a minute." There wasn't another of these for two weeks due to the July Fourth holiday. By then, Mrs. Crane could have changed her mind permanently. The ice was doing wonders for her skin. Faith pictured herself walking into the church with lima beans duct-taped to one side of her face. She started to laugh.

"What?"

"I don't know. This is so ridiculous."

A sound she remembered from her past blessed her ears. Mrs. Crane's laughter.

30

Heather

"Why do you always hang out with us instead of your friends?" I wished I'd kept my curiosity to myself when I saw the hurt on Nathan's face. We were plucking dandelions out of my yard while we waited for Faith so we could bike to the ice cream shop. If we picked enough of them, my brother might not be busted so soon for failing at his mowing duties.

"You and Faith are my friends, aren't you?" He twisted a stem and tied it into a green knot, dandelion milk oozing from the ends.

I kicked his foot with mine. "Of course we are, but you usually hang out with the guys. Is it because you have a crush on Faith?" I was never one to miss my target. Mom was always begging me to think before speaking.

"I like her, sure. But I needed a break from them, I guess."

I could understand that. Diane Hansen and I had been best friends in second grade, but by third, I couldn't listen to her snipping at her fingernails with her teeth for another second.

That was the end of that. We might still be friends if I'd taken a break, then gone back to her. And if we were still friends, Faith, Nathan, and I would be swimming in the fancy pool at her house this summer instead of cooling off in the mud-bottomed creek. Choices. "Do you think you'll all be friends again when school starts?"

"I don't know." He sounded tired, like my dad when the mill shut down for a long time and he wasn't working. The kind of tired that wasn't related to being sleepy, but more like being worn.

"Well, pal, it's good to have you." I elbowed him in the ribs.

Nathan shoved me over. "You're so weird." But he was smiling now, so I didn't mind.

That's when a dark blue car pulled up a house before Faith's. I could see her father in the passenger side, talking to someone with his hands, directing the conversation. Their words were muffled, but the anger made its way through the glass without distortion.

"I wonder what that's about," Nathan said. He ducked his head but kept his gaze on the car.

I did the same, trying not to look obvious so they'd keep going. Something like this was more entertaining to me than the television.

When Faith's dad pounded his fist on the dash four times, Nathan scooted closer to our house. I wondered about that. We weren't doing anything wrong, but he seemed like he was set to jump up and run.

Mr. Ferdon swung the door open so hard I thought it would fly off the hinges, then slammed it shut. Without ever looking our way, he stomped toward his house and disappeared inside.

From around the side of the house, Faith appeared. She grabbed her bike from the front of the garage and pushed it toward us. "Are you ready? I'm dying for an ice cream cone."

Nathan looked at her like she'd lost her mind, his mouth hanging fully open.

"What?" Faith kicked her leg over the banana seat. "Don't you guys want to go anymore?"

I gave Nathan the keep-your-trap-shut look, and we started off toward downtown.

31

Faith

Faith had nearly forgotten about the pepper spray and fiberglass pre-show until she walked into the foyer of Valley
Community Church. Every gaze took a brief landing on her.
It was the same on down the row. They'd see her, their eyes
would widen, then they'd look away, as if her right eye wasn't
nearly swollen shut.

"Good evening." A woman with a flowing blouse in muted
colors approached them. "I'm Hillary. I serve here at the church
in the counseling ministry. Are you here for our grief group?"

Mrs. Crane took a slow step back, as if she were contemplating a run from the building.

"We are." Faith reached over and held Mrs. Crane's elbow.
"I'm Faith, and this is Mrs. Crane."

"You can all call me Dora."

Recognition lit Hillary's face. "Oh, Dora. I believe you are
Brooke's mother, is that right?"

She nodded her answer.

"Brooke is such an amazing woman. I don't know how she
does all she does, but I understand she learned a lot from you."
She turned her gaze to Faith. "Brooke and Erik have been

helping us with the middle-school ministry. They are tireless. I wouldn't last in there for ten minutes."

"Neither would I." Faith had barely made it through her own middle school days.

"We'll be getting started soon. There's coffee and snacks on the table over there, because what kind of church would we be without food?" She grinned and moved to greet the next person.

Treats were the last thing on Faith's mind. She was thinking about an escape plan herself. She really didn't need to be here. Didn't Mrs. Crane have a friend her age who could accompany her to the group?

Dora filled a plate with cookies, then handed it to Faith as if she were an underfed child.

Hillary soon called the group together. Tables formed a square, with chairs along the outside and paperwork at each place. "Welcome. As many of you know, this is a twelve-week course, but we encourage participants to join at any time during those twelve sessions. We've found there is so much need for this ministry that we repeat it year-round with a one-week break at the end. What's different about our group is that we're not exclusively a bereavement support group. We discuss and work through all kinds of grief. That can be the loss of a loved one to death, a financial loss, loss of a relationship, divorce. Over our lifetimes, we all experience loss. Last week, we talked about taking our time through the process. Tonight, we're on week three, Identifying Your Experience. Before we start, does anyone want to share thoughts that have come up since our last meeting?"

A woman on Faith's right raised her hand, a prosthetic arm. "This was a good week for me in that it gave me a lot to think about. When I lost my arm, I wanted to force myself through the process of being sad and move on to living. I mean, my arm would have killed me if the doctors hadn't taken it. But it doesn't really matter how good the outcome. Accepting and living without something or someone that you're attached to"—she waved her arm in the air—"it takes time."

A man on the other side of the square gave her a thumbs-up.

"Excellent." Hillary's face beamed. "No one wants to be sad, but God doesn't give us the ability to have emotions without a reason."

Person by person, the group shared how their losses changed, at least temporarily, how they identified themselves. Faith had thought of herself as a wife and mother for so long. Then Neil walked away like it all meant nothing, as if her losing herself wasn't important. He'd taken one of her most valuable images and stripped it away. Every day, she made the choice to keep moving forward because of Harlow and Ava. But had she taken time to rebuild herself?

When Faith stepped into her house after walking Mrs. Crane to her door, something felt off. There was a coolness in the air, like an unperceivable breeze was weaving through the rooms. And the scent was different—not bad, but not what she'd grown accustomed to.

"Crouton? Here, kitty kitty." The cat didn't always come running when Faith came home, but he did usually check in from a distance.

Faith felt her key ring for the pepper spray, then remembered it was still in the attic. Just the thought had her rubbing her eye. She had never been a gun person, so the idea of having one in her home was frightening. For a reason she couldn't pinpoint, her views on the subject suddenly felt as though they needed more thought.

She left the front door open. If she were attacked by an intruder, at least she had a chance that a neighbor walking by may hear her scream and come to the rescue.

A crash rang out from the living room.

In all her planning for potential disasters, she hadn't counted on her feet becoming a fully-attached part of the flooring. Faith snagged a lamp and yanked the cord from the wall. Her heart beat so loud she couldn't hear if there were any noises in the kitchen.

With the cord ready to use as a whip in one hand and the lamp in the other, she stepped lightly toward the kitchen. What she found wasn't like any crime scene on the television. Her bag of bulk granola was torn open, the contents poured out on the floor. The flour she'd bought to bake cookies for the Fourth of July picnic looked like it had exploded.

She stared at the mess, letting her weapons down.

Something moved in the doorway. She swung around just in time to see the ringed tail scurry up the stairs into the attic.

Raccoons.

Faith flipped the stairs back into place and shoved the hatch closed, trapping the raccoon in the attic, or at least keeping it from visiting again. It had to get in and out some other way. Last she knew, raccoons didn't open and close doors. As a kid, she'd actually had a phobia of raccoons, thanks to a *Little House on the Prairie* episode. The healing of that fear hadn't been tested in her adult life until today. The way her body shook indicated a failing grade.

What was a person supposed to do about a raccoon in the attic? Her first thought, one she would be far too ashamed to admit to another woman, was to call Nate and have him deal with it. Instead, she swiped her phone to life and called Kendall. She'd grown up a farm girl, and the quality had never fully left her.

"Hey, there. How's life in the south?"

"This is hardly another region of the country. I'm still in good ole Oregon."

"Any more interviews with the hot detective?"

Faith sucked in a breath. "I never said he was hot."

"You didn't have to. I could tell."

"I'm hardly in the market for a man."

"Why not?" Kendall wasn't one to throw out a question without waiting for the answer, and Faith didn't handle the silence well. She usually blurted out her response before she could check it. Today wasn't any different.

"I'm married, or at least I was a minute ago."

"Your ex-husband just said 'I do' to another woman. And anyway, you have the summer without the girls. It's the perfect time to go on a few dates and see how it feels without having to worry about their thoughts on the matter. I'm not saying you should elope or anything."

"I don't think he'd be interested." The thought of Nate sitting at the bedside of the woman she'd seen in the photo was devastating. Despite the years, she found she still cared a great deal about the boy—and the man. "Anyway, that's not why I called."

"Doesn't mean it can't be talked about."

"You are ridiculous." Faith couldn't help but smile. Kendall was so different from her. Her spontaneity was like a complement to Faith's scheduled self. "I've got a raccoon in the attic."

Kendall busted into laughter.

"It's not funny. I heard something in the attic, so I went to investigate, but I must have left the attic open after I sprayed myself with pepper spray and rubbed fiberglass into my skin. When I came back just now, that thing had gotten into everything. You should see what it did to the kitchen."

"Oh, stop." Kendall struggled to breathe through her laughter. "You're killing me."

For the second time that day, Faith gave in to the craziness. Who could even make up this story? They laughed together long enough to ease away the stress and renew hope. "This is exactly what I needed. But I also need you to tell me how to get that raccoon out of the attic."

The roar of laughter on the other end of the call swelled again.

32

Dora

Dora held one cardboard box. It wasn't overly large—the size reams of printer paper came in—and that was plenty big. She stood outside Heather's room, knowing she needed to turn the knob and push to get in, but waiting for the energy to power that kind of strenuous motion.

She remembered the breathing exercise a woman had mentioned at the grief group. Breathe in for four, hold for seven, breathe out for eight. Dora worked through the series four times, then forced her hand to move forward.

The inside was exactly how she'd left it, exactly how it was every time she came in, but today was different. Today, she would fill this enormous box with items to donate. Somehow.

Dora had been an involved mother but not the kind who snuck into her children's rooms while they were gone to sneak peeks at diaries or other material that she herself would deem private. There was no way to accomplish this blasted task without invading Heather's space even further than the police had done in the process of their investigation.

The closet seemed like the easiest place to start. She tugged until the door accordioned open. Dora had been in here a thousand times, missing the scent of her baby and holding out hope that it still clung somewhere. It did not.

More than half of the rod was bare, the part that had held Brooke's clothing. She'd been in her fashion stage when she and Heather had last shared a room, while her little sister still thought of clothing as purely utilitarian.

Dora pulled the puffy jacket from the hanger. A coat would take up a lot of the room in the box, nearly all of it. She put her hand into each of the pockets, pulling out treasures. Three pieces of Trident were now as hard as marbles. One glove, no telling where its match was. She'd have to throw it out . . . but maybe it would be okay to keep just the one. Heather's hand had once fit snuggly into this knit. She set it on the bed, along with a rubber band and one of the forbidden Garbage Pail Kids cards.

All those rules, they seemed so pointless in the light of a missing child. She'd buy Heather the whole collection of disgusting images if she could have her back.

Holding the coat in her arms, Dora hugged it tight, felt the material minus her child, told herself this was only a thing. It wasn't needed anymore. If Heather had outgrown it, she would have donated this item without hesitation. Then she folded it in quarters and pushed it into the bottom of the box.

Dora felt sticky. Her shirt clung to her back. She needed a drink, a break, anything to stop the memories. Each item left in the closet was a piece of who Heather had been. Heather, who was likely long since passed, her body never to be recovered, her case never to be closed.

In a rush, Dora snagged a pair of moon boots from the floor and shoved them into the box. She sealed the top by overlapping the flaps and then picked it up. Leaving the room, she closed the door and kept going until she was in the garage, the trunk of the car popped open, and the box set inside to be left at the donation center. Dora slammed it shut and hurried back into the house. There she leaned over the kitchen sink, took a drink from the faucet, and held herself until the sickening feeling subsided.

Detective Covington was the man taking over Heather's case. Maybe Dora shouldn't have gone into the Potters' yard, at least that's what her attorney said, but the find back there was enough to force more eyes onto her daughter's case. She'd gladly go to jail for that win.

Dora had called the detective five times by noon, only able to leave messages. Why wasn't anyone telling her what happened with the pedal? Was there evidence? Could they determine if it was Heather's?

She'd been up well into the night, digging out every single photo that had Heather's bicycle in it. Then she'd made copies of each one. First thing that morning, Dora dropped the stack of copies at the police station, where she'd been told the detective was not yet in.

Waiting wasn't something she handled well. It took Dora back to the first days when Heather didn't come home. She'd done a lot of pacing back then, walking back and forth in front of the living room window, desperate to see her baby come biking up the road. But that never happened. Days darkened into nights, which formed weeks until years had passed, and Dora still spent long periods of time staring out that same window, waiting for a miracle.

Back then, she was a faithful believer. On her knees, she begged God to spare her child, to bring Heather back. Her Jesus had raised His own friend from the dead, restoring him to full health. She couldn't make herself understand how, if she was His beloved daughter, He could allow this agony to continue.

Why hadn't she taken a picture of the pedal when she still had it in her possession? Even knowing there'd only been seconds from her discovery to her apprehension didn't stop the scratching of regret against her soul. Evidence could be lost. Or, because she'd been trespassing, they could ignore the find. That was pretty much what Nathan had said.

If she would have waited, maybe the new owners would have allowed her access to the yard. Maybe they had their own little girl, and the story of Heather would have fallen on compassionate ears.

Potter's kid would have everything ripped out of there before any of that could happen. The man couldn't face the fact that his father was a monster.

Dora's phone rang. Detective Covington. "Hello? Did you get a warrant for the Potter house?"

"Mrs. Crane, would you be able to come down to the station this afternoon?"

"Of course. I can be there in ten minutes."

"That's not necessary. One o'clock would be a good time for me, and I'd appreciate it if you'd bring someone along with you."

Paul was the obvious choice, but not the one she'd make. "I'll do that. See you at one." Dora didn't even stop to run a brush through her hair. She headed out the front door, across the street, and right over to Faith's door.

33

Faith

Detective Covington was a middle-aged man with a head shaved bald and a scar that lined the side of his skull. His button-up shirt strained across his chest, and his face seemed molded into a permanent scowl. "Come on in."

Faith let Mrs. Crane go before her. As they walked down the bare-walled hall, she couldn't help but peek around corners to see if Nate might be there. At the end of the hallway, they were ushered into an office.

The stacks of paper and general mess of the room said the detective had worked here for a while, but there wasn't a single photo or personal item to attest to his commitment.

Detective Covington took a seat behind the desk. "Ladies, we need to talk."

Faith's spine went rigid without her permission.

"Mrs. Crane." He leaned forward, his gaze like a laser on poor Mrs. Crane. "I cannot have you breaking into people's yards and stealing items. Is that clear?"

Mrs. Crane crossed her arms across her chest. "Detective, I don't think you understand what it's like to lose a child. It consumes your life."

His chest expanded then deflated with a huff of breath. "I'm sure I don't understand. And you can't understand what it's like to be a detective. When you insert yourself into my case, you make it harder for me to find out what really happened."

"I got you evidence." Mrs. Crane stood from her chair.

Faith took Mrs. Crane's cold hand in hers.

"Please sit down." The expression on his weathered face never seemed to change.

She took her time, but Mrs. Crane sat.

"I looked into the pedal you found. It being stolen from the property, I have to tell you, we would never be able to use this in court if it actually was from Heather's bike. For all anyone knows, you took the pedal over there to bury it in the Potters' yard."

"I wouldn't do a thing like that."

"Listen, I talked with John Potter. He identified the pedal as one from his own childhood bicycle. And I compared it to the images you left here this morning, just to be sure. They are not a match. The easiest explanation is usually the correct one. Most likely, the pedal was left in the backyard, the rains came, and it ended up smashed into the mud. You've got to stay away from that house." He placed his elbows on the desk and set his chin on his folded fists. "I'm sure you're a nice lady. You don't want trouble. They are talking about suing you for dropping the value of the house."

"I don't care." Mrs. Crane's chin elevated.

"You will when they take your house in the settlement."

In a moment, the older woman aged another decade. "They can't do that."

He nodded. "Yes, they can. Please, I want to help, and I'm going to go back over everything we have in your daughter's case, but I need you to stay out of the way."

The pain Mrs. Crane must be feeling was contagious. It seeped into Faith's muscles, her bones, her soul. Motherhood cut short was a fate beyond comprehension, an agony that couldn't be lifted. "She'll stay out of the way." Faith stood, pulling Mrs. Crane up with her. "Don't worry. There won't be any more trespassing."

They left the office, Faith's mind running wild with ideas and plans. She was going to get to the truth even if she didn't sleep again for the entire summer.

Faith untangled a cord and set her microphone on the desk in the smallest bedroom. She couldn't re-create the studio she used at home, but this would work. Maybe listeners would find the slightly scratched sounds and the echoes from the attic to be a homage to the summer of 1987.

She'd stuffed and recut foam to fit into the window frame, blocking out the sounds but taking needed light with it. The bulb that hung from the center of the room cast shadows. Once again, she was thankful not to be on video. A messy bun and worn denim shorts weren't a problem for an audience that couldn't see her.

She'd need a lamp in here so she could read the notes she'd handwritten. Too bad the one from the living room hadn't survived the raccoon attack.

Today she'd start out with the trailer, getting her listeners ready for a new experience and hopefully pulling in a larger audience. Someone out there had to know what happened to Heather Crane. After all these years, there was no time to waste in finding them. A family needed answers. Faith needed them too.

As she sat in front of the computer, her headphones in place, the microphone aimed her way, Faith felt power come over her. For a lifetime, she hadn't known where she fit, but this felt like a match, like she was finally able to do something that would matter. Was it too much to ask God to bring Heather home, one way or another?

Faith opened her planner to Monday's page and started making notes on the schedule for recording. She highlighted each task with the color she recognized as its twin, then ticked off the checklist in the back of the book. If all went as planned, she'd record her report, then start editing in the clips from interviews.

Setting that all aside, she looked at her reflection on the darkened computer screen. A middle-aged woman looked back where the young girl used to be. Deep Valley made her feel like a child again. It tore open her heart with grief while, at the same time, allowed her to think she still had time to do great things with her life.

The computer whirred awake, running her through prompts until it was time to make the trailer and change this from a silly trip down memory lane to a serious effort to find a missing friend.

"Do you know the name Heather Crane? The people of Deep Valley, Oregon, do. Every last resident has something to say about the girl who has been missing for thirty-six years. Follow along and hear the story. Maybe you hold the key to bringing Heather home."

Faith ran through the words three or four times, changing the effect of her voice, adding or removing pauses, hesitations. When she had it the way she wanted, the real work began.

She added a page to her website, titling it *Special Series*. After staring at the words for ten minutes, she changed the title to *Bring Heather Home*. This was where photographs and other documents would be posted for listeners to peruse. It added another layer of familiarity to a story when the public was able to take a visual tour through the lives of the victims. It made them real, took away the plastic wrap protection of distance and allowed the story to permeate hearts.

That's what had to happen with Heather's story. There was someone out there who had information. That person could be long gone from Deep Valley, maybe long gone from Oregon. If she could reach them . . . It was a long shot, a bet not worth taking, but she had to do whatever she could to help Heather and her family.

Faith began scanning the photos, watching Heather's freckled face appear on the screen before her. How could anyone take her?

The lights flickered and the computer snapped off.

Faith leaned under the desk and found everything securely plugged in. The ceiling light was steady again, and she could hear the hum of the dishwasher in the kitchen. Pressing the power button a hundred times did nothing to solve the problem. She stood and walked around to the other side, as if she could diagnose a computer malfunction any better than she could perform brain surgery.

An odd sound vibrated through the ceiling.

Somewhere in this house was a fuse box. She searched her memory for any clue to its whereabouts but came up with nothing. Might as well start with the garage.

Once there, she spotted the breaker box and eased her way around her father's old car—a mystery in itself. If Faith remembered correctly, the vehicle had been left here due to some mechanical issue. But why, after all these years, hadn't the thing been hauled away?

It reminded her of Neil's college baseball cap. He'd put it on the bookshelf who knows how long ago, and there it remained, blending into the living room until no one even noticed it. The thing must have been there for years, until Neil moved out and took it with him. It was actually the removal of the hat that called attention to it having been there.

The car, though a great deal bigger, was probably like that for her grandmother. After her father's death, she could only imagine her mother didn't want to deal with any additional memories. Mom had been a mess for so long after his death,

184

moving between utter anger at his choice to leave them and pure, unresolved grief. And Grandma, well, it was hard enough to lose a son, but the way he'd died, by taking his own life . . . the car was probably too much to deal with.

This was something Faith could do. She didn't hold a lot of sentimental attachment to her father's belongings. It wouldn't take much to find a new owner for the car. It looked like it was in great shape, aside from whatever problem landed it here. She could even give it to a local teenager in exchange for some work around the outside of the house.

As she switched the flipped breaker back to on, she made a mental note to bring this up with her grandmother on their next call.

Her phone buzzed, a text from Ava.

Can I call?

Instead of texting back, Faith touched the call icon.
"Hi, Mom."
"Hello, sweet girl. How's paradise?"
A pause. "It's good."
"Really? Is something wrong?"
"No. How are you?"
The quick change of subject and a mother's understanding of her child filled in the blanks. "Ava, it's okay to be having a great time."
"I know. I just wish you could be here with us too. I went surfing, Mom. Like really surfing with a full board and everything. Dad hired a guy to teach us how. It's amazing. And I think I'm better at it than Harlow. She says it's not interesting to her, but I can tell it bugs her that I'm getting the hang of it faster."
"I'm so excited for you, but be kind to your sister, okay? It's not easy when your younger sibling outdoes you."

"I know." Her voice was soaked in satisfaction.

"How about Grandpa? How's he doing?"

There was a beat of silence as Faith waited for Ava's response. "He's okay. He's smaller than I remember."

"I'm glad you and Harlow can be there with him this summer, even if I do miss you like crazy."

"Tell me more about what you're doing." Interesting. It took a separation of hundreds of miles, or a subject Ava wanted to avoid, but maybe her youngest was seeing her as a human rather than the one who provided food and rides.

"Well, right now I'm dealing with a raccoon issue. There's one in the attic, and it did something to flip the breaker. I guess I'll need to call in an exterminator." She knew she'd made a mistake as the words fell from her lips.

"Mom, no! Did you know raccoons go into attics to have their babies? It's probably a mother up there, just trying to protect and feed her young. Please, Mom, don't kill her."

The pleading in her daughter's voice broke Faith's resolve. "Okay. No exterminator. I'll work this out in a humane way."

"Promise?"

"Yes, Ava, I promise."

"Dad is calling me. Will you send me pictures of the raccoons if you can get some?"

"Of course." Faith smiled as she hung up. In an instant she'd gone from a semi-dignified podcast host to an eccentric raccoon photographer. Anything for her daughters.

34

Dora

Dora had made excuses for years to not attend Brooke's Fourth of July celebration. The whole neighborhood joined in, and it was too reminiscent of Dora's own days as a young mother of three. But this year, she was going to make an effort for the other people in her life.

The decision had been made the moment she finished the day's assignment in her grief journal. She was to list the people she loved and come up with a statement of how she would show that love to them and another on how she would allow them to care for her. She'd been a disaster on both fronts.

Her grandchildren knew she loved them. They had to. She never forgot a birthday, and she went to most of their school activities. The jobs required to be seen as a good grandmother were the easy part. It was the more intimate tasks—the knowing them, knowing what they liked, where they struggled, who they cared about—that she'd kept herself distant from. It was never intentional, but her heart battled to keep a barrier between herself and the kind of love that could end in devastating loss.

Dora put the last strawberry in place, creating a flag cake

with blueberries and strawberries. She hadn't done this in years, and to her surprise, it hadn't cost her anything to make the effort. It was only a cake. *Enjoying this day, any of it, does not take away my sweet memories of Heather.* This was the mantra she repeated, a broken record that gave her legs the strength to keep moving.

On the wall of the garage, she found the lounge chairs she and Paul had used each year. Those were some of their best times together, sitting side by side, hands clasped in each other's while the neighborhood sparkled with flashes of lights and flames. Dora packed both into her trunk. It seemed sinful to separate the two chairs.

Brooke's house was only about a mile from Dora's. If she were the fit kind of grandmother, like her friend Chloe who still ran 5Ks at every opportunity, she'd head over there on foot. That wasn't her. Dora felt every ache and pain throughout the day, reminding her that time was short. If she wanted to know what happened to Heather, she'd need to hurry.

Outside Brooke's, the kids were already setting up a table by the curb. They displayed their fireworks like a miniature storefront. Sybil waved with one arm, her other in a cast Dora had known nothing about. "What in the world happened to you?"

Sybil looked from the fireworks to her arm. "Oh, that's nothing. I wrecked my bike when we were going over jumps."

A smile grew on Dora's face, wrinkling flesh that had grown unused to the motion. Sybil was so much like her aunt. Heather would have done the jump too, and then been proud to show off her injury. "Well, I hope your big brother and sister are taking good care of you while you recover."

"Ha." Connor came around the corner with another table. "She doesn't need help. She's all empowered and independent."

Sybil giggled. There was a joke here that Dora wasn't part of. Charity and Erik followed Connor, arms full of camp chairs.

Brooke had done well here. Had Dora ever told her daughter that? Probably not. The smile faded with that burden. She had to do better for her children. Pull her son back into the family, tell them both how much they were loved by her.

Retracing a few steps, Dora popped the trunk, then reached across the seat and picked up the cake. The sweet scent was overwhelming, making Dora long for a tart glass of lemonade. She carried it toward the door as Connor jogged up. "Let me take that for you, Grandma."

"Oh, no. I've got this, but if you wouldn't mind getting the chairs out of my trunk." She glanced back at her car, finding Paul there staring into the open back. Dora hurried inside.

"Mom?" Brooke stood in the kitchen, wiping her wet hands on the front of her red, white, and blue apron. "You came."

"You invited me, didn't you?" *Enjoying this day does not take away memories of Heather.*

"Yes, but . . . never mind. I'm glad you came. Would you mind giving me some help with the potato salad? That is, if you're feeling up to it." Brooke's gaze did a quick sweep of Dora, making her feel a bit too decrepit for her liking.

"I feel just fine." She went to the sink and washed her hands, trying to remember a time when she'd helped out in Brooke's kitchen but coming up empty. She set to work cutting the cooked potatoes and depositing them into a large glass bowl. "Brooke, I'm proud of you."

Her daughter's arm stopped mid-stir in the Kool-Aid pitcher. "What?"

"I'm proud of you. I don't think I tell you that enough."

"Mom, you never tell me that."

Heat rose up Dora's neck. "Okay, that may be true, but I'm saying it now."

"Thank you."

The sounds of the two women's hands at work filled the silence. She'd done it, made a move forward. It wasn't a miracle, but it was a step. That was another thing she'd read about in the grief literature, to celebrate small accomplishments.

When Faith walked in, Sybil chattering on beside her, Dora took a deep breath. It was like God dropping a much-needed distraction in the middle of a room tight with tension. "Mrs. Crane, I can remember the taste of your potato salad. I've tried for years to re-create it with no success. Would you please write down the recipe for me?"

"I would love to, but only if you stop calling me Mrs. Crane. Call me Dora. I mean it."

Faith tipped her head and winked at Sybil. "I'll give it a try."

Dora took in the scene, gave it thought, and purposefully placed it in her memory. If it was true that humans only used a small portion of their brains, she could find room in her cobweb-addled skull attic for a few more memories.

By the time the sun started to set, Dora was starting to turn back into a pumpkin. She took a seat in the old lounge chair and put her feet up. They throbbed with relief, while the muscles in her calves chose to scream. Dora let one hand dangle in the cool grass of the front yard. All around, the air was filled with whistles and explosions. She shut her eyes and let the sounds take her back, trying to see her own children as they had been, remembering what it was like to have Paul by her side.

When she blinked her eyes open, she found one part of the fantasy wasn't imaginary. There, beside her in the twin chair, was her husband, his hand hanging in the grass near hers.

35

Heather

Dad let us sit on the roof to watch the fireworks. He and Mom were sprawled out on lounge chairs in the driveway. All up and down the road, smoke billowed, sparks flew, and sparklers drew names in the night air.

Faith and I ate chips and drank pop from bottles while keeping our feet planted on the roofing. I'd seen plenty of movies where people fell from the tops of houses, and I had no intention of being one of those clowns. My sister would never let me hear the end of it.

A high-pitched whistle drew my attention to the Hastings display. They had three young boys, and I was pretty sure one of them would wind up burned by the end of the night. Brooke babysat for the Hastings. She always came home looking like an escaped war prisoner.

"Do you ever wonder what life will be like when you're grown-up?" Faith was laying back on the roof, her gaze on the stars rather than the show below.

"Nah. What's the point?" From where I sat, I could see Faith's grandmother and mom sitting in their own driveway. Mrs. Ferdon kept her face tucked into the top of her pregnancy

T-shirt while waving the sulfur smell away. I wasn't sure what the big deal was. I kind of liked it. That was the scent of summer and celebrations. Brooke said it smelled like the Hastings' dog when it had a bellyache.

"Do you want to be like your parents?"

I'd nearly forgotten what Faith had been talking about. "Sure. I guess." They were good people, why wouldn't I want that . . . eventually. "That's after I retire from archeology, though. First, I'd like to be the female version of Indiana Jones."

The way Faith giggled made me wonder if she was laughing with me or at me. There was no reason I couldn't search the world for treasures, escape evil plans, and be the hero of the story. After that, I'd settle down into a mom life. Until they called me to save the world.

I was losing myself in my daydreams when Faith's father walked out the front of the house. He was dressed like usual, the image of a politician, never found without a collared shirt. He put his hand on his wife's shoulder, and she shivered like it was a spider rather than the palm of her husband. "What about you? Do you want to be like your parents?"

Faith didn't hesitate. "No way. When I grow up, I'm going to marry a farmer. We'll live on a beautiful farm with all kinds of animals, and we'll have a houseful of kids. I'll make him breakfast in the morning, and he'll kiss me on the way out the door to check the cows. He'll come in for each meal, and we'll sit together watching television at night."

I wasn't sure I'd ever heard Faith string that many words together at one time. "It sounds like you've made a plan."

"I can't stand my parents." There was venom in her tone.

My mouth fell open. I'd heard Brooke say things like that, but it was usually her way of disagreeing with a rule Mom and Dad had set. But Faith was different. The way she spoke, I believed she really felt that way. I watched the couple below, both sitting now with a distance between them. I shimmied to the edge of the roof and gazed down at my own parents. The arms of their chairs touched. Mom's hand was wrapped in Dad's. They seemed to relax when they were together, as if nothing could touch them as long as they had the other one.

I wasn't sure what to say to Faith. Looking back at her parents, I had a weird feeling in the pit of my own stomach. I wasn't sure I could stand them either.

36

Faith

With the trailer recorded, edited, and sent to Kendall for her opinion, Faith filled her water bottle and grabbed a banana, then headed to the car to see what had become of Mr. Potter's cabin.

So many people raved about the Oregon Coast, but to Faith, it was in the mountains where her home state truly shone. Not many miles outside the Deep Valley city limits, the road began to climb, and the trees grew dense on either side of the road. She opened her window and let the sweet scent of Douglas fir and forest undergrowth fill her lungs. There was an ever-present dampness in the air, a relief after the unusually hot summer days.

She only grew restless as the navigation in her car announced a turn that brought her off the main road and heading directly toward the address she'd discovered had belonged to Mr. Potter.

The pavement turned to gravel and went on for what seemed like too many miles until the final curve brought a large newly built log cabin into sight. Out front, a woman knelt near the foundation, her hands covered by gardening gloves.

She turned as Faith pulled the car into the parking area and shut off the engine.

A wave of nervous energy spun down her arms. This wasn't anything like what she'd expected.

"Can I help you with something?" The woman, somewhere in her thirties with a simple beauty unaided by makeup, pulled the gloves from her hands and stuffed them into one of her pockets.

Standing on the sloped driveway, Faith dug her toes into gravel. "I'm . . ." She hadn't thought about what she'd say if someone was here. "I'm here to do some research."

The woman's features changed in the way the landscape did when a dark cloud passed by the sun. "We don't tolerate people who come out here to gawk."

"It's not like that." She managed a few steps closer. "My name is Faith Byrne. I'm a podcaster."

Hands turned to fists and anchored on the woman's sides.

"Wait. I'm not some stranger looking to make trouble. Heather Crane was my best friend the summer before she went missing. I'm trying to get attention back on the case one more time in hopes of giving Heather's mom a way to move forward."

"I'm not sure how I can help with that."

Two identical boys, somewhere near kindergarten age, came running around the house, followed by a dog who looked to be record-book old. "We're hungry," one of them announced.

Faith made her way up the steps into the yard. She held her hand out to the woman, who had little choice but to shake it with her boys watching.

"I'm Elenore. My husband and I bought this property and tore down the old structure." She tousled the hair of one of the boys. "I can guarantee you, there was nothing here. Boys, go on inside and wash up. I'll be right in."

When they didn't obey, she tipped her chin and gave an impressive mom stare until they jogged off, the dog following.

"Listen. I get what you're doing, and I'm very sorry for that family. We had cadaver dogs out here, just to be sure. The handlers assured me this land is clear."

"So you knew about Heather when you bought the place?"

"We did. The owner was honest with us from the start." She curled her bottom lip between her teeth. "I just don't believe that this place had anything to do with that girl's disappearance."

Faith let her gaze sweep the wooded property. "Would it be okay if I had a look around?"

Elenore crossed her arms. "No. It would not. It was nice to meet you. Please show yourself out."

Tingles of embarrassment crept up Faith's neck and heated her cheeks. "I'm sorry to have bothered you."

By the time she was safely buckled into the car, Faith was sweating, and her heart thundered. The feeling of being in a place she wasn't wanted had a familiar grasp. She'd felt it claw at her neck many times as a child, and again as her marriage came to an end.

37

Heather

I had the day all planned out. Faith, Nathan, and I were going to bike into town for ice cream since I'd earned some money taking care of Mr. Potter's cat, then we'd hit the creek for a swim and finish the day watching reruns in my living room. My dad had other ideas altogether.

In hindsight, I should have told him I was going out when I was closer to the door, making my escape before he could catch me. The task he gave me felt like the kind of thing I should be paid for, but the last time I brought up payment for chores, Brooke about took my hide off. It wasn't that I didn't understand we were in a financial pinch. I just figured with Mom working now that we would be fine.

Dad gave me a large envelope and directions to Mom's office. I didn't tell him I knew already exactly where she was. I was to take the package to her, wait while she signed something, and return it to Dad.

Faith was waiting outside when I finally escaped the endless directions. It wasn't like I was heading out on an FBI mission. "I can't go to ice cream, at least not for a while. Dad is sending me out on a job."

"Do you want company?"

"Sure. It's actually at your dad's office."

Faith's face fell. "I'm not allowed over there. Dad will have a cow if I show up with you."

"Ready?" Nathan came to a sliding stop beside us. "It's already scorching out here." He wiped his hand across his forehead.

"Heather has to go to the development to take something to her mom."

"Bummer." I was surprised that Nathan actually seemed disappointed. It wasn't a very well-kept secret that he had a crush on Faith. "We could go with you, then get ice cream."

Faith shook her head. "Not if I want to have any freedom the rest of the summer."

"You two go on and get ice cream. I'll meet you at the creek. I have to bring this back to Dad anyway." I held the envelope in the air.

They agreed a little quicker than I would have liked, but the plan made the best sense. I took off, pedaling toward the development while my two friends went the opposite way.

By the time I reached the new houses, my T-shirt was stuck to my back and my mouth had gone completely dry. I followed the road past the house we'd had our dinner in and to the back where the trailer stood. On the door was a sign that said *Office* in bright red letters, but it was nothing more than a mobile container. I leaned my bike on the side and climbed up the rickety metal stairs.

The door opened directly in front of my mother's desk. "What in the world? Heather, what are you doing here?"

I crossed my arms and tried to look hurt, but she wasn't having it.

"Heather?"

"Dad sent me." I dropped the envelope in front of her. "He needs you to sign this and then give it back to me to take to him. I'm basically the butler today."

She cocked an eyebrow. "I don't think you understand what a butler does."

"Sure I do. I watch *Benson*."

Mom peeled open the flap.

A man thrust the door open, nearly taking me out. "Dorothy, I need to see Ivan immediately."

I don't think I'd ever heard anyone use my mother's full name. It was like she was living an alternate life over here.

"Just a moment, Harold. I'll see what I can do." She got up from her seat and knocked gently on the door positioned behind her desk, like she was the guard keeping riffraff from approaching the king. A second later, she ushered the Harold guy her way.

He slammed the door, but not before I heard him announce that they had some sort of problem.

"Now, let me see here." Mom read through each of the documents. She was never one to sign something without reading it first. As if Dad was trying to scam her. Each time I brought home a permission slip she gave me a talking-to about the importance of knowing what you sign.

As she read, I couldn't help but listen in as voices rose and fell behind Mr. Ferdon's door. The guy who came in was talking about the find as if this was an archeological dig site. That got my attention. I sidestepped closer to the end of Mom's desk.

"And what do you think you're doing?" Her eyebrows were halfway up her forehead, which meant I was being called out.

I shrugged. "Nothing."

"You were listening in on that private conversation. Heather, you should be ashamed. I've taught you better than to eavesdrop."

I wasn't sure what to say. How was I supposed to not hear them? It's not like I could turn off my ears just because I found myself in a situation where I wasn't supposed to listen.

Mom slid the papers back into the envelope and handed it

to me. "I think you'd better get these back to Dad. No stopping anywhere on the way home, you understand?"

"Yes, Mom." I gave her a quick hug and went back outside into the scorching heat. As I pushed my bike toward the end of the trailer, the voices became clear.

The man, the one who wasn't Faith's dad, had a raspy voice, like he smoked most of his waking hours. I probably would have kept going, but the way he talked had an edge to it, almost like a threat, and well, he was talking to my best friend's dad and all.

"Listen, Ivan, I can make this all go away. No one will need to know, but I won't be putting my reputation on the line without compensation."

"Do it."

My hand rested on the siding, allowing my ear to be close without the obviousness of a snoop. That's how I felt the vibrations that came with the door slamming shut. I pushed my bike upright and was swinging my leg over when the guy came out the door behind me. I could feel him there, staring at me.

"Hey, kid."

I turned.

"What do you think you're doing?"

I forced myself to look clueless. "Getting ready to bike home."

"You been listening at that window?"

My skin felt like tiny bugs were crawling all over me. I looked up at the window, forced a shrug. "No, not at all."

"You better be minding your own business." He stuffed a hard hat onto his head, lit a cigarette, and started toward a pickup truck.

Air wove slowly from my lungs. Minding my own business had never been one of my talents, but this felt like a very good time to practice.

38

Faith

After another morning of recording, and a phone call with her grandmother, Faith contacted Sheila and set up a time to talk with Detective Masters, then went into town in search of a live trap.

Three blocks down from where the ice cream shop had been was an old hardware store. By the looks of the place, it had been there in 1987 and many years prior to that. Inside, the floors were made of planks, old nails were visible, and the spot in front of the cash register sunk in with the wear of customers.

Faith let her feet settle in the grooves and bounced her index finger on the bell.

A voice called from somewhere in a back room. "I'll be there in a minute." A moment later, a woman who was at least Mrs. Crane's age, her gray hair cut into a short bob, appeared. She was covered with a leather apron, her fingers darkened with the evidence of work. "How can I help you?"

"I've got raccoons in the attic."

"Sounds like a personal problem."

It took Faith a second before realizing the joke. "Yeah. But I need them out. Do you carry live traps?"

"We sure do." She came around the counter and headed toward a room off to the side. As she passed, Faith caught sight of a worn name on the apron. *Fiona.* She came to a stop in front of a wall of shelves, all stocked with cages from the size of a mouse up to the size where Faith couldn't imagine what would be caught in that kind of contraption.

Fiona pulled one from the middle. "This is probably the one you're looking for." She set it at her feet. "You're going to want to be sure you get all the babies. This time of year, they should be pretty mobile, but that doesn't mean they'll climb into the trap with their mama. Chances are the gate will swing down on her, leaving them outside."

"How do I get them all at once?"

Fiona scratched her chin, as if whiskers were growing in. She shook her head. "Well, if you just waited a few weeks, they'll be moving on."

A shiver zapped across Faith's skin. Could she wait? No. It was time to stop cohabitating with the creatures.

"And then what do I do once they're in the trap?"

"Where I come from, we'd poison 'em. Sorry. I don't know much more about livetrapping."

There was always Google. "Thanks. I'll take it."

At the register, Faith handed over her credit card.

"Now make sure you seal off their entry point, or you'll just have a new batch next year." Fiona held it in her hand a moment longer than typical. "You're the podcaster, right?"

"I am."

Silence fell between them like an iron gate slamming shut.

When the transaction was complete, Faith thanked her for her help and walked out the door, the trap banging at the outside of her knee. The door jingled as she stepped on the sidewalk.

"Wait."

Faith turned to find Fiona standing in the doorway.

"I don't think there's a connection, but you should know there were a lot of things going on that summer that weren't on the up-and-up."

Setting the trap at her feet, Faith swallowed. "Like what kinds of things?"

Fiona looked up and down the street. "I don't want anyone knowing we talked about this, you understand. No mention of me on your show."

"Okay. No problem. What was going on?" Her heart beat against her rib cage as Faith struggled to maintain her casual appearance.

"The development on the hill. My sister's no-good husband worked there. They found something and they covered it up."

"What?"

"I'm not sure, but it was big. Money exchanged hands. My brother-in-law was . . . well-off after the development was complete."

Her father's development. What had he been up to? "Do you think your brother-in-law would talk with me?"

"Not likely. He's been dead for five years. That's all I know. I just thought it might be important." She scanned the surroundings again, waved at a woman across the street, and went back into the shop.

For Faith, Deep Valley had been a paradise. How could she have been blind to the evils that lay so close to her? Her father, the man she wanted so badly to impress, the one who'd died without letting her know if she'd made him proud, was just another money-grubbing developer. Who had he taken advantage of, and what would the people around here think of her when they remembered she was the daughter of Ivan Ferdon?

Faith pulled the ladder down with her gloved hands. She wore her hair stuffed into a cap and some coveralls that must have belonged to her grandfather. She hadn't been able to locate safety glasses, but she had found a pair of swimming goggles, which she pulled down over her eyes. They pressed into the skin, but protection was key for this mission.

Two steps up the ladder, she remembered the headlamp. After pulling off a glove and switching on the light, she reconfigured herself and started again. Faith pushed the trap through the opening in front of her. It clanged and crashed so much she'd either scare the raccoons away or give the mother advanced notice so she could attack at Faith's first appearance.

Pushing her head through the entry, Faith forced herself to keep both eyes open as far as she could manage with the goggles pressing them closed. She turned her head slowly, evaluating the environment. There wasn't a sign of the raccoon or these babies everyone insisted must be part of the package.

Maybe they'd left on their own. If she found their entrance and plugged it, that would solve the problem without Faith ever having to come near the filthy critters.

She climbed the rest of the way in, standing to her full height. Above her hung a swinging lamp, the switch near the bulb. It illuminated all but the deep edges along the sides. Faith removed her headlamp.

Faith set up the trap, then cracked open a can of cat food, somewhat expecting Crouton to run up the ladder at the sound. Placing it in the metal prison, she stood back, evaluating the space.

All around her were boxes, pieces of old furniture, and shelves. By the looks of this place, her grandmother had held on to everything she'd ever owned, just banishing what she no longer needed to the attic.

Along one wall were two Rubbermaid tubs sitting side by side, both labeled *Ivan*. Prickles ran across the surface of Faith's skin. Her father was in many ways a mystery. He'd never been the kind of man who tossed his daughter in the air or pretended to become the tickle monster. Ivan Ferdon had been steady but distant until what would be his last year. Even when her parents endured another loss of a baby, he'd tempered his grief with increasing separation, but not the physical kind. It was the way a person can tuck into themselves until they might as well be thousands of miles away.

When he took his life, Faith hadn't felt the passing as she thought she should. It came with a numbing that didn't finish fading until sometime after Harlow's birth, when the rush of love she felt for that tiny little being superseded her mind's need for separation from pain.

Scanning the room again for little rodent bandits, she moved toward the bins. The lids were covered in dust and droppings. Only Faith's raccoon roommate had been near these tubs in the last many years. With her fingers under the rim, she pushed off the lid without making contact with anything disgusting. It shifted over the back and fell to the plywood floor.

Faith switched the headlamp on again to get a better look at the contents. Ivan Ferdon had been a textbook Enneagram one and ferocious about the removal of all unneeded belongings. High school yearbooks sat spine up in order of year, a shoebox holding them in place. Inside this, she found letters addressed to her father from her mother. She didn't peek into any of these envelopes but pulled the container free and set it by her feet to take downstairs. Her mother should have had these things to remind herself of good times, all of which seemed to have happened before Faith was born.

From where she'd pulled the box, Faith saw a key ring. She picked it up, finding two keys stuck together. Her imagination created an image of her father as a teen behind the wheel of his first car.

While her grandmother may have been a closet hoarder, that trait wasn't passed on to her father. The fact that he'd saved the letters from her mother meant more than a houseful of sappy trinkets could. So, why had he saved these keys? She set them on top of the shoebox, figuring if they belonged to the car in the garage, she might need them when she found a buyer.

True to his nature, the second box was nearly empty. Inside, she found a miniature photo album, but not the kind anyone would display on their coffee table. This book held only a few pictures, each one of a tiny baby, and labeled with a name. Sarah Marie Ferdon—October 8, 1978. Bethany Jane Ferdon—April 19, 1982. Cameron James Ferdon—September 25, 1987. He'd come back up here to add the photo. The man who seemed not to care may have been more tender than many who shared their hurts.

Decades of anger failed to hold back the grief she'd never allowed to seep out. A tear spilled over, splashing onto the plastic sheet covering the photo. She quickly wiped it away, tucked the album into the shoebox, and carried the treasures to the stairs. Good pieces existed in everyone, though loss was easier to keep under control when those heart-deep memories were kept shut tight.

The trap could wait. Everything could wait. Faith's body ached with the remembering. She'd forgotten so much of her father, blaming him for everything that went wrong in her life, but not giving credit when he'd been the one to hold together their fracturing family.

A phrase from the grief class came to her. *"Grief is not something you can work your way through step by step. It comes in waves that can't be tamed by logic."*

Her father had been gone since before she'd become a teenager, but here came the wave.

39

Faith

Monday morning, Faith packed up her stuff to have a second interview with Detective Masters. She'd checked in the night before, and Sheila let her know they'd gathered a few things for her, clipping from the newspapers and stuff like that. They weren't likely to be anything she hadn't already acquired from the newspaper archives, but along with his actual memories, they were what could move this case forward. If Masters was eager to talk, Faith was just as eager to listen.

She'd come within a few houses when she realized the dark funeral home car was parked in the driveway of Sheila's house. Faith had arrived too late, missed the chance with another person who'd been there. The urgency of finding out what happened to Heather permeated every strand of Faith's DNA. If there'd been someone out there who could tell Heather's story, would it be too late? Were they already gone?

Nate's car pulled up behind hers. He got out and came to Faith's window. "Sheila called. She said she'd tried to get in touch with you, but her calls went to voicemail."

Faith picked up her cell and checked. Three missed calls, two from Sheila and one from Nate. She checked the volume, probably off since her last recording session. "What happened?"

"Died in his sleep peacefully." Nate braced himself with one hand on the top of her door. "I'm sorry you weren't able to talk with him again."

Her head bobbed along with his words, as if she were taking in the conversation without thought.

"You look pretty shaken. How about we get a cup of coffee?" The dimple he'd had in his left cheek as a boy flashed with his sympathetic smile.

"Okay. I have a bit of free time on my hands." She could go in and offer her condolences to Sheila, but Faith was basically a stranger to the woman. "I'll follow you."

Nate went back to his car and pulled up in front of Faith. A few minutes later, they were at the diner. She'd foolishly assumed he'd lead her to a hidden Starbucks somewhere on the outskirts of town.

She stepped out and onto the sidewalk. "This really is the only coffee in town, isn't it?"

"Unless you have a taste for gas station coffee." His face wrinkled in an expression of disgust.

"I think the diner sounds great."

Inside, the collection of people didn't seem to have changed much in the last month, but the looks they gave her as she walked in the door certainly had. Those who hadn't been staring were quickly nudged or whispered to until all eyes were on her.

Nate leaned close to her ear. "You sure draw a lot of attention around here."

She turned her head to him, their faces a bit too close, before she stepped back and rolled her eyes. "I'm a regular celebrity," she said with dry humor.

Peggy scooped two menus from the holder and waved them over to a booth in the back corner. "Well, how are you folks doing today?"

"Good, thank you." Faith took the menu and scooted in.

"Carl is making his German pancakes today. Can I get you both a helping?"

She looked over the laminated page at Nate. German pancakes were one of those breakfast items that seemed to take forever.

"I'd love that, Peggy." Nate handed back his menu. "That and a nice hot cup of coffee."

They both looked to Faith. "Do you have bagels?"

Peggy shook her head.

"Toast and an egg?"

"Would you like sausage or bacon with that?"

She didn't want either. "I'll take the bacon. And coffee for me too."

Peggy made a few scribbles on her notepad and handed it to Carl through the open window. She was back in under a minute with steaming coffee. "So, how's the investigation going?" Her eyes were on Faith. "You sure have this town's attention."

Faith ventured another look around the room. Not all expressions appeared friendly. "Is that good or bad?"

"Don't let them bother you. People get stirred when the past is dug up. It's not that these folks have anything to hide. They're just protective of the community. You can understand that, I'm sure."

Faith wasn't at all sure that she could. If a child had gone missing, and the town seemed more concerned about reputation than uncovering the truth . . .

"I didn't come here to make friends." She poured cream into her coffee and swirled it around with her spoon. Defensive tension stiffened her arms and jaw.

"All right then. Is there anything else I can get you while you wait on those pancakes?"

"Nope. Thanks, Peggy." Nate winked.

She wasn't far when he let out a low laugh. "What in the world was that about?"

Her mouth fell open. "Are you kidding me? Ever since we walked in here, people have been staring at us. I'm not the enemy."

He wiped at his mouth, probably more to cover his smile than to clean his face. "Does life in the city suit you?"

She held both hands out in front of her. "What does that mean?"

"Well, you clearly haven't been living small-town life. I'm only wondering if you like the city living."

"It's hardly a city. There are maybe two hundred thousand people in my town. Yes, it's different, but I don't have to justify whatever I do to the rest of the population."

"Is that because most of them have no idea what you're doing?" He rubbed his finger along the rim of his white porcelain mug.

There was an anonymity to her life that made it easy to disappear within her own community. It meant no one calling her out when she was in the wrong, except maybe Kendall, but it also felt lonely much of the time. She didn't want to try and answer his question. There were too many variables, so she gave him an all-inclusive shrug.

"I think most of the people around here want this case solved. It was a horrible time for Deep Valley. Parents didn't know if it would happen again, so they were afraid for the safety of their children. I'm not sure that ever completely went away."

Faith picked at the edge of a Splenda packet. "Do you remember the development my dad was working on?"

"Of course. We had some good times there."

Faith's stomach did the same tickle it once had when Nathan Nobbles gave her a smile. Somewhere under their exteriors hardened by life's hardships, they were still those two kids, acting like grown-ups. "Someone told me there'd been issues out there. Do you know anything about that?"

"What kinds of issues?"

"I'm not sure."

His eyes widened. "I know it never became the kind of upscale residence it was supposed to be, but that's about it. I can ask around if you'd like."

"That would be great."

"Who told you about this?"

"I can't say. I promised." Her stomach ached under a layer of harsh coffee.

"Is this one of those protect-your-source kinds of things?" He crossed his arms and leaned forward on the table. "You're like Lois Lane, and I could be Clark Kent."

Faith covered her mouth as she laughed. "You flatter yourself. Clark Kent? Really?"

He rubbed his knuckles back and forth across his chest. "I don't see why not. I'm not a bad-looking guy when I'm out of my daily disguise."

Peggy returned with their plates. "Here you go." Without her usual chatter, she turned and went about her business. Faith would have to make amends. Activating the town scuttlebutt by being rude to the nicest waitress in the United States was not going to help her get people talking.

Nate stabbed at his bowl-shaped pancake. "Did they give you any names of people who might be involved? Your father?"

Faith swallowed. "My informant didn't mention anything about my dad directly. They knew a person who may have been part of some kind of cover-up. But I don't want this to affect my focus. I'm here to investigate Heather's disappearance, not corporate espionage. I'm not sure why I'm even bringing up the development." She tipped her head back and looked at the planked ceiling, then back at Nate. "I was up in the attic, trying to catch a raccoon, and I came across some of my dad's things. I wish I understood who he had been better than I do."

"Did you catch the raccoon?"

She tipped her head to the side. "That's not the point."

"So, I'll take it that's a no." He grinned, then returned to business. "Is your mom still alive?"

"No. Even when she was, she lived in Guatemala most of the time, and we never talked about Dad. Not since his death. He . . ."

Silence, shame, and regret wove a circle around her. It always happened this way, even when she'd finally told Neil the truth about his death. It took away a piece of her each time she shared it, like an announcement to the world that she and her mother—their family—weren't enough to fight for. Instead, he left them with nothing, barely able to survive, every cent that remained going to pay off debt her mother had known nothing about.

"What?" Nate covered her hand with his.

"My dad killed himself."

"I'm so sorry. That must have been devastating." His eyes didn't look away and his hand remained on hers, a warm cover on her chilled skin.

She could have stayed like this, drawing in comfort from a man she hardly knew but somehow felt connected to, but the stares of two women at a nearby table drew her attention to them like a magnetic field. Faith pulled her hand back.

"It was tough, but he made his decision." The old walls were back, providing the comfort that came with their confinement. "It happened a long time ago. I've moved past it."

His eyes narrowed. "Are you sure about that?"

Faith sat rigid, her spine tight against the seatback. "I think I'd know."

He pinched his lips together and cut away at his dwindling pancake. "Sorry. I'm sure you would." But his words didn't match the tone they rode on.

She'd hurt him. It was a new response, something she'd never gotten from Neil. "No, I'm sorry. That was rude and insensitive. It's a topic I don't handle well."

He finished chewing and wiped a napkin across his face. "Don't get mad at me for saying this, but I'm glad you're going to the grief group with Heather's mom."

Going sounded like a continual thing. Faith had really hoped to ease herself away as Mrs. Crane grew more comfortable. She didn't need a support group. It's not what she'd come to Deep Valley to do, and attending didn't bring her any closer to finding the truth about Heather.

The coffee had grown cool without a refill from Peggy. Faith would be tarred and feathered by the end of the week if she kept offending people. "It's a good class. I think it's already helping Mrs. Crane."

40

Dora

"Are you sure this isn't going to be too much right before the grief class?" Faith sat down at the end of Dora's sofa. "We can do this interview tomorrow."

Dora tapped a finger on the edge of her mug of tea. "I think this is better."

Faith set her phone in the center of the coffee table and tapped it. "Okay, we're recording now." She ran a finger down her notes in the black book she carried everywhere. "We've talked about the night Heather went missing, but I'd like to understand more of what the police did to help. What can you remember from the first days?"

Breathing in and out, each one with a count attached, Dora focused on remaining in the present. "We were angry at first. It didn't seem like they were taking it seriously. The first officer who came to the house insisted that Heather had probably lost track of time and would be home any moment. Then he started asking questions about her happiness here, if we had family issues. It didn't take long to realize he thought she may have run away."

"Paul wasn't home for much of this. He and Greg were out looking for Heather and getting no help from anyone in the department. My son's friends joined the search early on too, then some of the neighbors. Paul would call in from payphones every thirty minutes to see if Heather was home. I remember the defeat in his voice growing deeper with each call. When I told him the police weren't taking it seriously, he was enraged. I've never seen my husband so mad. He stomped in the front door. Detective Masters was here by then. Paul grabbed him by the collar and got right in his face."

Faith tucked her hair behind her ear. "That must have been scary."

"I guess, but a person can only be so frightened, and I had reached the highest level just thinking about my baby out there in the night. I was actually a bit disappointed when Paul didn't punch the smug man, but that would have done even more damage."

"What do you mean by that?"

Dora took a long sip of her tea, allowing herself a moment to pull her thoughts together. "That outburst put Paul on the top of the suspect list when morning came and there was still no sign of Heather."

The way Faith tapped her pen on the tip of her chin had Dora wondering if she shouldn't have skipped this portion of the story. "It wasn't Paul. I never thought for a moment he could have done anything to one of our children."

"It had to be difficult with the police looking at him."

"Oh yes." Prickles of memories bit at Dora's skin. That night she hadn't thought there could ever be a worse feeling for a mother to endure, but so many of the days, weeks, and years since had uncovered new levels of agony. "Word travels fast around here. It didn't take long before the rest of the town started talking. There were many close friends who stood beside us, people from church and our neighborhood, but the parents—especially the moms we didn't know well—they were the worst. Even when the investigation moved toward Potter, the rumors didn't stop."

"What led the police to Mr. Potter?"

"I'm sure you have all this information already." Dora rubbed at a tight muscle at the hinge of her jaw.

"It will really help to hear it all from your perspective." She leaned forward. "Are you doing okay?"

Dora nodded. She could get through this for Heather. "When Potter returned home, I think it was the second day that Heather was missing. He pulled up to his house, and I remember that Heather was taking care of his cat, or maybe that was Brooke. I can't be sure." She covered her mouth with her hand and closed her eyes, seeing it all again. "That's right. Your dad was there. He said he'd seen Heather bike up to Potter's house, but he didn't remember seeing her come out. He said Potter had come home that night around the same time."

"I thought he'd come back two days after the disappearance."

Dora waved a hand in front of her. "That's the thing. He did, but your dad was the one who saw him on the day she went missing. Potter had come home, then left again."

"Were they able to find out where he'd been?"

Old anger seared Dora's thoughts. "No. He claimed he hadn't come home early, and that he'd been at his cabin the entire time. Potter allowed the police to search his house. That's where they found her flannel shirt." It was probably packed away in some box at the police station to this very day, never come home to where it should have been. "But he refused to let them search his cabin."

"But they did."

"Yes. The police got a search warrant. They didn't find any evidence, but there was also no one who could even say that's where he'd been. It was a perfect alibi. No neighbors for fifty miles."

"But they found nothing out there in the cabin or the surrounding areas?"

"He could have been anywhere. It makes sense that he would say he was at the cabin and take her somewhere else." Just like 1987, the stories swirled around without landing on solid ground.

"Before this, what did you think of Mr. Potter? Had there been any concerns?"

She shrugged. After decades of knowing the man was a filthy devil, she couldn't remember with any kind of accuracy how she'd felt about him before. "I don't remember. You were here. What did you think about him?"

Faith rubbed the back of her neck. "He'd always been kind to us, never showing any kind of attention that created alarm. If anything, he was sad and lonely."

"I should never have let her work for him." Tears burned her eyes.

"There was no reason for you to worry. You can't blame yourself for any of this."

That was where Faith Byrne was very wrong. Dora had been blaming herself for all of it, for every single decision that led to losing Heather.

They weren't alone at the support group that night, not that the other members didn't matter. But not long after they took their seats, Paul walked in. He kept his head down, avoiding eye contact as if he were either ashamed or afraid of his wife. They were still very much married, even if he did choose to live elsewhere.

A childish urge overtook Dora, and she nudged Faith, tipping her head toward Paul like he was the new boy in the class, and she thought he was kind of cute. At seventy-five years old, Paul Crane wasn't bad to look at, Dora had to admit. His looks had changed over the years, nearly perfecting his rugged face with the mature look of salt-and-pepper hair. While other men seemed to have shrunk by inches, Paul still had his height and his hair.

He might be a nice sight to look at, but Dora couldn't share her feelings with her husband in the room. This was her safe space, and he added a level of danger to it. She reminded herself that the man had already left her. What more could he do?

The leader started the session with prayer. It soothed Dora's body in a way it hadn't in years. She'd stepped out of the life of faith about a year after Heather left them. Each Sunday felt like a reminder that God hadn't chosen her family for a miracle. She couldn't sit in the row they'd shared with all three of their children and listen to the promise of hope when she had none.

Dora never meant to leave forever, but time kept moving, and each year the thought of walking back into a church service felt harder than it had before. Paul had been a sporadic attender until Brooke's senior year. The two of them started back every week, even attending Bible studies on other days. That was another wedge driven between them.

"Tonight, we have a tough class, but it's always one of my favorites." Hillary wrinkled up her face. "That didn't come out right. Let me start again. Tonight, we're going to talk about what we have to look forward to, the joys that are still available to us even after going through a period of grief and even in the midst of grief. Would any of you like to share, especially those who've been through the course before?"

Dora's hands squeezed together until she felt pain through her knuckles. When Paul raised his hand, she squeezed tighter.

"I'm Paul Crane. Most of you probably know that I lost my daughter Heather many years ago." He kept his gaze on the leader. "I was really challenged by this subject the first few times I went through the grief classes."

The first few times? Dora's mouth fell open. Why wasn't once enough?

"Feeling joy . . . it was like giving up on Heather. It felt like if I was excited for something, I was forgetting her. But that wasn't fair to the rest of my family." His gaze clicked over to Dora, then back to his original target. "I have the most beautiful and amazing grandchildren. My remaining daughter works so hard to keep me connected with them. And my boy, he's an adventurer through and through. He's been trying to get me out on the Appalachian Trail. I think I'm going to give it a try."

"That's wonderful. What makes you feel like this is the right time to go hiking with your son?"

Dora resisted the urge to murmur about getting rid of his anchor of a wife.

"Because I realized how much Heather would have loved to go. That used to hold me back, but when we talked about what we were looking forward to before, it occurred to me that I take a piece of my little girl with me wherever I go. If I choose not to live my life because she's not here, I'm not serving her memory well. I know not everyone is the same, but that feels right to me. I need the love I have for Heather to find landing places. My grandkids and my children provide those for me. I think it's what Heather would have wanted."

She couldn't sit there and listen to him spouting words that were clearly meant for her ears. Dora stood, gathered her purse, and left the room. She reached the front of the building and stepped out into the early evening. Looking behind her, Dora found a sense of surprise that no one had followed her out here. What had she been expecting, the entire class to end because she walked out?

Tingles crawled across her skin.

The sun cast a pink-and-orange glow across the white building. In the distance, frogs croaked from the creek. A dog barked. A child giggled.

Dora was just one person on a huge planet, not the center but a member of the whole. If God didn't choose to give her the miracle she so desperately wanted, was it a mistake on His part or on hers, for thinking the resolution she longed for was the only outcome that held redemption?

41

Heather

I really wanted to ask Faith about her dad and the creepy guy, but I didn't want her to feel like I didn't like her family or thought they were bad. That's the kind of thing that could mess up a perfectly good friendship. On the other hand, my mother was working there, and she wasn't the kind of woman who would know how to deal with a dangerous situation.

I sat on the curb, my bike upside down on the road, and twirled the pedal round and round. The back tire spun and whirled. My mind shifted to inventing a flap that would transform a bike tire into a fan.

Kelly Beckman walked toward me with her little dog. It wasn't a very cute pet, with is mangy hair and endless eye goobers, but I felt sorry for the mutt. No one should have to live with Kelly. She was only eight but had the nastiness of a much older girl. Her sister was good friends with Brooke. Kelly seemed to have gotten her personality through genetics.

"I saw your boyfriend at the ice cream shop yesterday," Kelly said in a sing-song voice. "Oh, wait. I guess he's not your boyfriend. He was with the new girl. They were having such a good time."

"Isn't there a Barbie somewhere waiting for you to pull its head off?" I spun the pedals again, leaning back on one arm. If I wanted a boyfriend—which I absolutely did not—Nathan Nobbles would not be my choice. I'd known him since long before we started kindergarten. He'd been a scab-picker back then, and I wasn't sure that was something I could ever overlook.

Kelly rolled her eyes, stuck her nose in the air, and tramped on down the street.

"Heather, I need you to get the trash out to the curb." Brooke stood on our stoop, one of Mom's aprons tied around her waist.

My dad was back at the mill. Hopefully this time it would keep running. The only drawback was Brooke being in charge of me, as if I needed a babysitter. I turned my attention back to the bike. Inventors did not need to be bossed around by older sisters.

"Heather Marie Crane. Don't make me give Mom a call at the office."

My backside was beginning to ache. If it wasn't for that, I wouldn't have gotten up. Brooke knew better than to call Mom at the trailer she called her office. "Keep your clothes on. I'm getting to it." Flipping my bike over, I pushed it to the garage, where I flung the door up with enough force to see it slide to its resting place above my head.

My mother kept the trash can near the door from the kitchen to the garage. It had to be on the curb each week before the garbage trucks rumbled down the street sometime before dawn. Which meant I had all the time in the world to do my chore. It wasn't even dusk yet.

The good handle hung on by one side, while the other had disappeared months ago. Using both hands, I shimmied the tub down the driveway and to the sidewalk. It scratched and shifted like sandpaper on a block of wood. I got it all positioned for easy dumping like Dad had taught me, but I imagined our broken can was one of their least favorite along the route.

As I stood there, contemplating how the garbage man would take hold of the nearly handleless bin, Mr. Ferdon pulled up. He got out of his car holding some files, but instead of taking them into the house, he dropped them into the trash on the curb. It wasn't even the Ferdons' can. It belonged to the couple without kids who lived next to them.

People are always saying I have a curious nature. That night wasn't any different than usual. I ached to see what he'd thrown out. They had perfectly good garbage cans at the worksite. Why had Mr. Ferdon brought this stuff home to get rid of?

Brooke and I had pretended to be spies most of one summer after we watched *Cloak & Dagger*. This mission needed nothing more than dark clothing and a bag to disguise my take.

Mom pulled in as I was putting the finishing touches on the plans I formed in my mind. "There's my girl." She held her arms out to me.

I glanced around, finding the area clear. I was getting a bit old for all this hugging.

Mom led me to the trunk of her car and unlocked it. "Help me get these groceries in, will you?"

No was not an acceptable answer, so I agreed. Inside, I set my bags on the counter.

"What are you doing?" Brooke looked over from where she stirred something at the stove. The scent wasn't one I'd ever smelled when Mom was the one cooking.

"I'm trying not to gag." Stepping up beside her, I looked into the pan. Macaroni noodles stuck up from red sauce like they were crying out to be saved. "What is this?"

"It's Italian." She sniffed the air, as if she were smelling something very different than what I experienced. "Now, get those groceries unpacked and the bags off my counter."

"You may be cooking tonight, Brookie, but this is still very much my kitchen." Mom kissed Brooke on the cheek. "I can't wait to eat this delicious-looking dinner."

I noted that she hadn't mentioned the smell.

"Heather, please make us a salad to go along with Brooke's . . . food."

All during dinner, my mind was on that garbage can. What was in it? I imagined it to be the information that would break a case wide open, and finding it would make me the proud recipient of a cash prize. I wasn't about to take extra chances and miss my opportunity to get back outside without the eyes of my family watching. I ate everything on my plate and complimented Brooke on her cooking. My brother, a boy who could eat an entire horse after football practice, didn't agree.

After we ate, Mom put me on kitchen duty—the worst chore in the history of childhood labor, and also a job my brother never seemed to be assigned. I didn't dare complain or whine. That was a sure way to find myself scrubbing toilets or some other disgusting job that would keep me inside the house until someone sent me to bed.

With the last of the plates in the dishwasher, I poured in the soap, closed the door, and cranked the dial until the sound of spraying water filled the room. I could sneak out the back door without anyone hearing me over that machine and the television playing in the front room.

Outside, it was dark, but not the middle-of-the-night kind of blackness. We'd just passed the time when the sun went down far enough that kids were forced inside by their parents. I didn't spot anyone lingering around, but they would have been easy to miss. The most important thing was to be sure Mr. Ferdon didn't see me. Even if he did, I had a plan. I'd say I accidently dropped my retainer in that trash can along with a napkin. Of course, I didn't have a retainer. I hadn't even had braces yet, but I was confident that he would not know any of that. My mother would kill me if she heard that lie fall out of my mouth. Even I was becoming concerned with how easy it was getting for me to lie.

On the Ferdons' side of the street, I edged closer to the garbage can. When I was as sure as I could be that no one else was around, I tipped off the top and felt for the papers. My hand plunged straight into something squishy. My teeth clamped down on my tongue before I could holler. Almost immediately after, my fingers felt the edge of a file. I slid it out and pressed it under my T-shirt. There was a smell of something rotten on me now, and it wasn't only deceit. I shivered at the thought of what kind of trash was now smashed against my stomach. A dumpster-diver I would never be.

When I returned to my backyard, I pulled the papers out and rubbed them against the cool grass. This did nothing to cleanse my skin, but I thought it might temper the scent enough to get me by my parents.

With the stolen evidence tucked back underneath my clothes, I took a casual walk through the living room to the hall.

"Hey, kid, want to watch *Who's the Boss?*" My dad patted the couch beside him.

"Um, I would, but I need to take a shower." That was not the excuse to use. Every gaze in the room shifted to me. It made me think I should shower more often. "I'll be right back." I jogged off toward my room, unburdening myself of the papers and shoving them between my mattress and the box spring.

In the shower, I scrubbed away the sticky goop that stuck to my skin and belly button. I think it might have been gravy at one point. All in all, I got the job done in record time, then plopped onto the couch, snuggling into my dad's side. I was far too old to do this when my friends were around, but that wasn't the case tonight. Covert operations were a drain, and my dad had a way of filling me back up.

I blinked my eyes, trying to make sense of my surroundings. A blanket lay over my body, and the glow from a streetlight streamed in through a slit between curtains. This wasn't my room, but I'd been so sound asleep that the hand I'd had tucked under my cheek was wet with slobber.

The cushion below me was rough, not like the sheets my mother changed on my bed each week. I felt around, my fingers working the edging. I was on the couch.

It all came back. We'd been watching television, and I must have dozed off. This wasn't all that unusual. What was strange was that my dad didn't carry me to my bed.

Sitting up, I took in the room I'm not sure I'd ever been alone in after dark. Growing up wasn't so great if it meant I'd be waking up in strange places from now on. I stumbled down the hall, now fully awake. Brooke snored from her side of the room. She never believed me when I told her about it. I pulled out my flashlight and the tape recorder from the shelf and pressed down the two buttons to make it record, then set it on the floor near the head of her bed.

After a good nap, there was no way I'd be falling asleep anytime soon. Instead, I'd see what Mr. Ferdon had thrown in the trash.

I found the papers then climbed into my bed, making a tent with the light summer blanket. The smell was still clinging to the outside of the file. I breathed through my mouth, hoping I'd get used to it soon. Switching on the flashlight, the beam reflected around the small space.

Page after page was filled with words I'd never seen before and graphs of numbers, many with long tails after the decimal point. There was something about soil samples and readouts. It was honestly boring, not the kind of spy game clue I'd anticipated.

The last page was a black-and-white photocopy of a picture.

Dirt sat off to the side in a mound and a few large chunks of rock lay in the middle. Honestly, it was so grainy, I could hardly make out what I was looking at.

Written across the top of the page in red ink was the question, "What would you like done about this?" Scribbled in blue ink on the top right corner was *Marinoni* and a phone number.

42

Faith

Faith should have left when Mrs. Crane walked out of the group meeting. Anyone with a conscience would have, but Mr. Crane wasn't moving, and it seemed like it should be him to go after his wife. Wasn't that why he'd come to the class, to make some amends?

The thing was, Faith wanted to hear more. She was mesmerized by the way people talked about loss and turned it around until they were listing off a litany of blessings. In many ways, it was like her podcast, but their acts of heroism weren't the kind people stopped to look at. The people in the support group made decisions and steps every day that brought them closer to healing, that allowed their families to continue forward.

A woman named Laura stood. She was a single mother of seven children whose husband had walked out on the entire family in order to start a new one with a woman half his age. If that were Faith's situation, she would be stomping on the tables, yelling about the unfairness of her circumstances. And she wouldn't have been wrong.

Laura looked around the room, a subtle smile on her lips. "I'm seeing so many changes in my children. The toxicity of our environment came on slowly. It wasn't until Butch was gone that I realized the damage his anger was doing to the kids. When he left, I couldn't imagine anything good coming out of it. It's hard to support my kids both financially and emotionally, but I'm doing it, and I'm proud of that."

The class applauded, something that still seemed odd in a grief class.

When the session ended, Faith looked around, realizing Mrs. Crane had not returned. What was she supposed to do? Well, of course she should have gone after the woman to begin with.

Mr. Crane approached. He heaved a deep breath. "I was hoping she'd come back after she had a chance to cool off."

It was like they shared a mind. Why couldn't Paul Crane have been her father? They would have understood each other. "Do you think she went home?"

"I can get you the answer to that." He swiped away at his phone like a teenager. "We have the Life 360 app installed. Charity added it to Dora's new phone too." He tapped his nose. "She's halfway between here and there. If you don't mind, I'd like to pick her up."

Faith felt uneasy with his request, like she was inserting herself into a place she really didn't belong. "Of course. I'd like to stop at the grocery store on my way home anyway." She mentally searched her refrigerator, trying to come up with something that she was low on in case she had to answer more questions.

Mr. Crane scooped up three miniature chocolate chip cookies. "It was good to see you tonight. I hope you're getting something out of these classes."

He walked away, already putting the first snack into his mouth.

The grief sessions were supposed to be for Mrs. Crane. Faith was just the support person. Yet it was becoming clear that grief took on many forms, and it could either be an obstacle that led her to greater things or a barrier that stopped her from moving forward.

The sky was a peaceful shade of violet when Faith pulled up to her grandmother's house and parked the car. It was ridiculous to be parking on the street when there was a perfectly good garage with a door that went right into the kitchen.

She had her phone in hand before she reached the front door.

"Well, hello there. How's Deep Valley treating my favorite granddaughter?" Her grandmother sounded like a woman half her age, always ready to bounce up and take on the next challenge.

"Your only granddaughter," Faith replied automatically. "And you were right. Getting away from my place for the summer was brilliant. I would have moped around missing the girls, but instead, I've had the opportunity to reconnect with some wonderful people."

"That has been my prayer."

Faith unlocked and opened the door, always a little hesitant since the raccoon incident. "Hey, I was wondering about Dad's car in the garage. Is it still there for any particular reason?"

The long sigh on the other end of the line made Faith think again about her question. "No. It's just one of those things that never got taken care of. I wouldn't use it if I were you. It's been sitting so long, I doubt the old thing runs."

"I'm sure it doesn't. Wasn't that why Dad left it here in the first place?" Taking a step inside, Faith surveyed the area before letting her guard down. You couldn't be too careful when it came to raccoons.

"Oh yes, I'd forgotten. He was supposed to come back for it . . ."

Faith slipped into one of the dining room chairs. "Grandma, how did you get through losing Grandpa and Dad?" They'd never been the kind of family who talked about deep feelings, at least not with one another, but seeing the way grief could destroy people, she needed to understand how others walked through it.

Another long sigh wove through the distance between them. "That's a hard question, but the answer is simple. I leaned on my faith in God. It was so much harder with your father because I never could be sure where his heart was, but I know that God works all things together for His purpose with His people."

The Cranes had been devoted to their church that summer. They attended the same one her grandmother did, the church that sponsored the grief counseling group. Since arriving in Deep Valley, Faith hadn't heard a peep about God come from Mrs. Crane's lips. "What about people who don't have your beliefs? How do they get through hard times?"

"I can't speak to that. I can only tell you what I know in my heart. God sees us. He knows our pain and our suffering, and He takes no joy in our troubles. We can trust Him."

Faith used her free hand to tidy up her workspace. The box from the attic hadn't moved since she'd brought it down. "So . . ." She had a strong need to lighten the subject. "Would it be okay if I sold the car?"

"I wish you would. I'm afraid I left an awful lot of stuff that should have been repurposed years ago." Her grandmother paused. "I was going to wait to talk to you on your next in-person visit, but I've decided to go ahead and stay here at the village. The housing market is good, and selling the house will give me enough money to live out whatever days these old bones have left, then hopefully leave you something when I'm gone."

"I don't want money, Grandma."

"I'm not in a hurry to move on to the next life either, but it's going to happen at some point. I'll contact a realtor in town soon and let her know. I'll tell her not to touch it until this fall, but don't be surprised if she drives by and takes pictures."

Why was it so difficult to imagine this home in someone else's hands? Faith hadn't been here since her childhood, but the house held a connection with the best time she'd had growing up.

"I'd like you to take whatever you want," her grandmother continued. "I brought the most important things with me when I came to be with Gerdy. My plan is to let the rest go."

"Are you sure? There are so many memories here." Who was the one holding on now?

"That may be so, but I hold those memories in my heart too. And believe me, I brought along plenty. A friend here was talking about the burden we leave behind for those we love. I don't want you having to deal with all my old stuff. I never should have held onto things when I could have been holding onto relationships." A yawn followed. "I'm about whooped. I love you, Faith. You're doing a good thing."

"Thank you, Grandma. Good night." She ended the call and rubbed her thumb over the edge of the keys from the attic. She held them up and examined the ridges. Why had her father, a man who was the opposite of a hoarder, kept these?

The doorbell rang and Crouton zipped through the living room, sliding around the corner to his safe spot under the bed.

"Some guard cat you are." Faith opened it without remembering to check who was on the other side.

Nate Nobbles stood there, a sack in one hand and two pop cans in the other.

"Come on in." She moved to the side and let him pass.

"Do you usually open the door to just anyone?"

"Only when they come with food." She tossed the keys on the table. "What are we celebrating?"

He turned back to her from where he was setting the sack and drinks on the table. "No celebration, just an excuse to have burritos from the new food truck. They are so good. I got a chicken and a steak. Your choice, because I will gladly eat either of them."

"Steak?"

He handed her a foil-wrapped cylinder that looked to be family sized.

"I think there will be plenty of this one for you to have too."

"That's what I'm hoping." His dimple made a quick appearance.

They made casual conversation as Faith retrieved paper plates and napkins and set them on the coffee table in the living room. Nate wandered over to the butcher paper taped along the wall.

"I checked in on Potter's pickup," he said, tapping on a photocopy of Mr. Potter's green Chevy taped above a mark labeled *truck is gone*. "There have been no hits or sightings of the thing since the night he claimed it went missing."

"So, he disposed of it somehow. Obviously, there had to be a reason for that, and I'm having a hard time coming up with anything that doesn't tie him to Heather's disappearance. Unless Mr. Potter was telling the truth."

Nate sat down, took a massive bite, and chewed thoughtfully for a moment. "I'm not a math guy, but the odds of someone stealing his truck a couple days after Heather goes missing, well, that doesn't add up."

"Take me through that whole claim again."

"Mr. Potter was picked up by officers at his home somewhere around seven on the evening of September nineteenth. He was at the station for an interview until close to midnight, at which time officers returned him to his home. Sometime the next day, Mr. Potter claimed his vehicle had been stolen."

"Did the police department have anyone watching his house?"

Nate grinned. "This isn't CSI. I'm sure there weren't the resources to keep him under constant surveillance, but there were eyes on him most of the time, especially after they returned him to his home. Detective Masters had a note in the file stating he hoped to have shaken Potter up enough that he'd make a move that night. No one noticed the truck was missing because he had a habit of parking it inside the garage. The only place that I get snagged is this: How could Potter have driven off without being noticed by police?"

"Could he have been working with someone else?"

"I doubt it. You remember the old man. He was a loner, had been since his wife's death." He finished his burrito, stood up, and stepped closer to the butcher paper taped along the wall. "This is well done."

She lifted her eyebrows. "Thank you. I really appreciate that coming from a detective."

"If you ever get tired of the podcasting gig, we'll have a spot for you on the force."

Faith clamped her teeth together and swallowed before she burst out laughing. "That's what every police department needs, a middle-aged mother enforcing the law."

His body turned her way, the space between them suddenly sparking with electric tension. "I would never call you middle-aged. You look like I imagined you would in college."

"You thought about me?"

His gaze shifted from her eyes to the floor. "I thought about you all through the years. You never forget your first love."

She'd wondered about Nate too, but didn't have the courage to share that with him now, not when she was feeling things she hadn't thought she'd ever feel again. Faith cleared her throat and sat back on the couch, picking up a pillow and holding it like a shield between her and temptation. "So, do you have any theories about what happened to the truck?"

"The lake near his cabin was dragged. So was the river here in town. They even used a helicopter to search, thinking he may have abandoned it on some logging road, but nothing ever came of that."

"And Potter stuck to his story?" Faith jerked her hand back, clamping her finger in her grip.

"What happened?"

"I cut myself on the zipper."

The cushions sunk under Nate's weight next to her. He carefully unfurled her fist and examined the wound. "It's not too bad, but you'd better wash that out." He took the pillow. "I assume you're up-to-date on your tetanus shots."

"I hardly need a tetanus shot for a scrape with a zipper." She walked to the kitchen, where she rinsed the cut and wrapped her finger in a paper towel. "It seems like finding the truck would be key." She returned to the living room.

Nate was shaking his head. "I really don't see what would come of it. After thirty-six years, it could be anywhere. I doubt there would be even trace evidence to collect."

"My gut says otherwise."

"Great. But unless your gut has a location, this is pointless."

Her gut said she wished she hadn't eaten so much of that burrito. She rubbed her stomach. "Pointless? How can you say that? This town condemned the man because of that truck going missing."

"What about Heather's flannel shirt? They found it in his place."

"That hardly confirms anything. Do you remember what it was like to be ten? She could have left it there on accident. It's not like there wasn't a reason for Heather to be in the house."

Nate sighed. "I think you're looking for a needle in a haystack. Without a way to narrow down the search, it seems hopeless."

Everything in this case felt hopeless. So why not look for this impossibly hidden truck?

43

Dora

She shouldn't have accepted the ride from her husband. Paul was a man who spoke his mind, never keeping his thoughts buried where they sometimes belonged. He'd insisted on getting an ice cream from the drive-through, then parked in the lot as if they couldn't eat while he drove her home.

"I'm glad you're taking the class. I hope it's not just because Brooke is forcing you into it."

"Not just because of that, but it's a part." She bounced her leg up and down in a nervous rhythm. "I figured it wouldn't hurt anything but my heart to go through the course."

"What do you think so far?"

"I think this is not the kind of thing I'd like to talk about with the man who walked out on me."

His head tipped back onto the headrest. "That's not fair."

"Did you or did you not move out of our home?" She blinked hard to keep the tears from showing her emotion.

He stared out the window for a long moment. "You left long before that."

Cars passed on the street in front of them, people heading home from work or a baseball game, maybe a family picnic. It was easy to assume the lives of the passengers in those vehicles were whole, without broken shards that pierced them when they made a move without taking care to protect themselves.

"I wish you would have stuck it out through class tonight. Laura spoke. I'm always touched by that woman's tenacity."

Ice cream dripped from Dora's cone across her knuckles. She licked them clean, then wiped them with a napkin.

"I don't think anyone gets through life without hurts."

She sucked in a hard breath.

"I'm not trying to minimize what we've been through. Losing a child has got to be the worst kind of loss."

"No, losing your child and not knowing what happened to her—if it's still happening to her—that's the worst." The tears flowed over her cheeks. "You want me to live like Heather didn't exist, but she did. She was part of me. I can't fully be here without her."

"I'm not asking you to stop loving Heather. I just want you to remember that you once loved me too." His voice caught on the last words. When he continued, tears clouded his speech. "I love Heather. I will always love her. I want to be able to remember her with joy. There are so many things I'd like to talk about, but you get mad at the mention of her name. You assume that I'm over losing her if I laugh as I tell the story of her eating that bug off the sliding glass window or digging the hole in the backyard to make her own swimming pool."

Dora tipped her chin to her chest. "I think I know where she got that love for digging."

"I heard."

Her head shot up.

"You honestly think you can dig up a neighbor's yard in the middle of the night, get arrested for trespassing, and not have the entire town talking about it by noon the next day?" A tear clung to his upturned cheek as he smiled ruefully. "I do love the way you go into battle. I always have. I'd just like to be part of your army and not your enemy."

Dora slept late the next morning, having wrestled with sleep for hours after new thoughts barged into her mind. She'd always been afraid to doze off after a hard day. Nightmares took advantage when her defenses were compromised. But last night, having given up in the wee hours and dedicated her time to prayer, she'd had the best dreamless sleep she could remember.

The birds outside the window were loud, squawking away like they were waiting for Dora to feed them breakfast, something she never did. Then came the garbage truck, rumbling up the road, clanking and whirring with each stop.

She slipped her arms into her light summer robe and made a cup of strong tea, then went out to the backyard, where she sipped from her cup, not worrying about neighbors peeking over the fence and finding her in her nightclothes. This was a big day, and she was going to start it on her terms.

The backyard was Paul's territory, and he'd created a paradise back here. Trellises hung with flowering vines, and the air was scented with jasmine. When the kids were little, Dora had worked with them in a small garden. Heather loved getting her fingers into the dirt, digging out seeds to see their progress, and eating vegetables straight off the plants.

Dora had stopped gardening many years ago, and Paul finally ripped out the raised beds when the wood began to rot. He left a sunny space open in the event she decided to take up the hobby again, but she never had. Life went by quickly, missed opportunities and all.

The last sip of tea came with a great deal of disappointment, but she was resolved. Today, Dora had three medium-sized boxes to fill. Three cardboard containers that would move Heather's belongings into hands that could use them.

She breathed in another deep inhale of sweetness and got to her feet. Without taking time to change into her regular clothes, Dora tugged the boxes from the corner of the living room and tossed them into Heather's bedroom.

Looking at the bed, she thought she should probably wash the bedding before donation, then thought better of the idea. Hillary from the grief group was always saying to be kind to yourself. Someone else could wash them. Dora had enough to handle with the packing.

She left the case on the pillow and tucked it into the bottom of one box, covering it with the comforter and sheets. The bare bed changed the feel. Those four walls were becoming a room rather than the desperation of a broken mother seeking to keep something of her child alive. She'd tried so hard to make this room a place where she could still feel her daughter. But these were things. They could never replace Heather. Dora knew this.

As she filled the second box, she wondered if she should have let Paul be part of this. Grief could be a selfish season. She'd failed to consider his needs, while in all these years, Paul had never stepped foot in this room to pack it up without her. He'd allowed Dora to continue tending Heather's room as an altar to the child they'd had, all the while gently asking her if it was time to move forward.

In Heather's top drawer, Dora found a stack of birthday cards. She thumbed through them, putting each back into its place. Her strength was waning.

She picked up a box and walked it out to her car. Across the street, the Millers' garage door opened. The wife was walking frantically around in circles, as if she were missing something. What was her name? Bethany? Beth? Barbara? No, it was Jasmine. She remembered now because it was like the Disney princess.

Jasmine stepped toward her car, then looked Dora's way. Their eyes met. Usually, this would be where Dora ducked her head and pretended not to notice the other person, but this time she waved. "You look busy. Is there something I can help with?"

Jasmine jogged across the street. Her smile stretched her skin and pushed her cheeks up toward her eyes. "I'm just in shock, I think. Declan and I got the most amazing news. We're getting twins." She shook out her hands. "Well, not for keeps, unless that ends up being the plan."

Dora placed a hand on Jasmine's arm, hoping to slow down the rush of words spilling out.

Jasmine took a deep breath. "We finished all the work to become a resource family."

"What's that?"

"It's the new way of saying foster family."

Dora nodded. How was she supposed to understand anything if the powers that be kept changing all the words?

"I got the call today that we're getting our first placement. Two three-year-old boys."

Dora wiped her fingers across her forehead. Had she ever been young and fit enough to take on that kind of challenge?

"I'm so excited to meet them, but we're set up for a baby or a child. We have a crib and one bed." She placed a hand on each side of her head. "Now we need a second bed."

"Is Declan home?"

"He'll be here any minute."

"Have him come right over. I'll call my husband and we'll pack up our extra bed." Her heart began to gallop as the word *extra* escaped her mouth.

Jasmine's mouth fell open. "Are you sure?"

"I can't think of a better place for it to go. You might want to get a new mattress, but the bed itself is in good shape." She punched Paul's number into her phone. That new car even answered his calls for him.

"Did you miss me already?"

"Don't get smart." Dora said, but a small smile danced on her lips at his teasing tone. She shook her head as the next words formed on her lips. "I need you to come hom—back. I need help moving Heather's bed across the street."

After too many seconds of silence, she looked at the phone to be sure it was still connected. The call timer ticked on. She put it back to her ear.

"I'll be there in a minute."

Paul pulled up to the curb just as Declan's Explorer drove into his driveway.

She led the men to Heather's room where the bed had already been stripped of blankets, sheets, and pillows. They moved quickly, at Dora's insistence. This task needed done before her heart could insist on a different plan.

Dora stood against the wall, doing her best to stay out of the way as her daughter's mattress was lifted and removed from her bedroom. Declan handled the mattress on his own, leaving Paul for the box spring.

"What's that?" He reached down with a gloved hand.

Dora came closer. She took the file from Paul, flipping through papers from Ivan Ferdon's office. "Why in the world did Heather have these?"

"Mom?" The voice came from the other side of the house.

Dora jumped back, throwing her hand over her heart. If they didn't want her to have another episode, they should be more careful about surprising her. She ushered Paul out of the room, set the papers down on Heather's dresser, and closed the door behind them. "I'm back here."

"There you are." Brooke gave Dora a quick scan and her father a quick hug as he headed out the door. "I was wondering if you would be interested in having Sybil here for the afternoon. The big kids have activities, and she's bored at home. But if you're not feeling well, we can do it another time."

Dora glanced down at her pajamas. "I'm fine. I was getting

some work done and hadn't bothered getting dressed. I'd love to have Sybil." Brooke had never once asked her to take one of the kids alone. Maybe that was something Dora should have asked to do, but there was something about it that made her feel like she was moving into a danger zone.

"Great. I'll go get her. She's playing a game on my phone out in the car." She twisted her lips as if she had something else to say but thought better of it.

Dora hurried into her room. She washed the dust from her hands in the master bathroom and slipped into a pair of shorts and a T-shirt, then went out to the living room.

Sybil sat on the couch, still playing with her mother's phone.

Brooke looked between the two of them. "So, Mom, what do you have planned for the day? I just saw Dad leave."

Dora tipped her head. A plan was forming, but Brooke didn't need the details. "I'm sure we'll find something to do."

"Okay. I'll be back in an hour or so?"

"How about I call you when we're done?" An unusual tickle of excitement was building in Dora's stomach.

Brooke nodded, but she seemed uncertain, then hugged Sybil and took her phone back.

Once Dora was sure her daughter was gone, she held a hand out to Sybil. "I've been thinking about getting a dog. Want to do down to the Humane Society and take a look?"

Sybil burst from the sofa. "Are you serious?"

"I absolutely am." Dora slung her purse over her shoulder. What better way to move forward than to find a little critter who needed some of the extra love Dora had been hoarding? "We may not find the right one today, but we can look. After that, we can get ice cream."

44

Heather

The first week in August meant two things. The first was the county fair, a place where kids were allowed to run free and eat as many sweets and fried food as they could fit into their bellies, then ride the carnival rides until all that eating made them sick. I loved that part.

The second thing was not so good. It meant we were only a month away from school starting again. I liked to think I was a pretty positive person, but this got to me. I wasn't sure there's a point in all this education. What if I wanted to spend my life on a beach, eating crab I pulled in with my own nets? When I asked my dad that very question, he said I'd have to buy my own crab traps because he wasn't sharing his with a girl who dropped out of school to be a beach bum.

Faith's mom wasn't feeling well again, and her grandmother was taking care of her. My dad had an extra shift at the mill. And both my mom and Faith's dad were already at the fair, setting up a booth for the new development. We could have asked Nathan's parents to take us, but he was the kind of guy who liked to tell his folks where he'd been rather than asking if he could go. The only ride I could swing was from my brother, and he made it very clear that he would not be bringing us *kids* home. Luckily, Mom would be able to help us out then.

The three of us—Nathan, Faith, and me—were all squished in the back of my brother's Nova. Two of his friends flanked us, and another rode in the passenger seat. I ended up on top of Faith, who was smashed into Nathan. To say it was awkward was an understatement.

"So, Heather, what are you and your little friends going to do at the fair?" Greg revved the engine. It hummed and vibrated beneath my feet.

"We're not little kids." I rolled my eyes. I'd threaten to tell Mom about the cigarette smell in the car and the bottle I saw peeking out of Shawn's pocket, but I knew that would end my ride to the fair tonight and any time in the future.

The guy to our right chuckled. Something about him made me ease back the other way. "I think your little sister has a boyfriend back here. Don't you think we should give him some brotherly warning?"

"Nah. He's not after Heather. He likes the other one."

Faith's face bloomed into shades of red. Tears filled her eyes.

I squeezed her hand with one of mine, then used the other to pull myself close to my brother's ear. "You better knock it off," I whispered. "Or I'll tell Mom what you're up to even if it means missing out on rides."

Greg swerved around a corner much faster than the speed limit, nearly knocking me into Shawn's lap. "Take it easy, guys. They're just kids."

He was pretty fond of that word. As my dad would say, my ire was up, and I'd be tattling on him the first chance I got, regardless.

I knew we were there when my head started banging into the roof of the car. The fairgrounds used a neighboring field for parking. It had recently been harvested, and the ground was bumpier than anywhere we could go off-road.

Part of the deal for the ride was I had to hand over the parking fee. I pulled out the three dollar bills but had to convince my fingers to let them go. As soon as Greg parked the car and Shawn climbed out, the three of us tumbled over like Weebles, but we were free. We ran off toward the ticket seller.

"Stay out of trouble," my brother hollered after us.

"Same to you," I yelled back.

The smells of animals mixed with cotton candy overwhelmed me. I could hardly stand the wait in line while some kid counted out his change. Once we were paid and through the gate, we were able to do whatever we wanted, and the fair gave us options.

"What do you want to do first?" My head turned side to side, taking in the crowd.

Faith was already heading toward a barn. "Do you think there'll be goats?"

Nathan shrugged, but I jogged to catch up with her.

For an hour we went pen to pen, talking to the cutest critters, then we moved on to the arena where booths were set up. This was a great place to get free samples and to enter giveaways. It was also where we could see about getting a few extra dollars from my mom.

Nathan dragged us to the dairy booth without even looking at what he was passing. That boy needs a lot of calories, and apparently the ride over and the long tour of the barns had left him empty. We drank our fill of strawberry, chocolate, and plain milk, then went off in search of Mr. Ferdon's area.

We found them in the corner. They had a large setup with a tiny model home front and center. A large sign behind my mom said *Welcome to the Next Generation of Housing*. I pictured homes with robots and computers like on *The Jetsons*, but we'd been inside quite a few of them by now, and they didn't seem any different than the other homes I'd seen around Deep Valley.

"Hello there, kids." Mr. Ferdon wore a pink polo shirt with a sweater around his shoulders. He looked like George Michael's father, or at least what I pictured him to look like. "Are you enjoying your time at the fair?"

We all nodded.

My mother dipped into her purse, then leaned toward me, wiping a tissue over my upper lip. I was mortified. "Mom, stop, please."

"Well, you had something on you. You didn't really want me to let you run around like that all day."

It wasn't a question. If it had been, I would have told her I'd rather be seen with a milk mustache than have my mother give me a spit bath. "Could we have some money? I had to give Greg three dollars for parking." I did my best to look pathetic, but she never bought into that kind of thing.

"What happened to all the money you've made taking care of Mr. Potter's cat?" Her eyebrows did that thing where they inched up her forehead and made me feel like a fool.

"It got used."

"On what?"

There was only the truth. "Ice cream."

To my surprise, my mother grinned. She started to dig around in her purse, but Mr. Ferdon put his hand on her arm. "Let me take this one." He pulled a wallet out of his back pocket and retrieved three twenty-dollar bills.

I'm sure my mouth hung wide open because it was dry by the time he handed one to each of us. My parents never parted with that kind of money for entertainment purposes.

"Thank you, sir." Nathan looked from the money back to Mr. Ferdon.

I'm not sure why the act seemed so surprising. I guess I figured they were tight on money too, since they were living with Faith's grandmother and all.

"Ivan," my mother said. "That's far too much."

"Nonsense. Your family has been wonderful to all of us. I

couldn't do my job without you, and I'm very aware that we're not paying you nearly enough for all you're doing at the office."

My mom blushed, and it made me feel uncomfortable. "Thank you, Mr. Ferdon." I looked to my mom. "We're going to get out of your hair now." I took Faith's hand and tugged her.

She shrugged me off, then gave her dad a quick hug.

We were in the food court three minutes later with money to burn and so many ways to light that fire. I'd been wanting to try a deep-fried Twinkie, so I took the opportunity to do just that. Faith got a caramel apple, and Nathan came back to our table with the longest hot dog I'd ever seen.

Hours later, without a cent left between the three of us, our stomachs sore and our fingers sticky with sugar, we dragged our tired feet back into the area where we were to meet my mom.

"I need to use the bathroom." Nathan's face had a green tinge, but I didn't mention it.

Faith and I sat on the bench between the girls' and boys' bathrooms. My feet throbbed with the relief of being off them. Two men came out of the bathroom. I recognized one as the guy who'd fought with Mr. Ferdon at the office. Not wanting to be seen again, I ducked my head.

"So, what do you think?" the unfamiliar man said. "Do you think Ferdon will hire me, even with my record?"

"You don't worry about a thing. I've got that fool wrapped around my finger. He does what I want, when I want." The guy shrugged. "I could get him to hire the Son of Sam if I wanted."

They kept going without looking our way. That was the benefit of being a kid. Adults often didn't even notice we were there.

The look on Faith's face made me rethink that benefit. She was blinking back tears. "Hey, don't worry about those guys. They're just talking big. Men do that all the time. You saw your dad with my mom. He's no fool."

247

I thought about telling her what I'd overheard and about the papers I'd taken from the garbage can, but I couldn't stand the idea of my best friend more upset than she already was.

Nathan stumbled out of the bathroom. "I'm done in." He looked a little better than when he'd gone in. "I think I'm going to sleep until Monday."

Maybe by Monday the bad feeling I was getting about my mom working for Faith's dad would wear off, but probably not.

45

Faith

The DMV records confirmed what Faith already knew. There'd been no sign of Mr. Potter's pickup all these years, no sale and no registrations. Faith lay her phone on the table and walked to the kitchen window. The backyard was overgrown with weeds and plants that had not been tamed in years.

She stepped out the back door and knelt near the fence, pulling at a mound of grass where there had once been a neatly defined flowerbed.

When Heather had disappeared, Faith's dad was still here in Deep Valley most of the time. He had moved Faith and her mother north about an hour, and he did most of his work by commuting. Her parents said this was to get her established in the school she'd be attending, but a year later, they'd moved again. So much for promises.

The year before, Faith had interviewed a diver named Larry for her podcast. He'd lost his wife and two young daughters when the car they were in slid off an icy road and into a river. The car had been submerged, and it took three days before rescuers found it. Twenty years later, Larry was trained in search and rescue as well as river and lake diving. He'd been the one to bring closure to many missing persons cases. Faith wondered if his knowledge might be of service here.

As much as she knew that pickup had not evaporated into the atmosphere, there was hesitation in making the call to Larry. The man reminded her a bit of her own father, but only in the way he held people's attention with his authority. How much had she really known her dad aside from his professional exterior? He'd never hurt her, at least he hadn't done so physically, but what if there was another side to him, something that went along with what Fiona had said?

Faith yanked and yanked at a dandelion. Her lower back protested, but she wouldn't give up. Finally, the weed broke free, and she tumbled back on her rear.

She picked up the broken dandelion and hurled it toward the fence. What had her father done that was underhanded? And how could he have taken the easy way out, leaving her to find the truth and try to mend the hearts that were crushed, including her own?

There wasn't a choice. Faith had to keep going. Being here in Deep Valley, she couldn't help but let the questions she had about her dad rise to the surface. Faith needed to remain focused. The Cranes deserved to know the truth. She got to her feet and went back in the house, scrolling through her phone's contacts with dirt-smeared hands.

"Podcast lady. What can I do you for?" His voice had a backwoods drawl that came with heart and compassion. "I didn't expect to be hearing from you again."

"Well, Larry, I have a case that could use some of your expertise. Any chance you'd be able to come to Deep Valley, Oregon? I'll be paying your fee." Somehow.

She heard him flipping through paper, then he cleared his throat. "For you, I could be out there next week. What do you have for me?"

Faith laid out the case piece by piece.

"I'd bet my mother we'll find that pickup in water. Everyone thinks they can hide the evidence that way. I'll start on my research here and be ready to hit the drink when I arrive."

"Thanks, Larry."

She was either about to break the case open or slam face-first into another dead end.

In the bedroom, she pulled up Google Maps and ran her finger along the blue lines within a hundred miles of Deep Valley. There were so many places that pickup could be. If she didn't find a way to narrow the search—more evidence, a witness or something—she'd sink her entire savings into Larry's paycheck.

If Potter returned to his house at midnight and reported the pickup stolen in the morning, he could only get so far from the house. But how did he get back? Could there have been someone else involved?

Faith showed up at the police department unannounced. No need to give anyone a chance to blow her off, especially if Nate was still set that the search for the truck was a waste of time.

She walked up to the window, the man at the desk now a familiar face. "Hello. I need a minute with Detective Nobbles or Detective Covington."

"Okay, Mrs. Byrne, I'll see if either of them is available to meet with you." He punched something into the computer.

A moment later, Nate was in the waiting area, much like the first day when she'd been overwhelmed by the way he'd grown into a man. "Hey. What can I do for you?"

"I need a bit of information."

His eyebrows tightened. "Look, I heard an earful this morning. The boss is not at all thrilled about you being in town. He thinks your podcast could make the department look foolish for not having solved this years ago. If a podcaster comes up with answers, what are we even doing here?"

His words stung, but she understood. "I'm not going to cause any trouble," Faith said. "I want to find out what happened to Heather now more than ever. If you could tell me exactly when Potter called in and reported his pickup stolen, that would really help."

"Let's go back to my office." When the door was closed behind them, he looked her straight in the eyes for a long moment. He ran his fingers through his hair, repeating the action three times. After a deep breath, he started searching a database on his computer. Ten minutes passed before either of them spoke. "Here it is. Potter called and made the report at seven in the morning."

"That's only seven hours after he'd been brought back to his house. That leaves a lot of time for him to dump the truck and get back to the house."

"Seems like he would be taking a big risk coming home any time after five. Too many people starting to wake up, heading off to work. All it would take was one person spotting him, and it would be all over."

Faith leaned forward. "What if he—and I know you don't agree—but what if Potter had an accomplice? Or what if his truck really was stolen?"

"I promise you, we will look into every angle."

Faith knew a dismissal when she heard one. "Thank you, Detective. I hope you have a very nice day." She stood and walked to the door.

"Faith, please."

There was nothing left to say, and the stillness in the room bore witness to that fact. He could work the police investigation, but she was going to uncover the truth with or without his help. She lifted her chin and forced her gaze to stay on Nate, giving him one last chance to say something.

They lingered like that, neither one willing to break the

connection until another officer sidled up to Faith, poking his head into Nate's office.

She took her opportunity then and left. What had she expected from Nathan Nobbles? They'd been childhood friends for three months. They owed each other nothing. Still, she couldn't help but be disappointed.

Faith reached down and took hold of the garage door handle, then lifted with all her strength. Wheels screeched over rusty and unused runners. Inside, the light shined on tools and other assorted items that probably hadn't seen daylight in a few decades.

The garage was narrow, meant for only one car, but a workbench lined the right side. Above it hung tools on a pegboard, their outlines drawn with Sharpie to ensure they were put back in the right location.

Grandpa had been as neat and organized as Grandma was sentimental. Even forty years after her grandfather's death, only a thin layer of dust dared to settle on his work area. Faith wondered if he'd parked his car in here, or if this had been a sacred place for creating the woodwork she'd heard he was so passionate about.

It would be good to reclaim this space by getting the car towed away. The summer was more than half over, and she wanted to help her grandmother clear it for sale before she returned home.

Faith scanned the walls and searched through the drawers, hoping to find a key to her father's car, but there was none, though the car was unlikely to start even if she found it. She grabbed the passenger-side handle and yanked. Nothing happened. Faith bent down and peered through the tinted window but couldn't see much. The door was locked, and so were the other three. She pounded her fist on the hood. This was irresponsible and rude, leaving a car in someone else's garage, locking the doors, and neglecting to leave the key. It's not like anyone was out to steal it. Even in 1987, a 1986 Camry wasn't all that special.

Faith fished her phone out of her pocket and dialed her grandmother, but to no avail. She waited a moment, then tried again. Her grandmother picked up the phone right away, her voice edged with concern. "Faith?"

Apparently two calls this close together was enough to set off the alarm.

"Hey, Grandma, do you know where the keys to Dad's car are?"

"Oh, for heaven's sake." A minute ticked by. "I'm afraid I don't have a clue about that."

"No worries. I was just wondering."

After saying good-bye and feeling a good deal of guilt for scaring her grandmother, Faith scanned the room one more time, then returned to the house. Sitting on top of the boxes from the attic were the keys she'd found. It didn't make sense that her father would pack the car keys away, but neither did anything else associated with her father.

In the garage, Faith shoved each key into the lock. Neither of them would turn.

She sighed. She'd need to hire a locksmith just to get inside of a broken vehicle that was probably much worse off than it had been when it was parked there. She entered the house through the door into the kitchen and Googled locksmiths. Only one name came up. Apparently, the hardware store also did lock work.

It was Fiona that answered the call. "How can I help you?"

"Hello, Fiona, this is Faith Byrne. We met the other day."

"I remember you. You're the podcaster with the raccoons."

"That's me. Say, I've got a car I need to get into, but I can't find the key. Would you be able to help with something like that?"

The sound she made was nearly a growl. "You got proof it's your rig?"

"Well, not exactly. It was my father's car, and it's in the garage of my grandmother's house. That seems proof enough that I'm not trying to steal it." She looked out the door at the car she'd once thought to be cool and modern. Now it looked like an antique, but not in the good way.

"I suppose so. Ryker gets in at three. I can come out after that."

It's not like there was another locksmith to choose from. It was either Fiona or taking a rock to the window. Faith weighed the two options for a moment. "Okay. That sounds good." She rattled off the address, then ended the call.

She checked the time on her phone. One thirty already. The day was slipping away from her. Just that morning, the first episode dropped. She'd need to spend some time gauging the response from her listeners. Would they follow her along this journey, or would they turn to one of the other two million podcasts available? Losing her audience would mean losing her income. Just another reason for Neil to gain custody of her girls.

Sweat trickled down her hairline. It was too hot today to let her fears take over and turn up the flame.

Faith poured a glass of limeade and went to the computer in the back bedroom. It always seemed ten degrees cooler back there. The analytics page took a moment to load. Lightning-fast internet was not a concept that had come to Deep Valley yet. When the page appeared, Faith had to blink and reexamine what she saw. Downloads were up by forty-three percent from her last typical episode.

She liked to give listeners the opportunity to share their thoughts and questions directly with her without clogging up her email inbox, so she'd set up a Google form. Clicking through to that, she felt the overwhelming desire to both cheer and hide.

Heather's story was finding an audience, and they were vocal. It seemed people all over the country wanted to bring Heather home.

———

Fiona finally arrived at close to four thirty. Anywhere else, this would call for a negative review, but in Deep Valley that would only serve to upset the community over her attacking one of their own. Faith had about given up, even deciding on the best rock from the backyard to bust through the glass.

"What's the deal with this car?" Fiona asked, setting her tools at her feet and shoving her hands into her overall pockets.

"My dad had some issues with it, so he put it in here and apparently never got back to it."

Fiona's look was one of complete skepticism. "It's not easy getting a car up these inclined driveways. Seems like he'd leave it on the street or have it towed to somewhere they could fix it. But I guess old Ivan had a lot on his mind back then."

Faith's spine tightened. He may not have been perfect, and Faith had plenty to despise the man for, but he was still her father. A flash of memory came back to her, being at the fair when two men walked by talking about how her father was a fool. It felt so much like right now, with tears wanting to flow on her anger.

Fiona must have picked up on Faith's body language. "Sorry about that. I forget sometimes to take into account relationships and all that."

Faith nodded and cleared her throat before speaking. "Do you think you can get me into the car?"

"Sure. I could order you a key too, but that will take time. You could hotwire it in the meantime."

She shrugged, not knowing how to respond.

Fiona took out a long, thin strip of metal and a black square attached to a hand pump. She worked her way in between the weatherstripping around the edge of the door, then slid the square into the opening. As she pumped, it inflated and increased the space between.

"I talked to my sister about that no-good husband of hers," Fiona said casually as she worked.

Faith bit at her bottom lip. She wasn't sure how she could handle any more questionable information that pertained to her father.

"Barb said she remembered the last time they talked about your dad. That old scoundrel said he'd paid his debt. Your dad must have been making bank to get Harold off his back."

Faith pinched her lips together. If her father had access to a great deal of money, she and her mother surely hadn't seen any of it.

Fiona slipped the metal strip down to the lock and pulled it up. A second later, she had the door open.

Fiona stepped aside as if Faith should get in, so she did. Air trapped in a car for over thirty years was stale and had an oxygen-deprived feeling. Even though she was very aware that the door was open, Faith struggled with a claustrophobic reaction. Her heart pounded, sitting behind the wheel of a car she'd ridden in many times before. The dashboard was perfectly preserved, mixing outdated knobs with pristine presentation.

Her fingers went to the ignition without thought. A single key was stuck there, as if ready to ignite the engine and take the car for a spin. She turned it, but the car didn't as much as sputter.

"Fiona, would you help me push this into the driveway?"

Fiona's eyes went wide. "Girl, that might be harder than you think." She pointed to the cement floor.

Climbing out of the car, Faith looked where she'd indicated. The tires sagged. Apparently, air found a way out of rubber if given enough time to do so. She slammed the door shut again.

Time took advantage of everything, finding a way to age even that which was best preserved.

46

Dora

When she'd come up with the spontaneous idea to get a pet, Dora had been thinking about something that would bring a little life into the house, but Sybil found a dog who better fit her grandmother's personality. At least Finnegan fit somewhere. He certainly didn't fit in her car well.

If she hadn't taken her granddaughter to the animal shelter, Dora wouldn't have given old Fin a second look. But Sybil fell instantly in love with the old guy, a Great Dane that was estimated to be six years old. From what the shelter people told her, that qualified him for the dog equivalent of AARP.

Just like an old man, the dog seemed to feel cold all the time, except when he lay in direct sunlight. He also drooled and took over most of her bed. Living with Paul was looking better every day.

Dora sat on the sofa, scanning the television for old movies. Finnegan must have wanted to watch too. He ambled up beside her and set his rump on the couch, his front feet still stationed on the carpet.

"What do you think you're doing?"

He kept his line of sight straight ahead, as if waiting for

Dora to select something of interest to him while ignoring her at the same time.

This was what her life had come to. She was an old lady living alone with a humanized dog as her only companion. Brooke was going to pack her off to a nursing home if she wasn't careful.

Dora's phone startled her with an upbeat song that sounded like nothing she would ever choose to listen to. "Hello?"

"Hi, Grandma," Charity said. "Sybil keeps telling us about your new dog. Connor and I were wondering if we could come by and see him."

Had this ever happened before, the grandkids asking to stop by? She looked at the old guy sitting on his throne next to her. "Of course you can." A commercial for pizza played on the television. "I'll order a pizza if you'd like to stay for dinner."

"That sounds awesome. Can we have vegetarian?"

"How about a half-and-half? I'm guessing your brother will want meat."

"He's kind of gross that way."

Dora grinned. Charity sounded so much like her mother at that age. Brooke had been ready to take on the world and correct all the wrongs. When had that all changed? Or had it? "Do you need a ride?"

"No. Dad said he could drop us off. I bet Mom will pick us up after work, if that's okay."

"I can't wait to see you." For the first time, she really meant it. She'd always loved her grandchildren, but spending time with them came with a whole pile of regret and fear. It's hard to just be and let yourself sink into relationships when one had been torn away from you like Heather had been from Dora.

Dora set the phone down and looked at the dog. "Well, Fin, we're having company for dinner. What do you think about that?"

Drool formed along his sagging lips until it gained enough weight to become lines of spit reaching for the floor.

"This is not working." She stood up and headed into the kitchen.

His feet clomped along behind her.

Dora dug through her drawer of kitchen towels. It was stuffed so full it would hardly close, and rags often fell over the back and into the drawer of Tupperware below. She found a particularly well-used one, the floral pattern hardly recognizable, and laid it on the counter. Then she took scissors from another drawer, looked at Fin, then cut a hole about the size of his head. "I think this will help." She slipped the makeshift bib over his nose and past his large hanging ears.

He looked like one of those jacks in *Alice in Wonderland*, standing tall with a rectangular card over his chest. She used the long end of the rag to wipe his chin, then gave him a good scratch on the head.

Dora ordered the pizza using the phone number on the refrigerator magnet, then set out plates and cups. In the garage, she found Paul's stash of soda pop and brought in a few cans.

The doorbell rang, and Finnegan lost his dignity. He tore around the corner, sliding into the wall and collapsing, just to bounce up and lumber the rest of the way. If there was a pizza on the other side of the door, this might be her last delivery.

Dora put her body between Fin and the opening as she peered outside. Erik was the first to be seen. He stood with his kids behind him, as if he were unsure about the evening's plans. Looking back at the one-hundred-and-twenty pounds of drool, she could understand that.

She wove her hand under Fin's collar and yanked him back from the door. "Come on in."

"There's my sweet Finny Boy." Sybil pushed her way past her older siblings.

Erik caught her before she could reach the dog. "Let Connor and Charity see the dog. You've already had a chance."

Without hesitation, the two older kids wrapped around the

dog's neck. A moment later, Finnegan flopped onto his back, and high-pitched sounds of happiness filled the room from all three of them.

Sybil bounced up and down, looking from the dog to her dad.

"Okay. Go ahead. He seems to like the attention."

The little one dove into the pile of dog and kids.

"Erik, you're a very good dad." Dora kept her gaze glued on the joyful scene in front of her.

"Thank you."

She turned his way. "I'm really sorry I don't tell you that enough."

He rubbed a finger back and forth over one eyebrow.

"Sybil is welcome to stay too. In fact, why don't you and Brooke go out to dinner after she gets off work? I bet it's been a minute since your last date."

His head cocked.

"I'm learning the new lingo from Sybil."

"Well, it has been a minute. If you're really okay with all of them, I'll take you up on the offer."

"No problem at all. We can watch a movie. I haven't seen any of those new *Star Wars* programs."

"*Mandalorian!*" Connor shouted.

"Sybil is a little young for that one."

She bounced up, her fists on her hips. "I am not. I've watched a bunch of them already."

Dora put her arm around her granddaughter. "Don't worry, Erik. We'll find something age-appropriate for all of us."

47

Heather

On Saturday morning, Mom kicked me out of the house well before the cartoons were over. She and Dad had things to discuss. She even had the nerve to say it wasn't a conversation for little ears. Offensive!

Outside, I spotted Faith right away. She sat on the curb by her grandmother's house. I grabbed my bike from where I'd left it in the front yard and pedaled over there. I was a house away when I noticed the red splotches and swollen eyes. My first thought was that something must have happened to her grandmother.

Emotional situations were not my specialty, so I just sat down beside her. Mom always said that actions speak louder than words. It felt like eternity came and went as I waited for her to tell me what was wrong. Finally, I couldn't take it any longer. "What's the matter?"

She sniffled and wiped her eyes with the back of her hand. "We're leaving."

"What do you mean?" My heart started to beat all the way up in my throat.

She breathed out a long shuddering breath. "Dad is moving

us to Goshen. He wants to get me and Mom into the house before school starts, so I won't have to join late."

"Isn't he going?"

"The development isn't done. He'll be here most of the time. He says it's too expensive to drive back and forth every day. I guess the new place is an hour away." Her sobs started up again.

An hour. She might as well move to the moon. I shook my head. "This doesn't make sense. Why would you move to Goshen? There's nothing there." Of course I'd never been and I knew nothing about it, but if we couldn't be together, the place had to be horrible.

"He says there's a better hospital near Goshen. It's for my mom and the baby." Her shoulders shook.

"My mom had all of us here, and we turned out okay."

"It's not the same. My mom . . ." She hesitated. "She's lost a lot of babies."

"What do you mean?" The expression painted a picture of Mrs. Ferdon walking out of the supermarket with her child still strapped into the grocery cart inside.

"I'm not really sure why it happens. No one ever talks to me about it. They think I just don't notice or something. The babies die either right before they're born, or soon after. That's all they care about. It's like I'm not good enough, so they keep trying to get a new kid who might be better."

"No way. You're great."

She looked at me then, like she'd never seen how dumb I was until I said that. "Your parents are not at all like mine. You have no idea. Mine may seem okay when you're around, and even with Grandma here they've been better, but they aren't loving and caring and all the stuff your parents are. They fight, like, all the time. Sometimes my mom gets so mad at him that she breaks things. Dad will go days without even talking to her. It's miserable. I hate it so much."

I felt really bad. I'd spent countless hours with Faith that summer, but I'd had no clue what her family was really like. I wanted to barge back into my own home and hug my mom and dad. "Come on." I stood and offered Faith a hand. "Let's go hang out in my backyard." Sitting outside the Ferdon house was giving me the heebie-jeebies.

When we got to my house, I took her to the bathroom I shared with Brooke and Greg. There, I ran a washcloth under cold water and gave it to Faith to wash her face like my mom always did for me when I'd been crying—not that I was a baby or anything.

My parents were outside now, so we went to my room instead, and Faith laid on Brooke's bed while I took mine. Never had I felt such a quick ride into sadness. It didn't make any sense to me. The development wasn't finished. In fact, from what I'd overheard my parents say, it was months behind schedule. They kept talking about investors and interest and all sorts of things I would normally ignore if I wasn't already on this case.

I leaned up on my left elbow. "Maybe you can stay with your grandma."

"I already asked. My dad said that was out of the question. I'm supposed to be taking care of my mother while he's here during the week."

"But you can't do that from school."

She covered her face, and I could tell she was crying again.

"Don't be sad. We're still going to be friends. I'll write to you, and you'll write to me, and when you come to visit your grandma, it will be like you were never gone." I didn't even bother to say we'd talk on the phone. My dad had one thing he was adamant about: No long-distance calling. Brooke tried to get away with it last summer when she returned from church camp madly in love with some guy. She'd ended up grounded for a week and had to pay the bill. And with what

I got paid to feed Mr. Potter's cat, I'd be forty before I could afford a ten-minute call.

Brooke stood in the doorway, looking back and forth between us. She started toward her bed. I tried to get Faith's attention before my sister dumped her on the floor, but instead, Brooke sat down on the edge of the mattress and rubbed circles in Faith's back. She didn't even ask what she was blubbering about.

Faith stayed for dinner that night. She was a normal part of our family by this point in the summer. I couldn't help wondering what it was going to be like when she was gone. It seemed to me as if her dad was being cruel. We were best friends. Didn't he understand how important that was?

I squirted ketchup on my hot dog bun and scooped a large helping of macaroni and cheese. One of the best parts of this summer, aside from my time with Faith, had been the food. We weren't the kind of family that got to eat TV dinners and instant foods. Mom liked serving us healthy stuff as much as possible. The meal that sat before me that night was exactly what my stomach desired. Not a single vegetable on the table.

Afterward, my dad asked Faith and me to come into the garage with him. He'd been working on fixing some part of Greg's car while my brother was at work at the IGA. He lifted the hood and bent over the engine. "How are you girls doing?"

I shrugged, then realized he couldn't see me. "Fine."

"I understand that Faith and her mom are moving in a couple weeks." He held out a hand to me. "Can you get me that wrench?"

I picked up the tool and placed it in his hand. "That's right." Faith stood silently by my side.

"That has to be tough on both of you."

"It is."

He handed back the wrench and turned around, leaning

back on Greg's car. "Do you trust that God has a plan for your lives?"

This was a simple question for me, but Faith's family didn't attend church when they weren't staying with her grandmother. "Sure," I said.

Dad looked at Faith, waiting for her to speak up.

She nodded.

"A lot of times in life, it will feel like you're all alone and what's happening around you isn't fair. And sometimes, it really won't be fair, but if we trust in God, if we live our lives in service to Him because we trust our lives to Him, we can be confident that He will make even the hardest times produce good. Do you understand what I'm saying?"

I started to answer, but Dad held up a hand. "Let Faith answer."

Faith dug the tip of her sandal into a crack in the cement floor. "I think you mean that we will be okay even if this isn't what we want. That maybe God has another plan for us, and we should trust that?"

"Basically, yes. I'm really sorry that the two of you won't be living by each other much longer. I wish I could change that. But I want you both to be able to look back on this time and be happy for what you've gained. I think you two are not done being friends either. It's only an hour to Faith's new house. I'm sure we could make that trip once in a while."

I launched myself into my dad's arms. The scent of engine oil and hot dogs clung to him. No one in my world ever knew exactly what I needed to hear more than my dad did. I just wished Faith could have a father like that.

Before I was done hugging him, I felt someone else's arms join mine. Faith, my friend who had started the summer so quiet and shy, had jumped in and flung her arms around my dad and me. I didn't know what life would look like without her on my street, but my dad didn't lie to me. I knew it would be okay.

48

Faith

Larry and his new wife notified Faith that they had a location at Cramer Lake they wanted to start at. It wasn't the kind of thing Faith felt she needed to let any of the Crane family know. Lakes and rivers had been checked in the eighties and nothing had ever come of it.

She pulled up beside Larry's motor home, a sign on the side announcing he was a rescue diver, though she doubted many people knew what that meant. The back was covered in random stickers from places he'd traveled, usually to help out on cold cases. They'd already removed the small boat from the trailer attached to the back.

They'd chosen an early morning in the middle of the week, hoping to avoid too many people asking questions, but Faith had found there were few places she could be anymore without drawing attention.

"Hey, there. Long time." Larry shuffled up the side of the boat ramp, getting to Faith without losing his breath.

She reached out her hand, but he tugged her into a hug.

"Good to see you." Larry waved a woman over. She was tiny, not much taller than Faith had been in fifth grade, but she looked like life had worn some rough edges in her. "Meet Jean. She's signed on as my partner in life and in diving."

"It's so nice to meet you," Faith said to Jean.

"You too. I'm glad we could come out here and try to give you a hand. We'll do everything in our power to bring some closure to this awful situation." Jean nodded once.

Larry shifted in his life jacket that looked about two sizes smaller than comfortable. "Jean will be starting up the video soon. Do you need to run audio for your show at that same time?"

In lieu of payment, Larry had worked out a collaboration between his YouTube channel and Faith's podcast. By doing it this way, the cost had been waived and Faith could breathe without worrying how she was going to make her house payments.

"I'll take some audio too. We can share what we have when we're done, if that works for you."

A bright grin lit Larry's face. "Sounds good. Let's get moving on this."

Jean held up the camera and signaled Larry to begin.

"We're here today on the banks of Cramer Lake. My partner and I have come out to Oregon in search of clues to a thirty-six-year-old mystery. What happened to Heather Crane? The year was 1987. Heather had gone back to school, the fifth grade, when one night she went missing. A pickup that is suspected to have been involved disappeared two days later and was also never seen again. I've done my research, and within the time frame from the initial location, there are many bodies of water that could cover a vehicle, but Cramer Lake fits our criteria better than any of the others." He nodded, and Jean lowered the camera.

Larry rubbed at the back of his neck. "I'm going to go ahead and get out there with my sonar equipment. I'll let you know if I find anything."

Jean climbed into the boat, then Larry pushed it out farther and took his seat in front of her. The motor they used was nearly silent as they skimmed across the glassy water.

Faith walked to the lake's edge and sat on the cold earth. She pulled her knees up toward her chest and looked out over the stillness of the early morning. Fish jumped, their impact with the water forming circles that spread until they faded away. She could just make out the image of a fisherman casting his line on the far shore.

The big question loomed. What if they found something? What if they found *her*? The thought both terrified and fueled her. Was there any doubt that Heather was gone? Honestly, she couldn't bear the possibility of Heather still being alive, under the control of some kind of evil monster. To Faith, she was the constant and loyal friend she'd been all those years ago. Heather never stopped being that girl. She would remain the beautiful soul who brought Faith into her family without thinking twice.

She looked out again, watching the gentle waves of the water, smelling the sweetness of summer in Oregon and the hope that came with the warmth of the rising sun. Nothing could have prepared her for what God had in store for this summer. Just like the one in 1987, it was life-changing, healing. It was here she'd first understood the truth of God's existence, and here where she again felt connected to Him in a way that was tangible.

Without technology as a distraction, Faith felt the weight of every situation she'd been pushing down float to the surface. Heather was gone. "God, help me understand." Neil was gone. "Lord, show me how to accept this change." Her children were part of a new family that she didn't have a part in. "How is this supposed to work for my good?"

The fisherman pulled on his rod, moving his body back and forth until he eased a fish from the waters, grabbing the line with his free hand.

She watched as Larry and his wife motored slowly around

the edge of the lake, Larry's head down, likely keeping his eye on the sonar monitor. If they found the pickup, she'd have to make phone calls—not only to the police but also to Heather's family. She'd come here to find the answers and to bring Heather home. Now that there was a possibility of doing just that, she wasn't sure she had the strength to follow through.

The boat seemed to stall. Larry looked her way, scratched his head. They dropped something in the water, then worked their way back to Faith.

With each length they traveled, her heartbeat quickened. By the time Larry pulled the boat up to the shore, Faith could hardly draw a breath. She sat silently, her hands clamped over her knees, and waited for his pronouncement.

Larry stepped out of the boat, leaving his wife behind. He walked up to Faith and sat down beside her. "This one is really personal, isn't it?"

She nodded.

"Well, I'll get right to it. We did find something, but the image was blurred, more like what we see when we find a vehicle that's only been in the water for a few years. My guess is this isn't the pickup you're looking for, but I'm going to get my diving gear on and take a closer look."

"It's a truck, though?" Her neck screamed with the tension that tugged her muscles tight.

"It is. I don't think this is the time to call the family or the police. Let me have a look, then we'll get together and talk about what I find. I'll have a recording to share with you. You said you don't know if the license plate is still on the vehicle?"

"No idea."

"Even if it's not, we still have the year and the color to go by. If I can find anything that says Chevy or identify the color as the green you described, we'll take this further. Either way, the police will want to get involved, but that's not necessary now." He patted a gloved hand on her shoulder.

"Thank you."

Once again, she'd have to wait.

Over an hour passed before Larry returned.

Faith's breathing eased when she saw the license plate in his hand.

"It's not our truck," he called.

Tears streaked down her face, emotion held tight until this moment. "Could you tell much about it?"

"It's been there maybe a year or so. The plates were still attached, so I brought these up. I'll touch base with the police department and make sure this truck isn't connected to any other case." He sighed. "I know it's a relief when we don't find anything, but be prepared, you may find yourself disappointed before the day is up. It's hard to know a loved one is gone, but it's harder to not know."

Still, Faith's resolve was renewed. She would find these answers, and she would keep searching until she found Heather. It wasn't the truck they were looking for. Nothing had changed, but the stab of pain grew sharper.

Faith went back to the house. She had notes to compile and an episode to write. The wave of messages had become more than she could dream of tackling. Fortunately, Kendall had stepped up to take on the role of administrator, sending Faith regular compilations of tips, questions, and comments.

Her phone buzzed with a text from Jackson Sailor, a kid Mr. Crane had recommended to get the car working so she could send it on its way.

I'm out of work early today. Can I come over to get started on the car?

Faith typed back.

Sure. Anytime.

She went back to her work, but only five minutes had passed when she heard the rumble of an older engine pulling up in front of the house. A moment later, the doorbell rang.

A young man, probably older than he seemed, stood on the porch, his hands clasped together in front like a military pose.

"You must be Jackson."

He nodded. "Yes, ma'am." He might be small, but his voice was deep. His parents had taught him well to speak to even a stranger with respect. If only Harlow would look twice at boys who had more to offer than muscles and conceit.

She led him outside to the garage door. Before she could lift it, he jumped in front and threw it open. The boy wasn't weak.

He walked around the car with slow paces, checking every inch of the exterior. "Wow. This is in great shape."

"It should be. It's sat in here for over thirty years."

"Do you mind if I push it out to the driveway so I could have more room to work?"

She pointed to the flattened tires. "That might be a problem."

"Not at all. I've got a portable inflator in my car. The tires will need to be changed eventually, of course, but these might do while we're reviving this old thing." He patted the roof as though he were talking to a beloved pet, maybe something like the beast she'd seen Mrs. Crane walking the last few days.

Jackson jogged to his car and came back with a yellow box that had a tube running from one side. In minutes, he'd added just enough air to each of the tires to lift the car, but not to be fully inflated. "Would you mind being behind the wheel while I push?"

"Okay." Faith climbed behind the wheel and put the car into neutral. Giving Jackson the thumbs-up, she readied herself to get out and help, but the car started to ease backward. It bumped over the lip of the garage opening, then picked up momentum. She hit the brake just in time to keep the car from crossing the sidewalk.

Faith shifted the car into park and employed the emergency brake, then climbed out. Waves of memories came flashing in her mind as she stared at the car, the sun reflecting off the silver paint. Her dad had once told her she could have this car when she got her driver's license. That statement had given her reason to attach a kind of claim to the vehicle. But then, it was gone. She'd never known it was here in her grandmother's garage all this time.

49

Dora

Finnegan stared out the front window, his bark reverberating off the walls.

With a hand covering each of her ears, Dora went to him and nudged the dog with her knee. "Hush. You're going to break my eardrums."

Apparently, he couldn't hear her logic over his racket because he didn't even pause.

Across the street, a boy was fiddling with an old car in the Ferdons' driveway. Dora squinted. Her vision wasn't what it once had been. She could remember looking that way to check on Heather and Faith, seeing them easily though they were a bit down the road. Now, the images were blurred. In fact, she couldn't be sure what the kid was doing. What a fool she'd be if she stood here staring while her dog warned her that a crime was being committed right in front of her.

"Come on, Fin. Let's go see what's happening." She retrieved his harness and leash, knowing very well that she was making a spectacle of herself, an older lady walking around the neighborhood with a beast like Fin.

It was a workout getting his legs threaded through the

halter. If nothing else, this dog was getting Dora into shape. Before leaving the door, she remembered the trick she'd read on the Google. She filled her pocket with treats, then showed him what she had. Finnegan was a sucker for this. He kept close, knowing at any moment she could whip out a delicious prize.

She walked through the front door with Fin and a whole lot of confidence that was stripped away almost immediately. About the time they reached the sidewalk, the dog gave her a look, then broke free and ran to Milly Ferdon's old house.

The Great Dane was harmless, but the boy in Faith's driveway didn't know that. In a flash, he'd jumped onto the hood, then shimmied to the roof of the car.

By the time Dora got there, Faith was outside too, an amused look on her face.

"Mrs. Byrne, do you know this dog?" The boy made himself tiny in the center of the roof.

Faith took Finnegan's leash and pulled him away from the car.

"Oh dear." Dora panted. "I'm so sorry." She bent over, trying to catch her breath after jogging down the road for the first time in years. When she got herself calmed, Dora looked back at the car. The boy had climbed down but kept the vehicle in between him and poor old Fin.

Something was familiar about the Camry. It was old but seemed to be in beautiful shape.

"It's my dad's car." Faith answered the question before Dora thought to ask it. "It's been here in the garage for thirty-five years. Can you believe it?"

Dora's mouth fell open. "Why in the world would Milly have left it in there all that time?"

"She never was one to drive, preferring to walk where she had to go. And I think it was hard for her to get rid of something that had been my dad's. Maybe it was a connection to him."

That was something Dora could understand very well. She remembered hearing about Ivan's death. It was sometime in the first year after Heather disappeared. Dora hadn't been able to wrap her mind around her old boss dying and what that meant for her neighbor. All she could manage in those days was getting up, doing what she could to find Heather, and going back to bed at the end of the day. Had she even offered her condolences?

Faith stepped up alongside Dora, handing the leash over and kneeling to give Fin a good scratching. His mouth hung, and his ropelike tail wagged back and forth.

"What are you going to do with it?"

"I think I'm going to sell it." Faith shrugged. "Grandma is planning to sell the house. She's decided to stay on at Sparrow's Nest."

Dora placed her hand on the trunk. "All things, good or bad, eventually come to an end, don't they?"

"All things but God."

A chill spread out over Dora's skin. She'd turned her back on God when He didn't give her the desire of her heart—to have her baby back in her arms. But that didn't stop Him from being there, still waiting on His lost child.

Tears pricked her eyes. Maybe God did understand what she was going through. She'd been the one missing. The lost sheep, the prodigal son.

"Oh my goodness." Faith had both hands on the back window of the car. She pressed her face close to the glass.

"What is it?" Both Dora and the boy were giving her their full attention. Dora set a hand on her shoulder.

"I see something in there." Faith went around the car to the driver's side. She brought out a set of keys, then unlocked the door. A moment later, she stood, something shining in her hand.

"What's that?" Dora tried to see.

Faith came close. Her trembling fingers opened, and a necklace with half a heart appeared on her palm.

Dora touched her chest. "I remember those. You and Heather wore them every day. I'm glad you found yours."

Faith curled her lips over her teeth. "This isn't mine. This one belongs to Heather."

"Are you sure?"

She turned it over. *H. C.* was carved into the metal. "Mr. Crane helped us engrave them."

That sounded like Paul, always doing the little things with the kids that meant so much to them, things most fathers wouldn't think to do or take the time for.

"I don't remember Heather going anywhere with your dad," Dora said. "In fact, I had the necklace listed as one of the things she was wearing the day she went missing. I didn't even notice that she'd lost it."

"She hadn't." The color in Faith's face had drained away.

The boy hammered on something under the car. People walked by. Time stalled.

"What do you mean?" Dora finally whispered.

"Jackson, I need you to stop working on the car." Faith looked at her. "We have to call Nathan."

50

Faith

Dora, Faith, and Finnegan were sitting in lawn chairs in the front yard when Nate pulled up. "I came as fast as I could. What did you need me here for in such a hurry?"

Faith's eyes puddled before she could get a word out. She handed him the necklace that she'd placed into a sandwich bag. "It's Heather's."

"I was always a little jealous about these. Not that I wanted one or anything. Where did you find it?"

Faith pointed. "In my dad's old car."

"Maybe she lost it in there?"

"Follow me." Faith stood, leading the way into the house. She pointed to the last picture on the timeline. It was the one taken the day Faith had left Deep Valley. "Look close. She's wearing the necklace in the picture. This is the day I left town."

"That's strong evidence that she was in your father's car at some point after you left. I agree. That seems odd." He flipped the baggy over to the side with the initials. "Have you looked through the car any further?"

Faith shook her head. "I didn't think we should until you got here."

In the doorway, Mrs. Crane held tight to the knob.

"No one goes near it, okay? I'm calling this in, and I'm going to get forensic specialists in here right away." He went to Faith and pulled her to him.

His warmth and the beating of his heart near her ear were the only things keeping her from collapsing. Had she come all this way to find out her father was the one who took Heather away from her family?

Nate rubbed her hair. "I think it would be good if you stayed somewhere else tonight. Do you think your grandmother would let us look through the house?"

Faith's heart cracked a little deeper. How could she tell her sweet grandmother that the son she lost could have been the epitome of evil?

She looked to Mrs. Crane. "I'm so sorry. I had no idea he could possibly have anything to do with Heather's disappearance." Faith stepped away from Nate and toward Mrs. Crane, but the dog wouldn't have it. He stepped between them, his eyes on Faith.

Mrs. Crane held a hand up. "Excuse me." Her face was as hard as a Greek statue as she backed away, then turned and walked down the street.

Faith started to go after her, but Nate caught her arm. "You need to let her go. We'll call Brooke and have her check in, but until we know what's going on here, I think it's better for you to keep your distance from the Cranes."

She looked up at him. "I promise you, if I had any suspicion that my father could be involved in this, I would have said something."

He placed a hand on her shoulder. "I know you would have. This is complicated. Do you have a place you can stay tonight?"

Just then, Crouton ran through the house and out the door.

Faith ran out after him, catching sight of the cat going after Fin as if wanting to make it clear the dog was never welcome in Crouton's territory. Faith ran across the street and grabbed the cat by the scruff, pulling him into her chest. "I'm sorry about this too."

Mrs. Crane was on her porch, her eyes weary and wet. She turned the knob and went inside, closing the door behind her and the dog without uttering a word.

Crouton dug his claws into her skin, but the pain felt warranted, deserved.

As she turned, she saw Nate waiting for her. She was walking from the disgust of Mrs. Crane to the pity from Nate. There was nowhere she could be right now that felt safe. Where would she spend this horrible night? Everyone she had a relationship with was a Crane or part of the police department. She even thought about calling the gal from the hardware store. Could it really be that bad?

When she reached him, he tried to take the cat, but she refused the help.

"Listen, you're welcome to stay with me tonight. I can sleep on the couch, and you can have my bed."

"Not a chance."

"Why not? I'm on your side here." There was hurt in his words that trailed deep into the past.

"I can't stand the pity. I'm staying here." Her jaw was set but her gut was wobbly.

He looked from her to the house, as if it would give him another solution.

"You won't need to get a warrant. My grandma will give her permission, I'm sure of it. We won't be in the way of the investigation. I can sit in my car with Crouton while officers check out the house."

"Okay, I just—"

"You want to protect me. I can see that. But I don't need you to."

He touched her arm in a way she hadn't been touched by

a man in many years. It sent hope through her, hope that someday life could be whole again, but not today.

"I need to call my grandma and let her know what's going on. Can she give permission to you through the phone?" Stepping inside, she kicked the door shut and let the cat go. Blood left tiny red blotches on her white T-shirt.

Nate nodded. "But as the current resident, you can give permission for a search. I'll be in the garage, letting my boss know what's going on." How had the boy grown into a man who could sense her needs without her having to say a word?

She watched him walk away as she sank onto the couch to make a call that would break her grandmother's heart.

When her grandmother answered, her voice seemed older, frailer than before. "Hello, Faith."

"Hi, Grandma." She couldn't go any further.

"Spit it out, girl. Whatever is on your mind, it will be okay."

Faith pulled air in through her nose, releasing it out her mouth. "I found Heather's necklace, her side of our friendship necklace. It was in Dad's car."

She mumbled something Faith couldn't understand, something like a prayer.

"Is it okay if I give permission for the police to look through the house and the car?"

"Well, the car is yours to give, and I don't see any reason to keep them from looking in the house. If you feel this is wise, I'm behind you." Her words were slow and purposeful.

"I'll let them know."

"That's fine, but first I want to tell you something. It's important."

Faith's heart stalled. "What is it?"

"No matter what happened to Heather, even if your father was involved, he really did love you. Don't let that get taken away."

"Did he?" Faith ran her fingers through her hair. "I never really felt it."

"He was a tough man, very much like his father. Ivan wasn't the kind of dad who gave hugs and said, 'I love you,' but it was in his heart. I saw it when he looked at you. Just remember that, okay?"

"Okay." She could agree, if only for her grandmother's sake, but believing in her father's love was much harder than believing he may have known what happened to Heather.

51

Heather

We made the most of the next two weeks. During the day, we spent our time swimming and eating ice cream. At night, Faith slept over more times than not. I missed having my mom around, but if she hadn't gone to work for Mr. Ferdon that summer, I never would have had the freedom to have all the adventures we went on.

No matter how we used our time, the days kept ticking by until Labor Day weekend. Faith's dad planned to make the move on Sunday, giving them the holiday to get settled before school started on Tuesday.

That Saturday, Mom took Brooke to the mall in the next town over for new school clothes. I refused to go, and my mom didn't argue with me. I was willing to wear whatever crazy things they bought for me if it meant Faith and I could have one more day to hang out.

Faith and I had spent another night in the backyard, waking up to a cooler morning than we were used to. We went inside and filled our faces with Eggo waffles covered in syrup and sat in front of the television, watching Saturday morning cartoons.

At noon, Nathan arrived, a bag of sandwiches and three pops in his backpack. I left a note for my parents, leaving our location vague, then we biked off to the development.

Over the summer, we'd gotten bolder in our use of the half-built homes, but this was our first visit in the middle of the day. There were only a few houses near the center that we could still access. They surrounded an open area with fencing all around. It was like the heart of the neighborhood, but it looked like a broken heart. I could relate.

We climbed to the second story of a house that was half covered with plywood. From where we set up our picnic, we could look down on the area that was blocked off.

"I think that's going to be a swimming pool." Faith snapped open a pop and foam sprayed. She pointed it out the opening, but Pepsi puddled on the floor.

The three of us shifted to get away from the mess, giggling about what we'd just seen.

Nathan looked over the edge. He never seemed to have that wavy feeling I got when I looked down. "Do you know it's going to be a pool, or are you just guessing?" I could see the wheels turning. Nathan was already thinking about next summer and how we'd sneak in. But next summer it would only be the two of us. I couldn't hang out with a boy alone. That would be weird.

Faith set her pop down and looked out the opening. "I'm just guessing. I haven't heard Dad say anything about a pool, but what else could it be?"

I wasn't about to go to the edge, but I stood and looked from my spot a few feet back.

Below us, tarps and cement blocks covered the ground. I would ask my dad about it—he always seemed to know these things—but I wasn't allowed to be at the development, so I didn't dare. This conversation, just like most of the ones we'd had the last week, was our way of not talking about what we were all thinking of. Tomorrow, Faith would go, and our perfect friend group would crumble.

We circled around our food again, but with our time together now being counted in hours rather than weeks, none of us seemed to be able to muster any excitement.

Faith tore her peanut butter and jelly sandwich into tiny pieces, only occasionally plunking one into her mouth. "I can't stand it." There were tears in her eyes. "I don't want to go. How could my parents do this to me?"

"Would they let you stay with your grandmother?" Nathan took a huge bite and swallowed without enough chewing.

We'd talked about this a hundred times. He knew the answer as well as Faith and I did. "I asked again. The answer is always no. Dad told me yesterday that if I brought it up one more time, we'd never come back to visit. He was so mad. I mean, he's not the nicest guy, but he's never yelled at me like that before."

"You'll be back." Nathan crossed his legs. "I mean, your grandmother lives here, you have to come back."

Faith dipped her head. "This summer is the first time we came to Grandma's house that I can remember. She always comes to visit us. I don't think my dad likes being here."

I wrinkled my nose. My parents loved going back to their old hometowns. They'd make us hang out with the kids of their old high school friends while they sat around talking about the good ol' days. "Your dad grew up here, didn't he?"

Faith nodded.

"Doesn't he have friends here?" That was not the thing to say, and I knew it as I let the words out into the wood-scented space between us.

"I have no idea." Faith studied her hands. "I can't remember him ever having friends. I think grown-ups get married and that's that. They have each other."

I knew this wasn't right, but pointing out that my parents

had a large group of friends would only serve to make Faith feel even more like her family was weird.

Nathan jumped to his feet. "I have an idea."

"What?" Faith leaned back on her hands. "Does it keep me from having to move?"

"No, but it will give us another epic memory."

My attention was piqued. This was where Nathan and I had more in common than with Faith. We were the risk-takers. Faith was what my mother called the voice of reason. I waved Nathan on to tell us what he was thinking.

"We sneak over here tonight and have a look at what's behind the fences."

I rolled around, hugging my stomach as I laughed. "That's your big plan? It's probably nothing at all."

"Then why all the *Keep Away* signs and the chained fence?" He pressed his hands into his thighs and leaned forward. "I think they've found something like gold or oil, and they want to keep all the riches for themselves."

Faith shook her head. "I think there'd be clues if my family was about to be rich. I mean, I've seen the place we're moving to. It's lower middle-class at best."

I sat up, wrapping my arms around my middle as I remembered everything weird I'd overheard all summer about Mr. Ferdon and the development. "I don't think this is a good idea."

They both looked at me like I'd gone mental, which I guess made sense. I wasn't the one to bring reason into our plans. That job sat fully on Faith's shoulders.

Silence reigned between the three of us while my friends waited for me to explain my position. I wouldn't do it, no matter how much pressure they applied. Finally, I shrugged. "Okay, let's do it."

52

Faith

If it was possible for Crouton to be more upset than he had been on the drive to Deep Valley, it happened when Faith sat in the van in front of the house and watched police descend like she was the only unaware member of a notorious mob family. She understood. There could be evidence somewhere, and if Faith were a different woman from a different family, she might want to protect her father's memory.

Looking out the windshield gave Faith a sideways view of Mrs. Crane's house. She tried to avoid that view by shifting in her seat, but when Mr. Crane's pickup pulled into the driveway, quickly followed by Brooke and her husband, she'd seen it all. They stared her way with looks so broken and haunted, Faith's heart threatened to stop beating as a tribute to the pain that her father could have been involved with.

Two officers surrounded his car. There had to be another logical explanation for how the necklace got into the back seat.

Nate stood beside another officer as they put the key into the trunk lock. After messing with it for a few minutes, one of the officers returned from the garage with a can of WD-40.

The key finally turned, and they were able to release the latch. The lid sprung up, and Nate turned to Faith, his face ashen.

Before she could think, Faith was out of the van.

He jogged her way, holding up a hand. "You have to stay back."

"What's in there, Nathan?" His childhood name fell off her tongue.

He held her by the shoulders, but she looked around him and saw it. Heather's bike with the silver tassels, peering out of the trunk.

53

Heather

That night, my mother insisted on hosting a farewell dinner for the Ferdons. When she got something like this in her mind, there was no way out. She invited their entire family over, as well as Nathan.

I'd only talked to Faith's mother a handful of times. She was supposed to be resting because of the baby, and she didn't often come out of the house. I wondered how she was going to manage a household on her own, but I figured they had a plan, and it really wasn't any of my business.

Brooke stomped around, moping because her friend Joy was having a good-bye to summer party and, according to Brooke, *everyone* would be there but her. She was even more bent out of shape because Greg had been allowed to go see *RoboCop* at the drive-in with Angela and his friends.

Mom took us to Blockbuster earlier in the day so us kids could pick out a couple movies to rent. I really wanted *Back to the Future*, but she'd heard there were bad words in it, so she nixed that plan. We ended up with *Pee-Wee's Big Adventure* and *The Goonies*. Apparently, my mom hadn't heard anything about our second pick.

Nathan, Brooke, Faith, and I sat at a card table set up in the backyard, near the large picnic table where the adults were. If I wasn't so torn up about Faith leaving, I would have really enjoyed watching my sister squirm, outnumbered by us "immature kids."

Halfway through our meal, my dad stood and raised his glass of iced tea. "Ivan, I'd like to thank you for bringing your family to Deep Valley this summer. I know the development is going to do wonderful things for our town. We've been blessed by getting to know your daughter too. You will be missed." He looked to Faith with those last words.

We all lifted our glasses and cheered for the good that had come, as if tomorrow it wouldn't all go away.

The grown-ups quickly went back to their mumble of chatter while the four of us sat in awkward silence.

From inside the house, the phone rang. Brooke jumped up so fast her metal chair tumbled over backward. "I'll get it."

My mother rolled her eyes and said something to Faith's mother about teenagers and the phone.

It felt like we'd been sitting outside for eternity when Mom brought out the dessert, some kind of fluffy pink stuff that tasted a little like ice cream but wasn't that cold or filling and had the smell of strawberry Jell-O. We finished our bowls and excused ourselves to the living room while the parents and Faith's grandmother sat around the new firepit my dad had made from cinder blocks.

"No way we're getting out of here tonight," Nathan said. "Your dad told me he'd give me a ride home after our movies since it's already dark."

"I think that's for the best. We'd only be disappointed."

We started our movie, and the three of us lay on our stomachs, watching a group of kids go on an adventure the likes of which I would gladly join. My mind whirled with ideas, especially after Nathan told us they'd filmed this movie here in Oregon.

I woke in a panic. I was in my room, laying on my own bed. Brooke snored from her side of the room. Faith and Nathan weren't there. I couldn't remember anything after the kids in the movie entered the cave. I jumped out of bed and tore open the curtains, letting sunlight into the room.

"What in the world are you doing?" Brooke growled and flopped over.

"How did I get into my bed? Where is Faith?"

"Dad brought you in here last night. You fell asleep. So did Faith, so her dad took her home. Now hush."

I ran out of the room and down the hall, finding Mom and Dad at the kitchen table with coffee and the newspaper. "Did I miss Faith? Is she gone?"

My mom got up and came over to me, pulling me into a hug. "No, honey. They aren't leaving until after lunch."

Tears spilled from my eyes, a mixture of relief and dread. It wasn't fair. Faith was my best friend.

54

Dora

Dora couldn't stay away from the window, no matter how many times Paul, Erik, and Brooke tried to distract her. When they opened the trunk, she was watching, though she couldn't make out a thing at that distance. What she could tell was that something important had been inside.

"Brooke, come here." She waved her daughter to the glass. "What are they looking at?"

Brooke grabbed the wooden ledge around the window.

"What is it?" Dora asked louder this time. If Brooke couldn't tell her, she was going over to see for herself.

"I think it's a bike."

Paul and Erik were there beside them. They stood in silence, as if what was playing out across the street was too big for words.

She felt them coming closer, as if anticipating her collapse, but Dora's body seemed strengthened, ready for the battle of her life. Whatever came next, whatever horrible answers were about to be revealed, they were still answers, and that was something she'd had precious little of the last thirty-six years.

"Is it hers?" Paul pressed close to the glass. "I can't see from here."

"I can't be sure." A silent tear flowed down Brooke's face. "I'm . . . I don't know if I could tell anymore."

Paul grunted. "That's it. I'm going over there."

"No you're not." Erik stepped in front of the door. "We aren't going to get in the way. This is important, and the police are handling it."

"No way." Brooke's jaw was a hard line, so much like her father's. "I've seen them together all over town, Faith and Nate. I'm not about to trust him. What if he covers up the truth to protect her?"

"You hold up this instant." Finnegan came to Dora's side, alerted by the increase in her volume. "Faith was a child. She is not responsible for Heather's disappearance any more than you are."

At that, Brooke crumpled to the floor. "But I am. She was trying to talk to me about something that night." She buried her face in her hands. "I told her she was a pain and to leave me alone."

Kneeling beside her, Erik stroked her hair as he held her head to his chest.

"I knew she was having a hard time after Faith left, I just didn't care." She looked straight into Dora's eyes. "You were right, Mom. I made everything about me, and it cost Heather everything."

Dora and Paul exchanged looks, his accusatory, as if she'd really dropped the blame on their remaining daughter. "Did I tell you this was your fault?" She really didn't have any memory of such a hurtful outburst, but the first weeks were a blur, and she couldn't guarantee that she hadn't. "I'm so sorry you felt that way. I never blamed you."

Because she was too busy laying all the responsibility on her own shoulders. What if she'd been home that day? What if she'd never taken that ridiculous job from Ivan? What if that job, the increase in the connection with the Ferdons, had been the final piece that led her daughter to a monster?

Someone knocked at the door, and they all froze as if they'd been caught in the act of carrying out a crime. It felt like minutes ticked by as Dora stared at the knob, unable to move toward it.

It was Erik who took the reins for the family, first helping a sobbing Brooke to the couch and then answering the door.

There stood Nathan Nobbles, a man now, but still so much the boy who'd been brave enough to hang out with two girls that summer, who'd eaten everything Dora put in front of him and gladly accepted seconds. There, in her doorway again, but this time, he was all alone.

Paul sank onto the couch next to Brooke, letting his little girl melt into his side. "Come on in."

A chill from the cooling air wove into the house with Nathan. It washed over Dora and clung to her skin. "What did you find?" She breathed deep, practicing a few of the tips she'd learned at the grief group to ease tension. "Please, just tell us what's happening."

His head bobbed with determination. "There was a child's bike in the trunk. It would be good if one of you could come and identify if it was Heather's, but I'm sure it was." He pressed his fingers into his forehead and closed his eyes for a beat. "I rode alongside her for so many hours that summer, I'd recognize those silly tassels anywhere."

Dora moved toward him, hesitated, then closed the gap, wrapping her arms around the little boy in the man's body. "I'll go."

"No." Paul's voice was solid, demanding. "I'll do it."

Stepping away from Nathan, Dora looked into her husband's eyes. "This is something we should do together." She swept her view over to her beautiful Brooke, a piece of her heart, who had no idea how deeply her mother loved her. "Brooke, you don't need to come. You and Erik can stay here. I'm sure this won't take long."

Brooke's sobs grew louder again.

Without words, Erik took over the spot where Paul had just been, holding his wife tight into his side.

"There's more." Nathan fidgeted with the seam along the outside of his pantleg. "It's pretty busted up. We're going to need you not to touch it. There could still be evidence on it, especially since it's been in that trunk all this time."

"When you say it's busted up, what do you mean?" Paul asked.

"It looks like it was hit by a car or truck."

Paul reached for Dora's hand, and she let him take it.

The outside air had the crisp feeling of fall. Lights had been set up in Milly Ferdon's driveway. Police walked in and out of the house, and a large tow truck had pulled up, blocking the road.

Officers parted as they saw them approach, leaving space for Paul and Dora to look into the trunk of the silver Camry.

There wasn't a doubt. Dora had searched for this bike all these years, never seeing one like it. It was a hand-me-down from the daughter of one of Dora's friends. She couldn't remember who now. When they'd brought it home, Heather wasn't impressed, but after she and Paul spent hours painting, polishing, and adding the tassels, it was her dream bicycle.

Dora let go of Paul's hand to wrap her arms around herself. The chill was making her shiver. Then she heard the muffled sounds she hadn't heard for so long. Paul was crying.

55

Faith

Faith finally put her phone back in her pocket, though the conversation with her grandmother had been over for at least ten minutes. There were secrets held tight in Grandma Ferdon's mind, secrets Faith may never fully know or understand.

She rubbed her index finger over the scribbles she'd made on scratch paper while her grandmother had shared what she remembered of that time.

Faith's dad hadn't been at the house when the police came through for the second canvas. She could remember that weekend, though the sadness she attached to it seemed trivial now. It had been her eleventh birthday. She'd wanted so badly to make the trip back to her grandmother's and celebrate with Heather, but when her mother called to ask her dad, he'd refused.

Tears prickled Faith's eyes as she thought back over the anger she'd felt at her father. Not only had he denied her request, but he couldn't even bother to get home until Sunday night, when her birthday was nearly over.

The gift he'd brought her was a doll. It was her eleventh birthday, and he'd brought her a doll. She'd tossed it aside and run off to her room, slamming the door. Seeing her best friend was the only thing she'd wanted.

For years there'd been guilt attached to the memory, but all that time she hadn't known there were worse transgressions lurking in her father's heart.

After the car had been towed away and the Cranes were back in their cozy house, Faith was allowed to bring the cat and herself back inside. She sat on the couch and stared. What kind of things happened here in this house that she hadn't been old enough to understand? Should she have seen this coming?

Nate stepped in from the kitchen, a mug of coffee in his hand. "How are you doing?"

She rolled her eyes at him. "I can't believe you asked that. My father murdered my best friend. How do you think I'm doing?" That snapping she did when life felt out of control was in full force, and Nate was the target. He didn't deserve this attack. "I'm sorry."

"We don't have all the information. The way the bike looked, it could have been an accident. And we don't have . . ."

"A body?"

He nodded.

She pulled her knees to her chest. "I can't believe this is happening. I came here to try and help, but this is . . ."

Nate sat beside her. "You have helped. Even before you found the necklace, you helped Mrs. Crane move forward. No one had been able to do that in all these years."

"She'll hate me now. I watched them from the van. I saw everything as they stood there looking into the trunk." She grabbed a throw pillow and held it to her face, a buffer between herself and this horrible world she'd fallen into. "Any good I may have been a part of is blotted out by Heather's bike and the necklace being in my father's car."

The doorbell rang.

Faith blinked away tears until she could read the clock across the room. Who would be coming by at nine thirty? She looked to Nate. Did she really have to answer the door? Wouldn't they eventually go away?

He could still read her mind, stepping in for her when she didn't have the nerve. Nate got up and peeked through the window before opening the door. "Carl, this isn't a good time."

The man's eyes grew round. "Detective. I didn't expect to find you here. I have a few questions for Ms. Byrne. I think she'll want to talk with me."

Faith got off the couch but didn't go much farther.

"I don't think so, Carl." The hard tone of his voice must be the same one he used when dealing with criminals.

"Why don't you let her decide for herself? If I don't talk with her, I'll be forced to go to press with what I have."

She went a little closer, enough to see the side of his face. The man was at least six inches shorter than Nate and had a face so rounded she hadn't seen it on anyone aside from cartoon characters.

Nate crossed his arms. "What you're really saying is you have nothing, and you're willing to make up a story to keep your readers happy and the rumor mill producing. Is that really what you want to be saying to me?"

Carl flicked something out of his shirt pocket. "Give her this and have her call me. I can do a lot of good or a lot of bad for her image."

Nate slammed the door and tossed the card on an end table. "What a little weasel."

"Who was that?" She picked up the card. "The newspaper?"

"Carl is the entire newspaper. He does it all around here, which has to be a pretty boring job most of the time. Take my advice and stay away from him."

"He's only the first. There's going to be more by morning."

"Come stay at my house. The invitation is still open."

"You know I can't do that. How would that look?"

"Like you're staying with an old friend who cares about you." The lines between his eyes gave away his own doubt.

"Anyone with an ounce of imagination will make a juicy story out of it. It would look like I'm trying to get the police on my side—and a few other things."

"What if I slept on the couch here?"

She put her hand on his forearm and leaned into him. He still smelled like men's soap even after a long day. "Go home. I have my attack cat around here somewhere."

"I'm only a call away."

She stood back and looked up at him. "That's what I'm afraid of. I can't let you take care of every little thing for me. I need to stand on my own two feet."

Faith was summoned to the police department the next morning. It seemed that the night brought with it a whole new litany of questions, ninety percent of which she couldn't answer. By lunchtime, she'd gone over every detail and bit of information she'd collected since coming into town.

The only solid answer she got for her hours of questioning was a personal reminder that she needed to let Larry off the case. There was really no reason to find Mr. Potter's car anymore. Whatever happened to it, it had nothing to do with Heather's disappearance.

What had that poor old man been through, living his final years in a town that thought he was a kidnapper and worse? If only she could make it up to him, clear away all the awful suspicions her father had allowed to fall at that innocent man's feet.

That was why honesty would take priority. She still had the podcast, and she could use it to clear a man's name, even while condemning another.

56

Heather

Tuesday morning, I went back to school. I saw Nathan a few times, but we mainly just exchanged nods. He was back in the land of popular boys, and I was sitting alone at lunch because Amy's family still hadn't returned from their summer in Japan.

All the things I'd heard about middle school turned out to be true. By the second day, cliques were in full formation. I liked a couple of the girls I sat near in band and figured they'd make a fine group until Amy got home and we could figure out our future in the social scheme of Deep Valley Middle School.

The one good thing was the weather. The heat hung on. My dad said we were having an Indian summer. On Thursday, after school, I biked to the creek. I wasn't supposed to go there alone. My mom had made me promise that a hundred times over the summer. But I needed to get away from our street and sit in the quiet. I'd heard my mother talking on the phone the previous night about Amy's family not coming home until Christmas now. That was about all I could handle.

I prayed while I sat there, my toes in the icy water, the shade of the trees blocking out the sun. I asked God to make the year a special one, though I couldn't think of a way for Him to do that. Brooke said middle school was just something you had to get through. The thing was, I could have done that easily with one good friend. Maybe he would bring me another Faith or get Amy back earlier.

I was so deep in my thoughts and prayer that I didn't hear the approaching footsteps. I about jumped out of my skin when I felt a hand on my shoulder. Spinning around, I found Nathan standing there. I punched him right in the center of his chest.

"What was that for?" He stepped back, rubbing the spot I'd tagged.

"You scared the life out of me."

"Sorry. I didn't mean to." He plopped down on the bank. "You're awful jumpy today."

"I'm sorry too. I shouldn't have punched you. Are you all right?"

He cocked his head my way. "Of course I am."

I picked up a stick and started carving a line in the soft sand. "What are you doing here?"

"Same as you, I suppose. Wishing summer wasn't over. It's kind of unfair making us go to school when it's still so nice out."

"Why aren't you out with the guys?"

He picked at the seam of his jeans. I wondered how upset his mom was going to be when she saw the dirt he already had on his school clothes. "They're mad I decided not to play football."

"That's dumb."

He gave me a dirty look. "I don't like getting hit, okay."

"I meant it's dumb that they're mad at you."

He deflated a bit. "That's what I said. It didn't go over too well."

It could have been my own sadness, or I may have been becoming more mature, despite my dislike for the thought, but I held my tongue like Brooke and Mom were always begging me to do.

"There's no reason we couldn't still hang out, is there?" he asked tentatively.

There was one obvious reason, but I didn't want to say it because I didn't want to lose Nathan too. But he was a boy. Just the two of us would lead to rumors that could make middle school a nightmare. Plus, it was a reminder of how much I missed Faith. But I shrugged off my doubts. "Sure."

"I'm dying to know what they've done with that weird circle at the development. Want to go take a look?"

A glance at my Swatch said I had some time, though it wasn't much. "Let's go, but we have to stay away from the offices. My mom should have left by now, but I don't want to run into her out there."

"You got it."

We biked along the streets that were less used and came into the new neighborhood from the back. No one had moved in yet, and I'd heard Dad tell Mom he wasn't sure Mr. Ferdon would be able to sell them all. The computer company had changed their mind and was moving all their stuff to another country. Dad had gone on and on about American jobs and the economy, so I had naturally zoned out.

We came to the development and found it oddly quiet, the work crews gone for the day. With the days getting shorter, our vision was already hampered by the shadows of the mountains. Nate and I parked our bikes behind a house. The silence was eerie today. A fall breeze blew the heat away and left the air chilled.

I heard a jingle just as Nathan pulled me back.

"What are you doing?"

He held his finger to his lips. "There are people out there."

Pressing my body up against the siding, I peeked around the corner. Two men—the two we'd seen at the county fair—

stood near the gate. One was working the lock while the other leaned on the handle of a shovel.

A beep sent us scrambling around the other side of the house and crouching in the shadows.

"What was that?" I whispered in Nathan's ear.

His hand was held over his wrist. "My watch. I have to get home."

I had a whole lot of heebie-jeebies crawling up my spine, so it didn't take much to convince me.

We pushed our bikes along the back of the houses until we could get on the road where the two men wouldn't see us. I wasn't sure my heart had ever beat so hard.

57

Faith

Faith did all she could to avoid the house. Being inside felt like being trapped in a display case at the zoo, with people slowly walking by in hopes of getting a look at the dangerous predator in captivity. I didn't matter how many times Nate told her, or she told herself, that none of this was because of her. She still carried the stink of her father's choices.

She pulled into the campground where Larry and Jean were staying, found their site, and parked.

Larry sat back in a lounge chair, his feet elevated. "Well, hey there. I didn't expect to see you."

"I feel so bad that you came all the way out here for nothing." Faith opened the passenger side of her van and retrieved a *Welcome to Oregon* sticker. "I thought this might be nice with your collection."

Larry stood. He pulled the cuff of his worn plaid shirt over the heel of his palm and rubbed a clean circle on the back of his motor home between Ohio and Iowa. Taking the sticker from Faith, he peeled off the backing and pressed it into place. "Perfection." He stepped back, rubbing his hands together.

"It doesn't make up for getting you to come all the way out here from Arkansas."

Larry leaned his right shoulder against the RV. "My lady and I went into town this morning for breakfast at that diner. There's some real good eatin' in that place. But there's also a lot of chatter. I heard how it was your daddy's car they found the bike in, and I'm real sorry."

Faith dropped her gaze to the dirt.

Using his thumb, Larry lifted her chin. "Don't be doing that."

"What?"

"Takin' on shame that doesn't belong to you." He growled low in his throat. "I don't know what this investigation is going to turn up. Maybe your dad is as evil as folks are saying, but being kin to someone doesn't make you responsible for their sins."

Faith sunk onto the picnic bench. "You said it yourself. They're all talking about me."

"Whoa." He held up a hand. "That's not what I said. I said there's chatter. People have a habit of being curious. Most of the time this is a good thing. It brings about great advancements, and without curiosity, no one would seek the deeper meanings. But to everything human there's a dark side. Those folks in town are wanting answers. I think you can understand that. It's one of the things that brought you here."

Faith's arms felt as heavy as two anchors. "Maybe it would have been better if I'd stayed away."

"Nonsense. What you need to do now is keep digging. You promised that family you'd do your best to find out what happened to their little girl. From where I'm sitting, I don't see that job as done."

"I don't know how."

"Yes, you do. I've listened to every single episode of your podcast. Girl, you know how to find the heart of the story. Keep digging."

Faith breathed in the pine scent.

"Jean and I will head out today. We have a case to work on in Nevada, but I'm glad we came. It was good to see you."

Faith hugged him and said good-bye. Another friend she'd probably never see again.

———

Faith spread the transcripts from every interview she'd conducted on the floor around her. With an orange highlighter, she marked any reference that could play well with the new information they had.

The police had never interviewed her father. She was honestly shocked by that. He employed Mrs. Crane, lived nearby, and was the father of the girl's friend. Wouldn't it stand to reason he might have some kind of information? It was an inexcusable mistake. She'd believe that even if the bike hadn't turned up in his trunk.

What else had the police missed back then?

She remembered Fiona and her statement about Faith's dad and the development. She made a note to dig deep into that angle. It might not be an obvious path, but Faith was going to put the rest of this story together, and she only had weeks before Ava and Harlow returned from Hawaii.

She picked up the phone to call Fiona but decided it was too important to let her make excuses. Ten minutes later, she parked in front of the hardware store.

A customer stood at the counter, paying for a bag of nails.

Faith stayed to the side, picking up one item after another, as if she were interested in buying a toilet snake.

When the door closed and the store was empty aside from the two of them, Faith came forward. "Hello, Fiona."

"Oh no. I've been hearing stuff. I don't want anything to do with this."

"I just have a few questions."

She shook her head. "It's none of my business. I don't want to get involved."

"The first time I was in here, you said something strange happened at the development. Can you tell me more about that?"

"You don't get it. I don't want to talk to you." She picked up an old phone and held it to her ear, her finger hovering over the buttons. "I'll call the police."

Faith shoved her hands in her pockets and shrugged. "We can do it that way."

The standoff stood firm for so long, Faith started to wonder if she'd made the right move. Then, finally, Fiona settled the receiver back on its cradle. "I don't have a lot to say. My no-good brother-in-law worked for Ivan. He got a job out there for another winner, Jeremy Marinoni. They were real tight back then."

"Where can I find this guy?"

A slow smile crept onto her face. "Your best bet would be the jail. He's been in and out for as long as I've known about him."

Faith continued asking Fiona questions for the next twenty minutes but came up with no more information than she already had. But Jeremy Marinoni, that was a lead she could follow.

On the way out of the hardware store, she called Nate. He answered as she sat in the car. "Hey, how are you holding up?"

"About as well as you'd guess. Any new information you can give me?"

Nate cleared his throat. "I really shouldn't be talking to you about the case. I'd like to come out of this with my job intact."

"Have it your way. I guess I'll take the same approach."

The sound of a door closing came through the line. "What do you have?"

"You first."

"Is this going to be worth sacrificing my integrity?" His tone had gone light, almost as though he were flirting with her.

"You won't know if you don't play." Oh goodness. She was the one flirting. Faith held her forehead in her free hand.

"Okay. I have some news, but it's not great," he began. "The techs went over the car, and there's plenty of evidence that Heather was hit by it while riding her bike."

"So he didn't do it on purpose? He didn't kidnap her and . . ." Faith nearly choked on her emotion. Scenarios that had assaulted her mind, they weren't true. Her father had done a horrible thing, but she couldn't put words to her thoughts, not even in her imagination.

"There's no evidence to indicate it. Honestly, without her body, there are still so many questions."

"I know. And we need to find the answers. I have a lead on someone who might be able to help."

"Who?"

"Jeremy Marinoni. Have you heard of him?"

He grunted. "Oh yes. Mr. Marinoni is a regular around here. What makes you think he could have information?"

"He and another man, Harold, worked for my dad. I was told there was something underhanded going on at the development. I think the two of them were part of it, but Harold is dead, so that's no help."

"Where did you find out about this?"

She hesitated, looking through the windows at Fiona pacing behind the cash register. "I'd rather not say."

"Faith, come on. We're on the same side here."

"I know. I just get the feeling this person has been through a lot already. It's a small town. If you bring them in, rumors will fly. They could lose everything."

"I don't like this at all."

"Trust me, if there comes a point where I think telling you will add to the investigation, I will do it."

For a moment, all she heard through the line was the clicking of a keyboard. "Marinoni is in county lockup as we speak. I'll make contact and see about having a chat with our friend."

"Thank you." She meant it for so much more than following this lead.

Faith tossed the phone onto the passenger seat. If she'd just stayed at home, none of this would be happening. She would have remained *safe*, insulated from the truth and the consequences. But at what cost? This wasn't her story.

This was Heather's.

58

Dora

Knowing was supposed to bring closure, whatever that was.

Dora sat at the funeral home, making arrangements alongside her husband to bury her child—to bury the hope of her return, anyway. There would be no body to lay to rest, no place to visit that was more than a marker of stone. She kept telling herself that Heather's body was nothing more than flesh and blood, the vessel in which her daughter had lived, but she ached to know what had happened to that vessel.

The director placed a catalog in front of them, opening to a page with child-sized coffins. What did they even need one for? Dora flipped it shut. "This is ridiculous. A marker will be plenty. There's no need to bury an empty box."

"Some families find it therapeutic."

She looked at Paul. "Will this make a difference for you?"

He shook his head.

"No coffin."

"I understand." Yet his face didn't agree.

She had the sudden urge to ask him if funeral directors were paid on commission.

When they finished, Dora walked outside while Paul remained behind, participating in the socially mandated small talk.

The sun felt soothing on her face. It felt like there was hope for a future, even at her age. They may not know where Heather was on earth, but no matter what happened, Dora couldn't deny the truth of God. There was a great comfort in knowing her baby had a place with Jesus.

A glance down the street caught her by surprise. There was Faith, just like she'd been the last time Dora had laid eyes on her, sitting in her van. This time it was parked in front of the hardware store, rather than her grandmother's house while they peered into the trunk at Heather's mangled bike.

It wasn't her fault. Every ounce of Dora's soul knew this, but she hadn't been able to make a move toward Faith in the days since the discovery.

Paul came up beside her. "What are you looking at?"

She tipped her head toward the van.

"Is that Faith?"

Dora nodded.

"What are we going to do about her?"

She turned her attention toward him. "What do you mean?"

"She's a victim in all of this too. I'm just not sure I can make the steps to console her." The smallest part of his lip slipped between his teeth.

There were so many people who missed out when Heather was taken away. Was there a man out there who never found his soulmate? Would their daughter have made some great advancement that would have changed the world for the better? And what about her grandbabies? Who would they have been? It was all so senseless.

She and Paul had taken separate cars, and they drove away to their separate homes. Two more victims of the crime Ivan Ferdon had committed.

Dora pulled into her driveway but didn't put the car in the

garage. She engaged the emergency brake and stepped out, walking down the sidewalk until she faced a house that no longer had any power to hurt her.

Out front, John Potter watered what remained of the flowerbeds his mother had once cared for so diligently. He turned off the sprayer and looked at her, probably ready to boot her off his property.

"Hello, John. I owe you an apology." She blinked back the tears. This wasn't about the hurt in Dora's heart. This was about the hurt that the Potters had suffered. "I'm so sorry for all your dad went through. He didn't deserve it."

John's head bobbed in tiny nods.

"If I could go back and make it right, I would."

"He was a lonely old man. For the rest of his life, people saw him coming and turned the other way. And still, he refused to leave this house because it reminded him of my mother."

In all the years she'd feuded with John Potter, Dora had never looked past her own grief to notice the sadness in his eyes. "I'm so sorry." What else could she say? Dora couldn't fix the past. She couldn't bring her daughter home. She couldn't make her husband come back to her. She couldn't heal the hurts of the many people Heather's loss had devastated.

John's features seemed carved from stone. "I accept your apology, but that doesn't mean I'm ready to forgive you." He turned back to the flowers, his posture a clear dismissal.

59

Heather

My mom was always telling me that I was too curious for my own good. Well, that night my curiosity took tight hold not long after Nathan and I went our separate ways. I couldn't get the thought out of my head that there was something going on at that development that wasn't on the up-and-up. I might have let it go, but my mom was working there. What kind of daughter wouldn't investigate?

I stopped my bike and gave it a thought. I really did. Then, I went back to the development and parked my bike just where I had earlier. I got onto my stomach this time, thinking they'd never see me that low to the ground in the dimming light.

Both men were still there. They'd gone through the fence now and had uncovered a large hole beneath the tarps. "This should work." The guy who'd scared me before, Harold, pointed to a pickup with a canopy. "Back up as close as you can get."

It was hard to hear the other guy. He spoke soft, almost a whisper.

Headlights illuminated the street.

Both men went rigid.

Below me, the cold of the ground seeped through my T-shirt.

I wished I hadn't left my long-sleeved flannel at Mr. Potter's house.

Faith's dad climbed out of his car. "I've been thinking," he said. "This isn't a good idea."

"That's your problem, Ferdon. Too much thinking and not enough doing. Look in that truck." He pointed into the canopy. "Do you really think we have another choice at this point?"

Mr. Ferdon stuffed his hands into his pockets, looking deeply uncomfortable. "Just get it done."

I wiggled, trying to keep myself from shivering. A few more minutes and I'd know what was happening here. I could tell my parents and maybe, if the information was important enough, they wouldn't be too mad at me for coming out here.

My nose started to run. I sniffed as quietly as I could, but then a sneeze came out of nowhere. I couldn't stop it, and I wasn't known for my dainty sneezes.

"What was that?" I didn't look to see who had said it.

I jumped off the ground and ran for my bike. Throwing my leg over, my back tire spun out in the loose dirt as I tried to push off. Finally, I got myself moving, my balance coming with the motion. In a move I would have been proud of in any other situation, I jumped the curb and landed solid in the street. I couldn't go straight home. They'd know who I was, and I could hear them running behind me. My legs ached as I pedaled with all my might.

Suddenly, lights shone behind me. I glanced back. Two bright headlights were coming my way.

60

Faith

Faith woke to the early morning light filtering through the living room window. Something had pulled her out of sleep, but she wasn't conscious enough to know what.

Her phone beeped with a text.

When she opened it, she saw that it was the third one in a row from Larry.

> Jean and I made a stop on our way out of Oregon. We're about a hundred miles east of Eugene.

She yawned. That wasn't the way to Nevada.

> With the new information, we thought there might be some other places to look for the truck.

Faith blinked.

> We found it.

She had to remind herself to breathe, to not pass out on the living room floor. Faith pressed the call icon, and Larry picked up on the second ring.

"Hey there, crime fighter."

"Larry, you found it? You found the green Chevy? Are you sure it's the right one?"

"Positive. I've got a license plate here for proof. I'm sending you a picture."

Her phone vibrated. Faith switched the call onto speaker and opened the image. She walked to the timeline and carefully checked each number and letter. It was a perfect match.

"I wanted to give you a call first thing, but we'll need to bring the authorities in now. How are you doing?"

"I'm . . ." What was she? "I think I'm numb."

"It's a crazy drive out this way. I'm going to send you our location. I'd feel a lot better if you had someone else drive you."

Asking for help wasn't something she loved to do, but the week had taken a toll on her. "I'll call my friend and see if he can take me."

Faith knew this location with the sparkling water in the middle of the Cascade Mountains. She knew it not from her own experience, but from a photo her grandmother had in a frame of her grandfather and her dad when he'd been less than five years old. The two of them stood side by side, not touching, each holding a fishing rod and smiling at the camera.

She'd asked her dad about that photo once, and he'd told her it was the best time he'd had in his whole childhood. Now, another bit of beauty had been stripped away.

Nate stepped out of the car first. He stood near the hood, looking around.

She joined him. "It's beautiful, isn't it?"

"It sure is. I can't figure out how the truck got here, or why."

"I think detectives are supposed to keep thoughts like that

to themselves." She nudged him. "Maybe there'll be something in it that gives us a clue who took the truck." The clean air made her feel dizzy with peace. "This could be the thing that clears Mr. Potter completely. Even with so much evidence against my dad, the town won't give up Potter as an accomplice if we can't prove he wasn't involved. But there wasn't time for him to come this far from Deep Valley and then return by the time he called in the stolen vehicle."

Larry pulled his boat up to the bank and waved. He had somehow pressed himself into a wet suit that showed off his rounded center and thin legs.

Nate and Faith made their way to the water's edge.

"Everyone is gathering about a quarter mile past the north dock. Jean is there now, explaining everything and showing our footage to the sheriff. I'm heading back into the water now to attach cables. We'll pull it out with the truck they've got stationed on the bank, then it will go off to be inspected. The pickup is a mess, as we'd expect after all these years, but I'm hopeful we can get it out in mostly one piece."

"Larry." Faith twisted her hair over her shoulder. "Why did you keep looking?"

He winked. "I had a hunch that you'd sleep better at night if we had all the pieces of the puzzle that we could possibly collect."

She stepped up to him. "You are a dear man. Thank you."

His face turned a scarlet shade. Larry ambled back to the water, climbed in his boat, and then motored away.

As Nate and Faith approached the gathering place, the sound increased. A small group of spectators had gathered, but a deputy kept them from crowding around the people working to retrieve the old truck.

Finding Jean, Faith guided Nate toward her.

"There you are. I've got some footage I think you might be interested in." She stepped under the shade of a pine tree and held out an iPad. On the screen, the image went from above water to slipping through the haze of murky green water. Bubbles floated by, but nothing could be identified until a gloved hand reached out and patted something. It wiped away filth that danced around on the screen, then cleared enough to see a license plate. At another location, the color of the pickup was confirmed to be green. In a way, it reminded Faith of looking at her babies on the ultrasound machine while they still floated inside her womb. Bubbles filled the screen, and the image stilled.

"That's amazing. I can't believe you and Larry found it."

A proud smile lit Jean's features. "When Larry gets on a case, he has a terrible time leaving it before he's brought some closure to the people left behind."

"You found yourself a good one." Faith heard herself sounding a little like Larry.

She nodded.

Voices rose all around them as Larry's head popped out of the surface of the water. He held up two cables and swam them close to the shore, where another man attached them to a line. Climbing onto land, Larry shouted orders as a motor groaned.

Water dripped along the taut cables, running back to the lake.

Faith stood close enough to see the action but squinted as the lines cried under the pressure.

When a corner of metal appeared above the surface, the crowds cheered. Here was something that hadn't been seen in thirty-six years. A piece of history that had the power to set a man's reputation to rights, even after he was long gone. How had it gotten here? Faith hugged her arms across her chest as she felt the honor and responsibility of finding that answer.

They continued to lift the vehicle until it hung above the water, the axles barely attached to the disjointed body. Time moved in slow motion as the pickup was brought over dry ground, then set on the flatbed of a tow truck. Years of submersion had done unimaginable damage. If Faith thought seeing the truck would bring back memories, she'd been wrong. What sat before her was a mangled mess of metal.

A deputy climbed up beside the vehicle and searched inside, finally coming out empty-handed.

This was just another piece of information, a clue without solid reference. One thing was very clear: Mr. Potter hadn't done this.

61

Dora

When Nathan arrived, Dora wasn't surprised. He'd given her warning that he was on his way by text. It was the look of exhaustion in his eyes that she hadn't expected.

"Come on in." She moved to the side, and Nathan entered. Finnegan lifted his head from the couch cushion, then dropped back into sleep. What a watchdog. "Can I get you some coffee?"

"No, I'm fine." He looked anything but.

"Well, I'm having some, so you might as well join me." She led him to the kitchen, where she pulled a box of shortbread cookies from the shelf and poured them out on a plate. If Nathan Nobbles had any of the boy left in him, he'd need a snack too. "I was kind of hoping you'd have Faith with you."

He reached for a cookie. "She doesn't want to make you feel any worse by having her around."

"That's nonsense. Faith had nothing to do with this. She's been hurt by her father too. I'm guessing more than we'll ever understand."

"She feels responsible."

Dora sighed. "I know. I would too." She poured coffee into two mugs, sliding one over to Nate where he sat at the counter. "Every day I look down the street, planning to walk old Finnegan that way and at the very least wave, but then my feet turn left." She set out the sugar and cream.

"It's going to take time for everyone."

"But Faith leaves next week. There isn't a whole lot of time left."

His features sunk further.

"You know Faith has to go. She has her daughters to think of."

He nodded.

"But you love her." It wasn't a question. She could see the grief clinging to him, the impending loss of Faith all over again.

His shoulders bobbed.

"Don't make light of it, Nathan. What's keeping you here?"

His eyes shot wide open. "I can't follow her."

"Why not?" Maybe it was her age, but Dora couldn't bear the thought of missing another opportunity for herself or those she cared about. "Life is short—sometimes very short. Give it a thought."

"Thanks, and I will, but I'm not sure she'd want me to do that." He took another cookie and dipped it into his coffee. "I came by to tell you that we found Potter's truck yesterday."

"I heard a rumor about that."

"It was in the mountains, way too far for Mr. Potter to have taken it. We don't have a clue how it got there, but it's another checkmark for his innocence."

"That will mean a lot to his family." She leaned on the counter. "We've decided to hold a memorial service for Heather next week. I'd like to do this before Faith leaves. She should be there, if she's willing. Would you ask her for us?"

"Of course. I'm taking dinner over there tonight." He turned to face her in the doorway, a bit hesitant before speaking. "We've got a lead on a guy who may have done work for Ivan.

At this point, there's not much to tie him to a crime, but I wonder if you might've known him, working for Ivan as you did."

"What's the guy's name?"

"Jeremy Marinoni."

The name hit her square in the chest. "Wait." She ran into Heather's nearly empty room, picking up the enigmatic file. Back at the door, she thrust the papers into Nathan's hand. "I had forgotten about these. They were under Heather's mattress. I couldn't figure out why, but look." She flipped the pages to the back and tapped the name.

Nathan stiffened as he held the pages. "Do you have any other information to share?"

Dora shook her head. "I never met Jeremy Marinoni, nor do I remember any record of payment for him."

"Can I take these?" Nathan asked, tapping the file.

She nodded.

"Thank you." Nathan hugged her, then stepped away from the house.

62

Faith

Faith opened the door, and Nate stomped in. He dropped a cardboard box with bags of Thai food that gave off delicious spicy scents onto the table, then dropped into a chair.

"Looks like you had a good day." She peeked into a bag.

"I met with Marinoni."

Her fingers stilled. The healthy appetite she'd just had faded. "What did he say?"

"Not much at all. That's the problem. The guy says he wants immunity, and he won't talk unless"—he made quotation marks in the air—"'Unless Ferdon's kid who does that podcast is there.'"

She tapped her fingers on her collarbone. "Me?"

"I think he's hoping to get some notoriety. It makes me sick." Apparently, that didn't have an effect on his hunger, though. Nate tore open the bags, setting out containers of Thai food.

Faith went into the kitchen and collected plates and utensils, then set them by the food. "So, what's the plan?"

"I can't make him talk. That's never bothered me to this level with any other suspect." He scooped red curry onto his plate. "I'm sorry. Are you okay with praying first?"

Heat spread across her chest. She knew he attended church now, but this meant commitment. "Sure." He wasn't the same somewhat lost boy he'd been in 1987. This man had grown into himself, into his own faith, and he'd done it so much better than anyone could have predicted.

They bowed their heads, and he spoke out loud in a way that felt familiar and comfortable. When they looked up, their gazes caught, an intimacy in the air that felt like a magnet drawing them closer to each other.

Nate stood and stepped closer. He put his hands on her shoulders, then pulled her close, holding her against his chest. The only sound in the house was the ticking of the clock and the strong beat of his heart in her ear. "It feels like I'm about to lose you all over again."

She tipped her head back, looking up at him. "What do you mean?"

"I don't want you to go away again."

"I have my girls. I can't stay here." Would she, even if it was a possibility? There were so many memories here. Some were beautiful, but so many would haunt her the rest of her life.

He rested his chin on the top of her head. "I know. If you were the kind of person who didn't put your children first, I wouldn't be this heartbroken."

"I don't want to lose you again either, you know."

His hand ran up her back, along her neck, and stopped on her cheek. The beat of his heart turned to pounding.

She took a risk. Did something unplanned and not thought out. She lifted her face again.

And he kissed her. Faith could not remember ever losing her breath the way she did then.

Nate stepped back. He wiped a hand down his face and took a deep breath.

"You okay?" There was a laugh in her tone, a feeling that

even if the world was burning down, there were things so good it didn't matter.

He took her hand. "I'm not sure I'll ever be just okay again."

His phone buzzed on the table.

"You'd better get that." She took a seat, not trusting herself to not jump into his arms.

"We're sending uniforms around town, asking about Harold and Jeremy. Covington is sending me the photos of them from around that time." Nate kept watching his phone screen. His face went white.

"What is it?" She got up and stepped close, looking at the screen. A man stared back at them, but she couldn't say she'd ever seen him before.

"I remember something." He looked at her with wide eyes.

"What is it?" She itched to shake him until he told her everything that was going on in his brain.

"The night that Heather disappeared. We were at the creek earlier, not too long after school, if I remember right. When we were going to leave, it was getting dark earlier, but we made a decision to check out the center of the development again. Heather was full of curiosity about it."

"I remember."

"Well, we went. And we saw two guys. One of them was Jeremy Marinoni. I didn't realize it when I looked at his mugshot. He hasn't aged well at all. He and the other guy, I'm pretty sure it was Harold, they were up to something, but we left. We both rode out of there and headed home."

"Did you tell the police about this?"

"I don't know. Maybe." He shook his head. "I don't think so. It was thirty-six years ago. My memory is a mess when it comes to what happened to Heather. Sometimes I think I remember things that would be important, but I'm not sure if they were a dream or a real memory." He stuffed the phone into his back pocket. "I'm sure about this, though."

When Faith said she wanted to see Marinoni, she'd assumed Nate would be with her, but instead she had Detective Covington by her side. Nate assured her he'd be watching on a monitor from somewhere close.

The room was nicer than the ones she'd seen in movies, but the smell took her by surprise. It reeked of body odor mixed with Clorox, an unpleasant combination.

Jeremy Marinoni sat behind a table, his shaved head showing stubble. A tattoo of a dragon ran up the side of his neck, the tail disappearing behind his head. "So, you're Ivan's famous daughter. You're so much prettier than I had imagined, but of course, the ladies always thought old Ivan was a looker too."

Beside him, a woman who must have been his attorney cleared her throat in an obvious warning.

Detective Covington indicated a chair for Faith, then sat in the other. "Mr. Marinoni, we're here to find out what you know about a case we're working on. It seems you have personal involvement in the disappearance of Heather Crane in September of 1987."

Faith squirmed in her chair until she realized the joy her discomfort was giving Marinoni.

"I don't know what you're talking about." His gaze never left Faith.

"We have a witness who puts you at the East Valley development the evening the girl went missing. It seems that you and your pal Harold Walker were up to no good that night."

"What do I get for telling you what I know?"

"This isn't a negotiation."

The attorney leaned forward on the table. "My client and I have talked at length about this situation. He has information that is vital to the case but wishes to not be charged for his involvement if he indeed was involved."

Detective Covington crossed his arms. "You're kidding me, right?"

"No, sir, I am not. Mr. Marinoni will be taking a plea deal for another incident. In that agreement, he will spend four years in the state penitentiary. For the case involving Heather Crane, he committed no crime that would not include a statute of limitations that has already expired."

The room swelled with tension.

Faith looked from the detective to the attorney. He was going to get away with his part no matter what. It was sick. Unforgiveable. Didn't they realize that Heather had been a real person? She'd had a future that was taken away from her. Faith couldn't make herself understand how a woman could sit beside a man who'd been involved in a child's death and defend him.

"Then it sounds to me like you have everything you need," Detective Covington said gruffly. "Let's hear the story."

The attorney gave a nod, and Jeremy Marinoni began to talk.

"Harold got me the job with Ivan's company."

"Mr. Marinoni, can you please be specific and state Harold's full name?"

"Harold Walker. You see, Ivan Ferdon had a problem. When they were building that neighborhood up there, they ran into one of those little cemeteries. It must have been a family thing. There wasn't any record of it, and that movie about the houses built over the graves had just come out. From what I heard, the guy was up to his eyeballs in debt. And no one wants to buy houses where graves used to be. Ivan got Harold and I to . . . redispose of the dearly departed."

"When was this? Please be specific."

"September 17, 1987."

Faith's blood went cold.

"Ivan had a plan for a little park in the center of the neighborhood. The kind of place rich people hang out and barbeque while they gossip about whoever isn't there. We dug a nice hole and were about to place them in there when we heard something. Turns out it was the kid." He held up a cuffed hand. "I was confident she hadn't seen anything, but Harold was furious. He couldn't very well go after her, and we had . . . remains in the back of the truck. Harold jumped into Ivan's car and took off. I didn't know what to do. Ivan was spitting mad, but that was nothing compared to how he was ten minutes later when Harold pulled up again. He had the girl in the back seat." He had the good sense to look away from Faith then. "She was gone. He said it was an accident. I have no idea, man. I wasn't there."

"What did Mr. Walker tell you had happened?" Covington's voice showed no change in emotion.

"He said he'd been chasing her down. He was going to make sure she hadn't seen anything and that she'd keep her mouth shut. She lost her balance on her bike, and he couldn't stop in time. He hit her with Ivan's Camry."

It had taken time, but what Marinoni was saying started to make it through Faith's mind. Her father hadn't killed Heather.

"We didn't have much choice. Well, Harold didn't give us much choice. He said if me or Ivan said anything about the girl, we'd be done for, and that would include our families." He held up his cuffed hands. "I'm a victim here."

Faith's stomach turned.

"What did you do with the body?"

She wasn't sure she could handle this much longer. The room swam, the edges of her vision narrowing until she had to lean forward in her seat.

"Mrs. Byrne, are you doing okay?" Covington's voice had an edge of disgust in it. He hadn't wanted Faith in the room to begin with.

She forced herself to calm her breathing. "I'm good. Go on."

"He—Harold—made me and Ivan do the burying. He wanted us as involved as possible, but we didn't want to. Ivan was crying like a little girl, begging to go to the police."

"Where did you bury the child?"

"Right there in the neighborhood center with the other folks."

63

Faith

Faith stood behind a barricade put up by the police department. She could see Nate closer to the central area, where a man in a hard hat cut through cement, the blade of his machinery screaming nearly as loud as the cries in Faith's heart.

In a way, she wanted to be beside Nate. After all, it had been the three of them once upon a time, staring down at this very place and wondering what it would become. What they would become. It seemed right for her to be with Nate as the story came to an end.

The concrete saw stopped, leaving too much silence to weigh the air.

Two officers with shovels stepped forward as the last bit of concrete was pulled away. They didn't rush, removing small scoops of dirt until one stopped, knelt, and used his hand to uncover something. He waved Covington over.

Even from where she stood, Faith could see the corner of brittle black plastic. It turned her stomach, and she leaned on the barrier as her legs went weak.

Nate turned away from the scene and came to Faith's side. Maybe he felt the need to connect as much as she did.

A moment later, Covington looked their way. He nodded, and that was all that needed to be said.

Heather had finally been found.

64

Dora

Dora stood behind Paul as he opened the door to Detective Covington and Nathan. Down the street, she saw Faith standing in the driveway, her fluffy cat held in her arms.

The distance from one yard to the other had grown each day since the bicycle had been discovered.

Paul stood to the side, letting the two men inside the house.

A hum sounded through Dora's head, muffling the words around her. She sat on the couch next to Paul, who'd given his recliner to the detective. A reminder clicked in her memory that it was polite to offer their company a drink, but Dora couldn't form the words.

"Mr. and Mrs. Crane." The detective started off as though they were still the couple who'd lived here in 1987. "We have news to share with you."

Nathan picked at his cuticles, a habit he'd carried forward from his youth, but he didn't make eye contact.

"Did you find my girl?" There was a shake in Paul's voice.

Nate's head sunk further.

"We believe we have. Our interview with Jeremy Marinoni brought much into the light. If what he says can be trusted, and we do believe it can, Heather died that night as a result of being struck by a car."

A tear slid down Dora's cheek. "Then where is she? Why didn't Ivan come forward? How could he hide something like that?"

"Mr. Ferdon was not the one behind the wheel. It was a man named Harold Walker." Covington chewed at his bottom lip, as though he needed time to gather his words. "Walker ran her down because she'd seen him committing a crime."

The sound that left Paul was like a tire being punctured. Dora patted her palm on his leg. "Have you arrested this man?"

"We're too late. Walker is dead."

Wasn't that one of the reasons Dora had kept pushing to see the person responsible put behind bars? She'd never get that satisfaction, but it didn't really matter now. "If Ivan wasn't the one who hurt her, why did he have the bicycle in the trunk of his car?"

"It seems Mr. Ferdon was tied to these other crimes. Walker got him to dispose of Mr. Potter's pickup, to cast suspicion on Mr. Potter. The pickup was supposed to have the bike inside. The best we can figure is Ivan's remorse led him to keep the bike. Maybe he eventually planned to come forward." Detective Covington paused. "Marinoni gave us the burial location. We've uncovered remains, including those of a family that had been buried on the property over a hundred years before, and those of a child with remnants of cloth that match what Heather was wearing that day. The medical examiner is making a final determination, but we are confident we've found your daughter."

Dora clasped her hand around Paul's as his body shook with emotion. After all these years, Heather was coming home.

Dora stood for her first time to talk in front of the grief support group. Her legs wobbled, and she wished she could have Finnegan by her side, but she was there with both Brooke and Paul.

"We're having a memorial service for our daughter Heather this weekend. In a few weeks, we'll be properly laying her body to rest. I've cried so many times over the last thirty-six years, mainly because I was afraid of what could be happening to my child. It's an awful hurt to know she's gone, but I'm comforted by the knowledge that Heather is safe.

"For so many years, I fought grief. It felt like giving in to it was giving up on my daughter. I held it at bay, and with that, I kept my remaining family pushed back too. I was reading my Bible the other day, and I came to the part in Luke where Jesus wept because He saw the pain of Lazarus' sisters. As I read, I felt the assurance that God understands my grief, that it isn't a weakness, but a consequence of love. I don't know if that makes sense to any of you, but for me, it felt like permission."

She sat back down, looking from Brooke to Paul. He hadn't moved back in, and Dora hadn't finished boxing up Heather's room, but they were making movements toward the future.

Hillary tucked a loose curl behind her ear. "What do you all think about what Dora had to say? Have you ever needed permission to grieve?"

The room warmed with the utterances of agreement.

Across the square of tables, Laura wiggled her fingers in the air. "I was so busy caring for my kids and trying to make enough money to feed them and keep them in a home that I pushed off grieving the life I'd dreamed of. Dora, what you're saying makes so much sense to me. It wasn't until a friend insisted on taking my kids for an hour each week that I saw what I'd lost." She shrugged. "I didn't have the money to do anything, so I'd sit in my car. Sixty uninterrupted minutes a week is a long time when you're trying to battle back the sadness and disappointment. I finally had to start facing my losses. I know it's not the same as losing a child, but . . ."

Dora shook her head. "Don't downplay your hurt on my account. I'm glad you had a friend who helped you, and even more, that you accepted that help. You're a braver woman than I am."

Paul stretched his hand toward her, laying it over hers. He still wore his wedding band. So did she. And that was hope for a future together. Though their grief was expressed in different ways, they could support each other. They could stand alongside each other and march forward, knowing they wouldn't have Heather with them on this side of eternity but hoping for a sweet reunion when the proper day arrived.

65

Faith

The Cranes decided to hold Heather's memorial in the backyard of their home. According to the note left on Faith's doorstep, this would keep the looky-loos and reporters from interfering.

Faith would be leaving Deep Valley first thing the next morning. There was a familiar pain that tightened her heart as she finished up her packing, then removed the timeline from the wall, rolling it into a cylinder that she placed in a box. She'd done this before—packed her things, then walked across the way to say good-bye to her best friend. Just like last time, she held close the hope that they'd be together again someday.

She opened the front door and found Nate standing on the sidewalk. He wore a suit that fit snug across the shoulders.

"You look beautiful." He held out a hand to her and she took it. "I hope Mrs. Crane picked up a copy of *The Goonies*."

She couldn't help but chuckle. "I can't believe you remember that."

"I remember a lot about the three of us that summer."

"So do I." She tipped her head onto his shoulder and stood at the curb, watching time pass by before moving on to the next step, the good-byes.

Erik stood at the Cranes' front door, ushering people through the house to the backyard. Inside, Faith's eye caught on a familiar face. She nudged Nate. "Is that Greg?"

"I think so. He looks exactly like I remember Mr. Crane looking."

Out back, the yard was splashed with colors. Balloons rose from strings tied along the fence. Potted flowers sat along the ground. The barbeque sent summer aromas through the air, and a sign above two huge coolers indicated pop and ice cream.

Goose bumps popped out along Faith's arms. This was exactly what Heather would have wanted—a party that truly represented who she was.

Brooke set her phone near a speaker and eighties music sang out over the conversations and laughter of the invited guests.

Mr. Crane walked up to them, sporting an apron with pictures of his three children and three grandchildren. "Can I get you a burger or a hot dog?"

"Burger, please," Faith said.

Nate scratched his chin.

"Both for Nathan, I think." Mr. Crane grinned and stepped up to the grill.

"I'm glad you're both here." Faith stiffened at the sound of Dora Crane's voice.

They turned to find the woman behind them, her huge dog leaning on her side.

Mrs. Crane scratched Finnegan's ears. "I wish I'd had the guts to get a dog like this when the kids were little." She hugged Nate, then Faith, holding on tight and whispering into her ear, "No matter how this worked out, it could never be your fault."

Tears flowed over Faith's cheeks.

Mrs. Crane reached into her pocket and pulled out a tissue, dabbing it below Faith's eyes. She looked around the yard wistfully. "There's a house for sale right down the road from Brooke and Erik. Paul and I are going to buy it and sell this house. I don't want to miss another minute with my grand-babies."

"That's wonderful. I know it will mean a lot to them. The love you gave me that summer changed me. It allowed me to love my daughters in a vulnerable way. Having someone care about you as a child, even if it's only for a short time, makes a difference. You made a difference."

Throughout the afternoon, there wasn't a single mention of Heather's death, only the ten years of life she'd led with exuberance. Faith listened to stories that filled her heart. She'd record the final episode of Heather's podcast when she returned home and planned to share many of these stories with her listeners.

In the end, this was a story that fit right in with her theme. It rang out with hope, perseverance, and strength. When Faith drove away from Deep Valley this time, she could do it knowing the job she came to do was complete.

66

Dora

Dora and Paul parked on the edge of the development, which was now a neighborhood, of course, and walked toward the center. She could still picture the trailer that had been her office, where she'd so blindly worked alongside Ivan Ferdon. Had he thought she would be the perfect fool, a woman who wouldn't catch on to the corruption within his business?

She breathed deep. It was up to her to stop the past from making her a victim again.

As they approached their destination, she was stunned to see how fast the land had been turned from crime scene to sanctuary. A fountain sat in the middle of bright green grass.

Paul took her hand in his, and they completed the journey, ending at the stone placed to commemorate their daughter and the pioneer family who'd been placed here.

Even though Dora knew her little girl had been with Jesus long before she'd been laid in the ground here, there was a comfort in knowing her body had not been alone. There had been another mother with her.

Paul knelt in front of the plaque and rubbed his thumb over the words.

May they rest in the arms of their Lord.
William Ingram
Carol Ingram
Samuel Ingram
Rebecca Ingram
Heather Crane

67

Faith

Faith hung a *Welcome Home* banner across her garage.

Three days earlier, she'd released the third and final segment in Heather's special series. She'd felt closure knowing she'd completed the story, as if by doing so she'd finally found a way to thank her old friend for the summer that shaped the woman she was today.

The temperature had dropped, and she ran inside to grab a sweater. As she came back out, Neil's car pulled up to the curb. Harlow and Ava tumbled out and ran up the driveway, jumping into their mother's embrace.

The house hadn't been home until that moment when she felt her babies in her arms again. "I missed you two so much."

Harlow stood back. "We've been listening to the show. Mom, I'm so proud of you."

Faith bit her bottom lip, hoping to squelch the topic before Neil got started.

"You're a hero." Ava clapped her hands together.

"Girls," Neil called as she walked toward them. "Get your bags out of the trunk."

They rolled their eyes but turned to obey their dad.

"I've been listening too." Neil's face was typical for him—unreadable. "You did a great thing back there. Wendy and I listened to the show, and I feel like a real jerk for thinking you were being selfish." He scuffed his shoe along the cement. "I guess I'm saying I'm sorry."

"Thank you. I really appreciate that. I know it was hard for you."

He huffed, but there was a slight smile on his face. "Well, they are back in your care now. Enjoy." A slight dusting of sarcasm sprinkled over his words.

She would enjoy her girls, every minute she had with them.

Faith's phone buzzed. She looked down at the text from Nate.

There's a detective job opening in your town.

She responded without hesitation.

Apply!

Christina Suzann Nelson is an inspirational speaker and the award-winning author of five books, including *More Than We Remember*, *Shaped by the Waves*, and the Christy Award–winning *The Way It Should Be*. She is the mother of six children, an advocate for children in foster care, a substitute teacher, a conference director, and the wife of her partner in this crazy adventure.

Sign Up for Christina's Newsletter

Keep up to date with Christina's news on book releases and events by signing up for her email list at christinasuzannnelson.com.

More from Christina Suzann Nelson

Cassie George has stayed away from her small hometown ever since her unplanned pregnancy. But when she hears that her aunt suffered a stroke and has been hiding a Parkinson's diagnosis, she must return. Greeted by a mysterious package, Cassie will discover that who she thought she was, and who she wants to become, are all about to change.

Shaped by the Waves

You May Also Like . . .

Zara Mahoney was enjoying newlywed bliss until her estranged sister, Eve, upends her plans, moving Zara to take custody of her children. Eve's struggles lead her to Tiff Bradley, who's determined to help despite the past hurts the relationship triggers. Can these women find the hope they—and those they love—desperately need?

The Way It Should Be by Christina Suzann Nelson
christinasuzannnelson.com

After a life-altering car accident, one night changes everything for three women. As their lives intersect, they can no longer dwell in the memory of who they've been. Can they rise from the wreck of the worst moments of their lives to become who they were meant to be?

More Than We Remember by Christina Suzann Nelson
christinasuzannelson.com

After Ingrid Erikson jeopardizes her career, she fears her future will remain irrevocably broken. But when the man who shattered her belief in happily-ever-afters offers her a sealed envelope from her late best friend, Ingrid is sent on a hunt for a hidden manuscript and must confront her past before she can find the healing she's been searching for.

The Words We Lost by Nicole Deese
A FOG HARBOR ROMANCE
nicoledeese.com

BETHANYHOUSE

More from Bethany House

In 1865, orphaned Daisy Francois takes a housemaid position and finds that the eccentric Gothic authoress inside hides a story more harrowing than those in her novels. Centuries later, Cleo Clemmons uncovers an age-old mystery, and the dust of the old castle's curse threatens to rise again, this time leaving no one alive to tell its sordid tale.

The Vanishing at Castle Moreau by Jaime Jo Wright
jaimewrightbooks.com

With a notorious forger preying on New York's high society, Metropolitan Museum of Art curator Lauren Westlake is just the expert needed to track down the criminal. As she and Detective Joe Caravello search for the truth, the closer they get to discovering the forger's identity, the more entangled they become in a web of deception and crime.

The Metropolitan Affair by Jocelyn Green
On Central Park #1
jocelyngreen.com

During WWII, when special agent Sterling Bertrand is washed ashore at Evie Farrow's inn, her life is turned upside down. As Evie and Sterling work together to track down a German agent, they unravel mysteries that go back to WWI. The ripples from the past are still rocking their lives, and it seems yesterday's tides may sweep them into danger today.

Yesterday's Tides by Roseanna M. White
roseannamwhite.com

◊ BETHANYHOUSE